KITCHEN BOSS

ASHLEE PRICE

https://www.ashleepriceromanceauthor.com/

PROLOGUE

Cathy

Eleven years earlier...

It hurts.

My left leg feels like it's being squeezed off by some invisible tentacle. The water turns into a thousand ice cold pins and needles pricking every inch of my skin. My head spins with every thought that races through it in a flurry of panic. My chest seems like it might collapse around my heart and cause it to explode with every fleeting breath that I strain to pull into my aching lungs.

Is this... it? Am I going to die?

My life flashes before my eyes. Rushing to school. Classes. Homework. Dinner with Mom and Hal. Piano lessons. Soccer practice. Weekend sleepovers. Summer camping trips. White Christmases at Grandma's. Birthdays that usually take place on the coldest day of the year.

Wait. Is that all?

I've never even been kissed, never been alone with a guy. I've never driven a car. I've never tried sushi or kimchi. I've never tasted alcohol, because I'm only fifteen.

Only fifteen. And dying.

I can feel death creeping under my skin as I sink below the surface, my legs too numb and my arms too tired to keep myself afloat. Water gushes into my mouth. It seeps inside my nostrils and makes its way to my lungs. I can't breathe.

I guess this is it. I guess I'll die without getting married and having kids, without even knowing what sex feels like, without going to college or even to prom. So many things that I'll never get to experience. So much life I'll never get to live.

Such a waste.

I'd cry, but I can't. I have no control over this body anymore. Even my thoughts are starting to blur. I'm slipping away.

Yes, this is it.

I give in to the cold and the darkness. I have no other choice. This is the end. My end.

"Cathy!"

Trisha? My best friend's voice is the last I hear, her pretty face with those mischievous teal eyes and that carefree smile the last image my mind manages to conjure before the nothingness takes over.

~

When I wake up, the first thing I see are bright lights. Too bright. I blink a few times and squint until I finally see something else.

A pale green ceiling. Cream-colored walls. A watercolor painting of a bird's nest with eggs which doesn't look familiar to me in the slightest.

Where am I?

"Cathy!"

I hear the relief in my mother's voice and feel it in her arms as they wrap around me, lifting me off the bed and squeezing me tight.

My eyebrows crease. Relief? Why would she be relieved?

As I turn my head, I see a stocky man in a checkered shirt standing in the doorway past her shoulder. He gives me a smile and waves.

Hal?

"Hal, call the doctor!" my mother orders.

Hal runs off. Through the doorway, I see people walking past, some more hurriedly than others - nurses and doctors.

I'm in a... hospital?

I glance at my hand and see the needle buried beneath strips of clear bandage. I follow the tube to the bottle hanging by my bed and see the machine beneath it. Red and green lines move up and down in waves on the screen.

What the hell?

"It's alright, sweetie." My mother strokes my cheek as she gives me a smile. "Everything's going to be alright."

I shake my head. "What happened, Mom? Why am I...?"

My words drift away as the doctor rushes into the room. He looks like he's in his fifties, with salt and pepper hair and eyeglasses with a black frame and round lenses.

"Dr. Allen." My mother steps away from my bedside. "She just woke up. This is good, right? She's going to be alright now, right?"

Dr. Allen doesn't answer. He takes out his penlight and flashes it into my eyes. Then he gazes straight into them.

"How do you feel, Cathy? Does your head hurt? Does it hurt anywhere?"

I shake my head. "I feel fine. I'm just... confused."

"Confused?" Dr. Allen gives me a puzzled look.

I glance at my mother. She looks worried now, and I'm scared I might make her worry even more.

"It's okay, Cathy," Dr. Allen tells me. He grasps my chin so that I'm meeting his gaze once more. "Tell me why you're confused, or what you're confused about, exactly."

"I..." I swallow the lump in my throat. "I can't... remember why I'm here. What happened to me?"

I hear my mother gasp. Hal rushes to her side.

"Please don't panic, Mrs. Jeffries." Dr. Allen turns to her. "It's completely normal for her memory to be fuzzy considering she... considering what she just suffered. Besides, she only just woke up after being unconscious for nearly two days. It will take time for her brain to begin functioning as well as it used to."

What?

"Wait. What are you saying?" I touch the back of my head. "Are you saying I have... amnesia?"

"I'm saying your brain has been through a lot," Dr. Allen answers. "And that you should give it time to recover. For now, you should consider yourself lucky that you woke up. That's a huge step in the right direction."

Dr. Allen pats my mother's shoulder.

"The same goes for you, Mrs. Jeffries." He glances at me. "I'll send a resident to check on her and run some tests, but she is stable and everything looks good right now."

"Everything looks good?" I shake my head. "Then why can't I remember...?"

"Don't force yourself, Cathy." Dr. Allen grabs my hand. "Your body has done well to get you to a point where you are now awake. Do not waste all that effort."

He squeezes my hand.

"Besides, maybe it's better that you don't remember," he mutters.

I look at him. "What?"

Dr. Allen leaves my side. He gives my mother a nod before walking out of the room.

I throw my mother a questioning look. "What did he mean? What happened to me, Mom?"

She approaches my bedside and takes my hand but says nothing.

"Mom, please."

I'm just so confused right now. I feel so lost. I feel like I'm missing something important.

I look into my mother's eyes. "I need to know what happened."

She nods and draws a deep breath. Hal places his hand on her shoulder.

"You drowned," my mother tells me.

My eyes grow wide. Drowned?

"In a lake. You were vacationing with... with friends, remember?"

No. I don't remember. I don't even know the last thing I do remember.

Think, Cathy.

Well, I remember my mother, obviously, and Hal, my step-dad. I remember going to school. I'm in... ninth grade?

"What grade am I?" I ask my mother.

"You'll be starting tenth grade in a few weeks," she answers.

Right. So I am in ninth grade. I remember that much. I remember the last day of school, which Trisha and I celebrated by eating all the Ben and Jerry's we could afford.

Trisha. Yes, I remember her. My best friend. I remember her sleeping over. I remember us watching DVDs from Netflix. I remember us making our own pizza - mine with loads of cheese and bacon and hers with those olives she loves so much. I remember her birthday, which we spent at the mall - just the two of us because everyone else was already busy with their summer escapades. And I remember her jumping up and down as she told me we'd be going to her uncle's lakeside cabin with her cousin.

Lakeside cabin.

Lake.

I look at my mother. "You said I drowned in a lake?"

She nods. "Well, nearly. Or should I say you drowned but were resuscitated?"

No way. I can swim. Well, not as well as Trisha, but...

My thoughts skid to a halt.

"Where's Trisha?" I ask. "She was there, right?"

I'm sure she can explain everything to me. Why isn't she here, anyway? Back when I had my appendectomy, she was right by my side.

My mother doesn't answer. She just pulls her hand away and purses her lips as she bows her head.

My chest tightens. I've seen that look before, back when she told me that my father would never come back so that I wouldn't keep waiting for him.

What is it she's hiding from me now? What bad news is she trying to keep from me?

"Mom..."

Slowly, she lifts her head. The look of grief in her eyes makes tears well up in mine.

"Trisha... didn't make it, sweetheart," my mother tells me in a trembling voice which seems to echo from a world away as she places her hand over mine. "They... couldn't save her."

My jaw drops. No.

What is she saying? That Trisha's dead? Impossible. Trisha can't be dead. She's only just turned sixteen. She's perfectly healthy. I was just with her.

"You're lying."

"I'm so sorry, sweetheart."

It can't be. Trisha wouldn't leave me. We said we'd graduate high school together, go to college together, share an apartment in the city after we started working and then live next door to each other when we had our own families so our kids could be best friends and we could cook meals together and keep watching movies together and talk about our husbands while we drank wine.

I shake my head as tears trickle down my cheeks. Trisha can't be gone. She's my best friend. She's like a sister to me. She's...

I clasp both hands over my heart as I feel it break.

"No!!!"

CHAPTER 1

Cathy

I kick off my high heels and drop myself onto the couch. The worn out cushions sink beneath my weight. The old springs creak. I lean back but wince as I feel the teeth of my amber hair clip dig into my scalp. I take it out so my hair tumbles past my shoulders and try again. This time, I feel the cool softness of cotton against the back of my head and I let out a sweet sigh of relief.

Finally, I can relax.

All day long, I've been walking and waiting. I've been trudging around in two-and-a-half-inch heels from one building to another. I've been to corporate offices, a bank, a hotel, a department store and a cafe. And that's just today. I've been waiting in lobbies, corridors and yes, waiting rooms, for minutes and even hours just to hand someone a resume and then be told to wait for their call or worse, be turned away for not having any experience. How am I supposed to get any experience if no one will give me a chance?

I let out another sigh, this one of exasperation, as I prop my legs up on the coffee table. As soon as I cross my ankles, I hear the sound of nylon ripping. I glance at the back of my leg and frown at the gaping hole in my stocking.

Great. Another pair of stockings ruined. And I just bought this one the other day. Maybe I should start a pile so I can see how many I waste before I finally land a job. If I do land a job. The way things have been going, I've started to wonder if I can.

So many people are looking for jobs, after all. Not just me. And half of them are probably better than I am. They're younger, because unlike me, they didn't take sabbatical before tenth grade, or eleventh or twelfth. Or they're older and more experienced, wiser. Or just smarter, more confident, with a better dress or a brighter smile, the kind of smile you can only wear if you've never had anything bad happen to you.

Is it too late for me to have a future?

The sound of metal clattering to the floor jolts me to my feet. My heart hammers in my chest.

An intruder? Has someone broken into my apartment?

My thoughts stutter. What do I do? Should I head out the door? Should I call the cops?

Both sound like reasonable options, but first, I have to make sure that there is an intruder. The last thing I want is for the cops to think I'm crazy. Not that I haven't been called that before.

I tiptoe to the bathroom. After a few steps, I see the door. It's slightly open, but I don't see anyone inside. I don't hear a sound either.

I stop in my tracks. What if the intruder is waiting for me, getting ready to pounce on me?

That thought sends me looking around for a weapon. I need one to defend myself just in case.

My gaze falls on the knife block by the kitchen sink. It's too far away, though. Besides, I don't want to stab anyone by accident, or worse, get stabbed. I consider the pen on the counter before deciding on a book within reach. If the intruder tries anything funny, I'll just whack him on the head as hard as I can or hit him in the crotch with a pointy corner.

I hold it with both hands and proceed. Just in front of the door, I draw a deep breath.

One. Two...

At the count of three, I kick the door open. Greenish yellow eyes stare back at me in indifference.

I let out a breath of relief as I lower my book. The grey and white Birman goes back to licking its paw on the shelf above my toilet, completely oblivious and unconcerned about what it's just put me through.

"Trespassing again, are we, Molly?"

The cat doesn't seem to have heard me.

I glance at the bathroom window. Oh well. It's my fault I left it open. Again. I guess I should be glad it's not big enough to let a person in.

I close the window and pick up the can of scented wax cubes that has fallen on the floor. I place it beside the sink before grabbing my uninvited guest from its perch. It protests with a meow.

"Now, now, Molly. You know the bathroom is no place for you." I stroke her fur in an effort to console her as I carry her across the living room. "Actually, my apartment is no place for you. I don't even know why you like it. It's tiny and old. I'm sure your apartment is much better. In fact, I know it is."

Another meow.

"Let me guess. You snuck out while Mrs. Garland was having her nap. Well, I've got to get you back."

I place the pumps I discarded earlier on the shoe rack and grab my Keds so I can slip them on.

"I'm not a pet sitter, you know."

Pet sitter. Well, there's an idea, actually. Sure, I've got a degree from a respectable university, but what use is a college diploma if it can't get me a job?

I look at the cat in my arms. "At least pet sitting is something I've got experience in."

It blinks in agreement.

I'm about to open the front door on my way to return Molly to her owner when my phone rings. I make a 180-degree turn and rush to answer it. Who knows? It might be about a job.

The moment I see the name on the screen, though, my excitement vanishes.

Mom.

Okay. Not what I wanted. Still, I have to answer. If I don't, she'll just keep calling.

I tap the screen and hold the phone to my ear. "Hi, Mom."

"Cathy?" I hear my mother's soft, scratchy voice.

It's been that way since she had a tumor removed from her larynx five years ago, though she likes to say it's because she loves karaoke too much.

"You sound disappointed."

Of course she'd notice.

"What? Were you expecting a call from your boyfriend?"

I roll my eyes. What is it about moms and boyfriends? When you're thirteen, they get mad if you have one. When you're past twenty-five, they get mad at you if you don't. Well, not mad exactly. Just bothered. Immensely.

"Not funny, Mom. You know I don't have one."

I've never had one, in fact. Between all the struggles of my personal life and trying to get an education, I've simply never had the time. Maybe that's why my Mom is worried.

"Who knows? You might have been able to get one since the last time I called you."

"Mom, you just called me yesterday," I remind her as I set Molly down before I drop her or she jumps out of my arms.

"Who says you can't meet a guy and fall in love with him in a span of 24 hours? That's what happened with..."

"You and Hal." I sit down. "I know."

I've heard the story a dozen times before. My Mom's car broke down after she dropped me off at daycare. Hal, who was new in town - he had just agreed to take over his uncle's dental practice - drove by, stopped to help her and stayed with her until the tow truck came. Then he stayed with her some more while her car was at the garage. They talked. They ate snacks from the vending machine, shared a Snickers bar. By the end of the day, they were in love. They married a year later.

"You do know the chance of that happening is just one in a million, right? Besides, I have my hands full trying to get a job."

"Oh, sweetheart." I hear the concern in my mother's voice. "Has no one called you back yet?"

"Nope," I answer. "Not a single one."

I can almost see her frowning.

"Sure you don't want to come home? Maybe Hal or I can help you find a job here."

"I'm fine, Mom," I tell her.

If I go home now, I just know I'll never be able to leave, especially not with the massive effort it took the first time around. Besides...

"Don't you have other kids to worry about?"

Since I left, she and Hal have been taking in foster kids. They always wanted more kids, and they were already planning on doing it before I regressed into a baby and took up all their attention. Now, they have three.

"If you're telling me to stop worrying about you, Cathy Josephine Jeffries, I won't," my Mom answers. "I never will."

"And I wouldn't dream of telling you what to do."

"Though maybe if you got a husband and a job, I'd worry less," she adds.

A couple of minutes ago, it was a boyfriend. Now, a husband?

I exhale. "Given the fact that both are so hard to find, I think I'll only end up with one."

"A husband?"

"A job. Hopefully, I'll get one before the week ends."

Which is what I said last week. Maybe this week, that hope will turn into reality.

"I'm sure you'll get a good job soon," my mother says. "Anyone would be a fool not to hire you after meeting you."

The problem is I rarely even get to meet the people who have the power to hire me.

I tap my fingers on my lap. "Yes, the world is full of fools."

"Well, don't let them get the better of you. Just hang in there, and if you ever need anything, anything at all, you just have to call me, okay?"

I nod. "Okay."

"I love you."

I smile. "I love you, too."

The call ends. I set my phone down on the coffee table and stare at the screen until it turns dark.

True, I sometimes wish my mother didn't check on me every day, but there's a part of me that's glad she does. She said she never intended to take Trisha's place, and yet she has become my best friend. Without her, I don't know what I'd do.

I'm about to sink into the cushions when I catch a glimpse of Molly going to the kitchen.

Right. I still have to get her back to my landlady.

I pick her up. "Come on. Let's get you home."

~

"Thank you, dear," Mrs. Garland tells me as she presses the cat's head against her cheek. "And I'm so sorry that Molly broke into your apartment again."

I wave a hand. "Hardly. I left the window open and she came in. And she didn't break anything, so..."

She jumps down from Mrs. Garland's arms and struts off.

I take a step back. "I should go back to my apartment."

"Wait." Mrs. Garland touches my arm. "I actually have something to tell you."

"Yes?"

"I just spoke with my son and he said he would like me to stay with him and his wife," she tells me. "They're expecting their first child."

"How wonderful." I give her a wide smile. "Congratulations."

"It is wonderful, isn't it?" More wrinkles seem to appear on her face as it lights up. "I am so excited."

"So you won't be staying here anymore?"

"No," she answers. "And actually, no one will."

I give her a puzzled look.

"My son wants to have the building renovated since it's old and all. He has a friend who will be taking care of everything. He's already made the arrangements."

My eyebrows furrow. "Are you kicking me out, Mrs. Garland?"

She takes my hand. "I'm sorry, dear. I know you've stayed here longer than all the others, and truth be told, I've grown rather fond of you. Molly has, too. But it is my son's decision and he's made up his mind, so yes, you'll have to move out after two months."

My head drops along with my heart. I have to move out?

"Well, Charlie says you can move back in when renovations are done, though Lord knows how long they'll take," Mrs. Garland adds. "He said the rent will be higher, but I can ask him to give you a small discount."

I give her a weak smile as I start to walk away. "Thank you."

I'm not sure it's any comfort, though. If the renovations start in two months, I have to find a new place to stay as soon as possible, and doing that will take time, time away from my job hunt. And money, money I don't have right now.

How am I supposed to move?

My mother's face and her words immediately come to mind.

If you need anything, anything at all, just call.

I'm sure if I ask her, she'll be here by tomorrow and help me find a place by next week, even help me move. She and Hal will probably pay for it, too. But I don't want to. She's already done so much for me. For God's sake, I'm twenty-six now. I'm not a child anymore. I shouldn't be relying on my mother anymore, not for stuff like this.

I have to grow up and get a job.

As soon as I get back to my apartment, I turn my laptop on and start searching for employment opportunities again. I've already applied to most of them, though. Should I just email them again? Should I call? Or should I just get a part-time job in the meantime?

I'm contemplating all that as I fidget with the charms on my bracelet when the words on the side of the page catch my eye.

Interns Wanted. Hourly wages. Graduates welcome.

An internship. It's not the same as a job, of course. It only lasts for a few months and I'll get paid by the hour. Still, I'll get paid. And it might just give me the experience I need to land a real job.

I draw a deep breath and click on the ad.

Guess it's time for me to switch from job hunting to internship hunting.

~

Looking for an internship is nearly just as hard, though. Or so I've learned after two days of applying.

There are limited slots and plenty of applicants - not just college graduates but undergraduates as well. And while no experience is required, many of them have tedious screening procedures. No, thank you. I'm not going to waste a whole day taking tests and going through interviews for a ten percent chance of securing an internship which has just a five percent chance of becoming a permanent job.

I take one hand off the wheel to pop a Life Saver into my mouth. Afterwards, I glance at the piece of paper on the passenger seat.

Hopefully, the restaurant that placed the last ad on my list for today doesn't have too many applicants or a complicated screening procedure.

It's quite far, I realize as I keep driving towards Sausalito. Farther than I thought. I'm guessing it will take me more than an hour - maybe an hour and fifteen minutes - to drive from my apartment to the restaurant. That thought nearly makes me turn back. I've already come so far, though.

Oh well. I might as well take a look at this one.

Finally, I see the restaurant, or at least the house that's being renovated into a restaurant. There are workers on the roof and on the scaffolding. Planks of wood and piles of sand sit in the front yard.

"Excuse me," I say to one of the workers as I approach the building. "Would you know who I have to see to apply for an internship?"

He gestures inside the house. "Boss is in the kitchen. Just go around the back and go in through the smaller door."

"Okay. Thank you."

I go around the back just as he instructed. Sure enough, there are two doors. As I approach the smaller one, which is slightly open, the aroma of butter, spices and seafood drifts to my nostrils. My mouth waters.

I must be going in the right direction.

I follow my nose and walk through the door. I find myself in the spacious kitchen - spacious, but also rustic and cozy. The gleam of the polished wood, bathed in the sunlight drifting through the large windows, outshines the metal surfaces of the various equipment scattered throughout. Black pots and pans hang from sections of the ceiling like chandeliers. Jars filled with grains and powders of all colors line a shelf that wraps around the whole room.

In the middle of the room, a man towers above one of the stoves. His back is turned to me so I can't see exactly what he's doing, but I can tell he's the one responsible for the heavenly aroma that's whetting my appetite so intensely. I lick my lips.

Darn. That smells so good.

As the man turns, though, my senses are overwhelmed by something else.

His burnt brown hair is cut close to his scalp, just a tad thicker than the beard which fringes his chiseled jaw. His sleeves are rolled up above his elbows, revealing the ink on his left arm. Both arms boast massive, defined muscles which look like they could easily lift the stove. If not for his apron, a gray one with black stripes, I would have thought he was a soldier.

Something tells me he'd look absolutely yummy in just that apron.

As he lifts his head, our gazes meet. My breath catches. My cheeks burn. His eyes, dark like lumps of coal, widen with surprise.

"Oh, hello there."

Even his voice sounds intensely masculine, deep and strong and sending ripples of excitement down my spine. His smile makes my pulse flicker.

"Hello," I manage to squeak.

His eyebrows crease. "Are you lost?"

I swallow. "N-no."

Am I?

"I'm here for the internship," I proceed in a steadier voice as I regain my composure. "I was told..."

"Wait a second." He touches his chin as he takes a step forward. "I've seen you before."

He has?

"You're Cathy, aren't you?"

My eyebrows arch. How does he know? I'm pretty sure we've never met before. Yes, I know my memory isn't that great, but I have a feeling I'd remember perfectly if I ever met someone so... hot. Is he psychic or something? I glance at my blouse. I'm not wearing a name tag, am I?

"Cathy Jeffries," he says my full name.

Now I'm really freaking out.

I frown. "I'm sorry, but I don't think I know..."

"Jackson," he says as he takes another step forward.

I'm still confused. My thoughts flutter like rattled birds in a cage. Is that his last name or the city where we're supposed to have met?

"Jackson Holloway."

My heart stops.

Trisha's brother?

CHAPTER 2

Jackson

It is Cathy.

I didn't recognize her at once because... well, the last time I saw her, she was... what? Thirteen? She was just a girl back then. A girl with braids and braces who liked to wear long T-shirts and skinny jeans. A girl who liked to eat candy while reading inch-thick books. A girl who hated peanuts and cringed at the sight of blood. A girl who laughed at the corniest jokes and cried over the deaths of fictional characters.

She's a woman now. Her hair is swept back, tucked into a bun just above her nape, though some wisps have managed to escape and cascade over her ears. The fat in her cheeks which she used to hate is gone. Her braces are gone now, too. Instead, I catch a glimpse of perfect teeth between thin lips coated in pink gloss.

The midnight blouse she's wearing looks good on her. The color makes her hazel eyes seem a radiant gold, just like the deep blue of the Mediterranean makes the sun more dazzling as it rises above the horizon. A thin gold belt cinches it around her slim waist while the sleeves puff out gracefully around her elbows. The V-neck doesn't dip low enough to reveal any cleavage, and yet I can't help but notice those firm breasts pressing against the cotton.

I bring my gaze back to hers as I give her a smile. "It's nice to see you again, Cathy."

"Yeah." She tucks her hair behind her ear. "Same here."

She doesn't look happy to see me, though. Surprised? Yes, though that's fading now. Happy? No.

"How are you?" I ask her.

"Good."

Another automatic response that comes with a forced smile. Then again, I can imagine her life hasn't been easy, not after what happened to her and Trisha. Maybe just as hard as mine. She was just as much a sister to Trisha as Trisha was to me, after all. Thick as thieves, they were. Two peas in a pod. Looking back now, maybe I should have reached out to her right after the tragedy. We could have helped each other move on. But I was too... busy. At any rate, I'm glad to see her standing in front of me now. She may not be "good", but the fact that she's here means she's at least trying to get by. That's commendable enough.

"Well, you look good," I tell her as my gaze goes over her once more, this time taking in her cream-colored slacks and her pointy silver shoes as well.

"Thanks." She gives a sheepish grin. "You, too. You look..."

She pauses as she searches for the right words.

I chuckle. "It's okay. You can say it. I don't look like a creep anymore."

Cathy frowns. "I never said you looked like a creep."

That's because she never spoke to me much. She would usually only come over to pick up Trisha when they were going somewhere together. She'd wait for her as she gathered her stuff and we'd see each other, wave and exchange obligatory smiles and sometimes say "Hi" and "Hello" and all that, but we didn't really have conversations. The one time I tried to talk to her, I just scared her and then Trisha told me to stay away from her. I think she told Cathy to stay away from me, too. She was a moody teenager. Or maybe that's redundant. Anyway, one day she adored me and the next she couldn't stand to be related to me.

"But you thought I did," I say.

"No." Cathy shakes her head. "I just... thought you were a... nerd, which you were."

"Ah." I tap my fingers on my hip. "The truth comes out."

"Clearly, you're not one anymore." She glances at my arms.

I scratch my chin. "Sure about that?"

"Well, at the very least, you don't look..."

"Malnourished?" I supply the adjective.

"I was going to say thin."

I narrow my eyes at her. "Are you saying I'm fat?"

"No. You're..."

I wave a hand. "I'm just teasing you. I know what you mean."

I'm well aware of how many pounds I've gained.

Cathy gives another frown.

"So, how have you been?" I change the subject. "Are you married now?"

"No," she answers with an edge of impatience.

She must be asked that a lot.

"Boyfriend?"

Cathy rolls her eyes. "You're starting to sound like my mom."

I fold my arms over my chest. "How is she?"

"Good," she answers.

This time, she sounds more convincing.

"How's yours?" she asks.

"She passed away a few years ago," I tell her.

Her eyes grow wide. "I'm so sorry."

I shake my head. "She and Trisha must be spending lots of time together now."

I notice her flinch before she goes silent. Okay. Maybe I shouldn't have said that.

I clear my throat as I lower my arms. "So, what brings you here? If you heard of my new restaurant and came here to try my food, I'm afraid you're a few weeks early."

Cathy's eyebrows furrow. "Your restaurant?"

"Guess you haven't heard." I lean on the nearby counter. "I'm a chef now. And a restaurant owner. This one will be my tenth."

"Wow." I see the admiration in her eyes. "I guess you're a big shot now."

I shrug. "Big enough to give you a free three-course meal and a bottle of wine if you come back in a few weeks."

"Well, actually..." She fidgets with the strap of her purse. "I came here about the internship."

"Internship?" I scratch my beard. "Oh, you mean the management internship. Well, in that case..."

"But I'm not sure I want it anymore," Cathy adds quickly as she touches the back of her neck. "I didn't..."

"Did someone say 'management internship'?" Ken interrupts as she walks into the kitchen.

I glance at her. She looks like she's in a good mood today. The keys to the bike she proudly calls Cara jingle from the waistband of her jeans. Her hair, which seems to have a fresh coat of purple, is swept into a stylish mess. Her lipstick matches her red leather jacket.

"Let me guess," I say. "You sorted out the problem with the tables."

She gives me a wide grin. "Of course I did. Who do you think I am?"

I turn to Cathy. "Cathy, meet Kendra Moore, the best restaurant manager in the world."

"Almost perfect," Ken tells me. "Except for the fact that you said my name was Kendra."

"That is your name," I remind her.

She glances at Cathy. "Rule number one - don't ever call me that."

"She'll run you over with her bike if you do," I add.

"Call me Ken."

Cathy just gives a weak smile.

"Ken will be managing this restaurant," I explain. "And I do believe she's looking for an intern."

"The last one quit last night after just one day," Ken says. "Admittedly, it was not one of my best days. Still, think you can last longer?"

Cathy draws a breath. "Actually, I - "

"What's your name again?" Ken asks.

"Cathy."

"Short for Catherine?"

"No, just Cathy," she and I reply at the same time.

I remember my mom asking her the same question and Cathy giving the same answer.

"Well, just Cathy," Ken turns to her with a hand on her hip, "do you want the internship or not?"

She tightens her grip on the strap of her purse. "I'm... grateful for your offer, but on second thought, I don't think this will suit me after all."

Ken looks at me. "What did you do to scare her?"

"You're the one who scared her," I allege.

"Did I?" Ken asks Cathy.

She shakes her head. "It's just that while I was driving here, I realized that it's a bit far from where I live, farther than I expected."

"We did want to put the restaurant somewhere away from the city," I say. "I thought the diners would enjoy their meal better listening to the symphony of the waves rather than the discord of traffic."

"Where do you live?" Ken asks.

"More than an hour away," Cathy answers. "Besides, I don't really know what I'm supposed to do here."

"That's why I'm going to explain things to you," Ken says. "And mind you, I've been called a good mentor."

"Ken will teach you everything you need to know as you help her with her tasks," I tell Cathy. "If you have any questions or concerns, you can talk to her or me."

Ken narrows her gaze at me. "Since when have you taken an interest in interns?"

"Why not? They technically work for me," I answer.

"I thought you were busy."

"Not always."

Ken snorts.

I look at Cathy. "If you decide to do the internship, you'll get an hourly wage, free meals and allowances for clothing and transportation."

"Allowances?" Ken raises an eyebrow.

I ignore her. "And although the internship is only for four months, you can get a job here after."

"If you last," Ken adds.

That seems to catch Cathy's interest.

"You mean you'll hire me? For a real job?" she asks.

"If we think you're good enough," Ken says.

She means if she thinks Cathy's good enough. As for me, I think my mind is already made up. If Cathy is as smart and responsible as she used to be, she'll do just fine.

"You'll never know unless you try," Ken goes on. "Besides, you need a job, don't you? Isn't that why you drove all the way here in the first place?"

Cathy doesn't answer.

I place a hand on her shoulder. "Listen, Cathy, if you don't want to work here, I won't force you. But if you're just hesitating because you doubt your abilities, don't. I know you can do this."

She looks away. I can almost see the wheels inside her head turning as she wrestles with her thoughts.

Why is she hesitating? Didn't she come here for the internship? Is it because of me? Because she can't stand to be around me? Because I remind her of who she lost?

I squeeze her shoulder. "Cathy..."

"Daddy!" The high-pitched squeal of a little girl draws my attention.

I go down on my knees and spread my arms wide to welcome my daughter. "Hey, sweetheart."

She crashes right into me, nearly toppling me over.

"Whoa!"

"Daddy, let's go," Maisie tells me as she wraps her little hands around my neck.

I glance at my watch. Right. It's almost time for her tumbling class.

"Okay, okay." I carry her in my arms as I get on my feet.

As soon as I'm standing, I see the stove. Shit. I forgot about what I was cooking.

"Five minutes," I say as I put her down.

Maisie frowns. As I walk over to my pot, I hear Ken talking to her.

"Don't worry, sweetheart. Your Daddy won't take long."

I smile. Sure, she can be tough, but she's a softie at heart.

"Who is she?" I hear Maisie ask.

I glance over my shoulder to find her pointing to Cathy.

"Hi." Cathy gives the first genuine smile I've seen since she arrived. "I'm Cathy."

"Cathy is still thinking about whether she wants to work here or not," Ken says.

I suppress a grin as I turn my attention to my pot and stir the chowder. It still seems okay. Ken sounds like she's trying to get Maisie's help in convincing Cathy to take the internship. Clever.

"You're a chef, too?" Maisie asks.

"No," Cathy answers.

"Oh, she won't be working in the kitchen," Ken says. "She'll be in management, like me."

I hear a pause. "But she doesn't look like you."

Cathy chuckles. I grin as well.

"You're pretty," Maisie adds.

I glance again to catch the look of admiration lighting up her face.

"What? Are you saying I'm not pretty?" I hear Ken complain.

Maisie laughs.

"Why, thank you, sweetheart," Cathy tells her. "You're quite stunning yourself."

"What's stunning?" Maisie asks.

"It means you look like a princess from a fairy tale," Cathy answers.

"What's a fairy tale?"

Cathy gasps. "You don't know about fairy tales?"

I pause in the act of bringing a spoon to my lips and frown. I've bought Maisie a ton of books, but somehow I haven't found the time to read her a single story. Pathetic.

I taste the dish. It needs just another pinch of Szechuan pepper. As I reach for the bottle, I hear Cathy speak.

"Well, who knows? Maybe I can tell you one or read one to you sometime."

Maisie giggles.

My eyes grow wide. Cathy will do that?

"Only if you're around," Ken says. "So does this mean you're our new intern?"

I pause, waiting for her answer as well.

Cathy sighs. "Well, I do need a job."

I smile triumphantly. I'd throw my fist into the air if I wasn't holding the bottle of pepper. As it is, I sprinkle just a bit more into the pot and stir.

"Did you hear that, Jackson?" Ken asks me.

"Yup." I bring the spoon to my lips once more.

Perfect.

"Great!" Ken clasps her hands together. "Another intern."

"Hurray!" Maisie cheers as well.

I turn off the stove, cover the pot and walk towards her.

"Thank goodness we've got a lucky charm," I say as I lift her in my arms.

She squeals.

"She is charming," Cathy tells me.

"Hmm." I touch my chin. "I wonder where she gets it from."

Ken snorts. "Well, you go get that charmer to tumbling class. Cathy and I have business to discuss."

"As you wish," I answer.

As the owner of the restaurant, I'm supposed to be the one giving orders, and yet I somehow always find myself unable to disobey Ken's. She's just that good at managing people.

I look into Cathy's eyes. "I'll see you tomorrow."

"See you tomorrow," Maisie echoes.

"See you," Cathy replies as she waves her hand.

As I carry Maisie to the door, Ken whisks Cathy away. I sure hope she doesn't give Cathy a hard time.

I shake my head as I withdraw the thought. Why am I so worried about her? She's not my little sister.

"What's wrong, Daddy?" Maisie asks.

I meet her questioning gaze. Even at four, she can be so perceptive.

Just like her mother.

"Nothing," I answer before planting a kiss on her soft cheek. "How was your day, hmm? Did you have fun playing with your toys?"

She pouts. "I want Ella."

I frown at the mention of the nanny I fired for having sex with a cook. Well, technically, for having sex with a cook in the bathroom while Maisie was just a few feet away, sitting on the bed and watching TV all alone. And to think I was paying her three times the going rate. I thought she was good. I thought I could count on her to take care of the person who matters more to me than anything else in the world. Yet it seemed that she didn't care for Maisie at all. Who knows how long she'd been leaving Maisie alone to do God knows what? What if Maisie had seen her? Or worse, what if something had happened to Maisie while she was... busy? I still have to stop myself from cringing whenever I think of it.

"Ella isn't coming back, sweetheart," I tell my daughter as we leave the house.

She sticks out her lower lip and gives me a face that looks ready to burst with tears. "But I want someone to play with."

I stroke her back and press my lips to the top of her head. "I'll find someone, I promise. Soon."

Right now, with the new restaurant set to open in a few weeks, I just don't have the time to look for a nanny. I'm well aware it's not an easy procedure, and I have to do it myself. The last time I had a nanny sent by an agency, things didn't end well.

"What about Cathy?" Maisie asks. "She's nice."

I smile. I should have known Maisie would take to her. Maisie has always liked beautiful women, maybe because they look like dolls. Or maybe she's just looking for a mother.

"Cathy is nice, isn't she?" I agree.

All those times that I saw her come over to the house, I never heard her pick a fight with Trisha or say a single mean thing to her. And God knows Trisha could be a pain to deal with sometimes.

"Unfortunately, she'll be busy."

"Like you?" Maisie asks me.

I feel a pang in my heart.

"Hey." I touch the tip of her nose. "I'm never too busy for you."

It's true, sort of. If ever Maisie's life was in danger, I just know I'd drop everything. Unfortunately, unless that's the case, I can't just walk away from the empire I'm building. It's for her, too.

"Then maybe Cathy isn't too busy," Maisie says.

I shrug. "Maybe you can ask her if she can play with you when she doesn't have too much to do."

That brings a sparkle to Maisie's eyes. Ah, how simple things can make a child so happy.

I squeeze her tight.

And whatever makes her happy makes me happy.

"Daddy," Maisie complains as she wriggles against my chest.

"Sorry." I loosen my arms. "I got carried away. And you know why?"

Her ponytail sways to and fro as she shakes her head.

"Because you're so cute."

I pinch her cheek and then tickle her neck. She lets out an explosion of squeals and laughter.

"Dad...dy!"

I stop after she gives a particularly loud squeal. I may have been able to secure a permit to put up a restaurant in this neighborhood, but it's still a residential area, and I don't want any parents thinking I'm trying to hurt a kid, or any old couples scolding us for being too noisy. Best be on their good side, at least until the restaurant opens.

Besides, I can already see the car.

I'm almost next to it when my phone rings. I take it out of my pocket and frown as I see the name of my mother-in-law on the screen.

How can I even have a mother-in-law when I no longer have a wife?

I'd like to ignore her, but by now, I know that's not a wise thing to do. Best to get this over with.

"Betty." I force a smile as I hold the phone against my ear. "It's nice of you to call, but now's not a good time. I have to - "

"How's Maisie?"

Of course she's not listening. She never does.

"Good," I answer. "I'm taking her to tumbling class now."

"Tumbling class?" I hear the disapproval in her voice.

"Yes, you know, where they run around and jump and climb things for an hour. I told you this before."

"What? You couldn't find something more educational?"

I sigh. Of course she'd turn this conversation into another argument. Frankly, I'm getting tired of it.

"Daddy?" Maisie lifts her little eyebrows.

I set her down but hold her hand. "Just a moment, sweetheart."

"Jackson?" Betty's impatient voice prods me from the other end of the line.

"We have to go, Betty."

"To a class where Maisie won't learn anything and might break her bones?"

I should have known she wouldn't let me off the hook so easily.

"It's good for her," I say. "She's learning to get along with other kids. She gets exercise. And there are a lot of people watching her."

"How many?"

I suppress another sigh. "Enough."

"But why tumbling class? Why not piano lessons? Or violin? Or golf? Or chess?"

"She's not interested in any of those."

"How would you know if she hasn't tried them?"

"She's four, Betty," I point out. "If she was ready for education, she'd be in kindergarten."

"Well, have you tried getting her into one?"

"They'll take her next year," I say. "Most children go when they're five, not four."

"But isn't she almost five? Surely you can talk to the school. Or find one that will. After all, my granddaughter's a genius."

I glance at Maisie. Granted, she's smart. Sometimes, when I'm talking to her, I feel like I'm talking to a ten-year-old. But genius?

"She'll go next year," I insist. "I've read that sending children to school too young backfires later on."

Reading Smart Parenting is helpful after all. Take that, Betty.

She snorts. "Says who?"

"Experts."

Another snort. "You're just too busy to do what's best for her. If you don't have the time, I can - "

"Betty, I've got this," I cut her off. "We're fine."

I can put up with her condescending tone and her excessive "expert advice" because I know she cares about Maisie, but I won't have her say I'm not taking care of my own daughter.

"You say that, but are you really? It seems like..."

I stop listening as Maisie lets go of my hand and bolts.

"Maisie!"

She runs after the yellow butterfly fluttering in front of her, chasing it to the corner of the sidewalk.

"Jackson?"

I ignore Betty's voice and run after my daughter. "Maisie!"

To my relief, she stops at the corner - but then suddenly she screams and falls to the pavement.

"Maisie!"

As soon as I'm by her side, I see what scared her - a teenage boy on a bike, its front wheel just a foot away. The boy seems terrified as well.

"Shit," he mutters as he takes off his headphones.

"Watch it," I scold him as I pull a shaking Maisie into my arms. "And watch where you're going. This is the sidewalk. People are walking."

He puts his headphones back on and rides off.

"Hey!" I call after him, but he keeps pedaling.

Why, that son of a...

"Daddy," Maisie whimpers as she buries her head against my chest.

I decide to let the boy go and tend to my little girl.

"Are you alright?" I stroke her cheek.

She nods.

"Jackson! Jackson!" I hear Betty screaming from my phone.

I guess she's still there.

"I'll call you later," I tell her before hanging up.

Right now, Maisie needs me.

"Are you alright?" I ask her again as I look into her eyes.

Like before, she nods.

I place my hand against her cheek. "Don't ever let go of my hand again, okay?"

Instead of answering, she wraps her arms around me as she rests her head on my shoulder.

"Shh." I stroke her hair. "You're alright now. Everything's alright. Daddy's here. And I promise that I won't let anything bad happen to you."

I'm not the best father, I know, but I can swear that much. And I mean it. Whatever it takes, I'm not going to let anything bad happen to my daughter.

CHAPTER 3

Cathy

This is bad.

I slam the car door closed before running towards the restaurant - only to rush back and open it again because I've forgotten my phone on the dashboard.

I start running again as I slip it inside my purse. The heels of my shoes clack against the pavement.

Shit. Maybe I should just wear sneakers like Ken.

Better yet, maybe I should have left my apartment sooner.

I fully intended to. I got out of bed before my alarm went off. I had just toast and an apple for breakfast. I put on the clothes that I'd prepared the night before as quickly as I could.

The problem was that I spilled the last bit of my coffee as I was on my way to deposit the mug in the sink. Why do I have to be such a klutz sometimes? I had to change clothes, which took time. Then when I went out the door, I stepped on cat poop. Just my luck. I had to scrub the soles of my shoes in the bathroom so my apartment wouldn't stink, then change into new ones. By the time I got into my car, I realized I could be running late. I thought I still had a chance of getting to work on time on my first day, though... right up until I got stuck in traffic because of some stupid driver who somehow crashed his car into the front of a barber shop.

It's just one of those days when the universe seems to be conspiring against me. And it's only 8:20.

"You're late," Ken tells me as soon as I set foot in the yard.

She's standing on the front steps with her hands on her hips. The heel of her sneaker taps the wood impatiently.

"I know."

I stop in front of her and place my hands on my knees as I catch my breath.

"I'm so sorry."

"Sorry? You think customers will forgive a waiter for serving them the wrong dish if he just says sorry? You think a cook should be let off the hook for sending out raw meat if he says sorry? You think a supplier should be forgiven for giving us poor quality vegetables so long as he says sorry?"

I meet her gaze. Something tells me this is the real Ken - the one who means business, who demands nothing less than perfection. No wonder the other intern didn't last long. I have to say I myself am a little scared. Even so, I can't bring myself to dislike her. She's not wrong.

"I'll do whatever I need to to make up for it," I tell her with as much earnestness as I can muster.

Now that I've signed up for this internship, I have to show her I'm just as serious as she is.

Ken nods as she crosses her arms over her chest. "Good. You'll do that today. Tomorrow, come on time, though. Punctuality is of the utmost importance when you're running a restaurant. No one likes to be kept waiting, hungry people least of all."

"I understand. I won't be late again."

For a moment, she stays silent, her narrowed eyes studying mine as if she can see my soul through them or gauge the worth of my words. Finally, the tension on her face eases.

"Good." The corners of her mouth turn up slightly. "Now, let's get to work."

~

Just as I thought, working under Ken isn't easy. She never runs out of things for me to do, and if I lose focus for just a second, she's on me like a vulture on a carcass, pecking until I come back to life.

As I take my second break on the balcony, I kick off my shoes and stretch my arms. The breeze feels wonderful against my cheeks.

Note to self - tomorrow, wear something comfortable. And maybe bring another set of clothes. And a towel so I can wipe off all this sweat. And a pain reliever in case I get a headache. And a basin of water I can soak my feet in to relieve some of my stress. Okay, maybe not that last one, but all those other things.

I let out a deep breath. An internship is even harder than I thought.

Is a real job just as hard? No wonder some people get burned out or look like corpses by the time they retire. And yet, no one really has a choice. If you don't work, you don't get money, which you need to pay bills, to survive. But if you do work, you get tired all the time, too tired to have any fun. It seems like in order to survive, you have to give up living. Cruel, but nothing can be done about it.

I shake my head. Why am I entertaining such depressing notions when I've only just started working? Surely I don't want to hide in my room forever, to rely on Mom forever?

It's high time I live my own life.

The sound of laughter from below scatters my thoughts. I peer over the railing and see Maisie laughing and running in circles as Jackson chases her.

I smile. Children have it easy, alright.

My gaze goes over to Jackson. I still can't believe I'm working for him, or that I've met him again after so many years. And I still can't believe how... hot he's become.

Yes, I admit it. He's a hunk now.

He wasn't before. He was a pencil neck with thick glasses that kept sliding down his nose and hair that always looked like he just got out of bed. That's why I never paid him much attention. Now, though, he's got these movie star features and a body worthy of a gym ad.

As I watch him, my gaze is drawn like a magnet to his tight ass outlined by his tight jeans, and to his broad shoulders and his toned arms. And I don't normally ogle men.

I lick my lips. How on earth does someone so puny end up with a body worthy of being enshrined in spandex?

"Why so serious during your break?" Ken's question breaks into my thoughts.

I quickly turn towards her. "Serious? No. I was just..."

What? Drooling over an old acquaintance who happens to be my current boss?

"Admiring the view," I say for lack of anything better.

Ken peers over the railing. "Hmm. Some view indeed."

I blush. "I wasn't..."

"Save it." Ken lifts a hand. "I may not act like a woman most of the time, but I still am one. I'm well aware that Mr. Jackson Holloway down there is one premium piece of meat."

I lift an eyebrow as I look at her. "So you...?"

"What? Want to eat him all up like you do?" Ken snorts.

I frown. "I don't..."

"Don't worry. I'm not interested in him. Or men, for that matter."

I'd guessed as much.

"I'm not worried," I tell her as I square my shoulders. "I don't want to... eat him all up like you said."

What am I? A cannibal?

"Mm-hmm." Ken nods but doesn't look at all convinced.

"I was just thinking how much he's changed," I add. "Since I last met him."

"Right. I think Jackson did mention that you knew each other. Something about growing up together? Childhood friends?"

"Not us," I say. "It was me and... his sister."

My hand instinctively goes over my chest as I feel it tighten.

Ken taps her fingers on the railing. "I see."

I wait for her to ask me questions, but she doesn't. It makes me wonder if she knows about what happened. Does Jackson talk about it?

"How about you?" I ask her. "How long have you known Jackson?"

"About three years," Ken answers. "Since he put up that restaurant in Toronto."

So I guess she knows him well. Well, they do seem to get along.

"He may not look it, but he's an amazing chef," Ken adds.

I turn around to look at him once more. This time, he's lying on the grass, lifting Maisie on his knees and holding her by the armpits as she spreads her arms so that she seems to be flying above him.

"He seems to be a great father, too," I remark.

"Yup," Ken agrees. "He may not spend as much time with her as he should, but he tries his best. I think that's what's important."

I nod.

"Besides, it's not like it's easy being a single dad," Ken adds.

Single dad? That bit of information piques my interest.

"What happened to his wife?" I ask curiously.

Ken gives a deep sigh. "She died shortly after giving birth to Maisie."

I frown. "I'm sorry to hear that."

"It is quite tragic," Ken remarks. "Then again, things happen for a reason, don't they?"

"Do they?"

I still don't know the reason why Trisha had to die.

Ken pats my shoulder. "Some things end so that other things can begin. Jackson lost his wife and Maisie lost her mother, but who knows? Someone might come along to take care of them both."

"You think so?"

Jackson doesn't seem like he's looking for a new wife. Or is he?

"She might even come sooner than they think."

She turns to me with a meaningful grin.

Wait. She's not implying that I should marry Jackson, is she? That's the most ridiculous thing I've ever heard.

I narrow my eyes at her. "If you're saying - "

"Whoa, look at the time." Ken looks at her watch. "We should get back to work."

Before I can say more, she goes back inside. I let out a breath before following her.

There's no way I can fill the void Maisie's mother left behind. I may like kids, but I don't know the first thing about being a mother. Or a wife, for that matter. Besides, they seem happy enough. They have each other. They love each other. They don't need anyone else.

Then again, if Trisha were alive, she'd probably be the one taking care of them.

I gaze up at the sky, beyond the clouds.

Is that what you want me to do? Take care of them? Is that why you brought me here?

As before, I hear no answer, so I come up with my own.

No way, I think as I shake my head. Didn't she tell me to stay away from her brother?

Still, I can't help but wonder.

~

By evening, I've forgotten about it. With all the work Ken has dumped on me, I haven't had time to think about anything else. I'm still working, in fact. I've kept my word and decided to work overtime to make up for being late this morning. Ken has already left. My fingers tapping the keys as I put numbers into spreadsheets is the only sound in the office, but I can still hear some machines whirring outside.

I guess it's just me and the workers left here now.

Or so I think until the door opens. Jackson comes in holding two steaming mugs of coffee.

"I thought you might need this," he tells me as he sets one of them on my desk.

"Thank you."

I pick it up with both hands and close my eyes as I breathe in the bittersweet aroma of the roasted coffee beans. I lift it to my lips to take a sip. As the warm liquid flows down my throat, a sense of calm washes over me. I wasn't sure I needed this, but now that my mind feels clearer, I'm grateful for it.

"Do you like it?" Jackson asks me. "I wasn't sure how you take your coffee."

"I do," I answer.

As I take a second sip, I taste hints of vanilla, cinnamon and hazelnut, even a dash of mint. The combination makes the coffee on the sweeter side, but I can still feel the kick. It's just how I like it.

"Shouldn't the intern be the one bringing the boss coffee, though?"

Jackson chuckles. "You watch too many TV shows."

He pulls a chair near my desk.

"Mind if I keep you company for a bit?"

I shrug. "You're the boss."

He turns the chair around and sits on it with his legs on either side.

"Where's Maisie?" I ask.

"Sleeping in the next room. She got tired from playing all day."

"Better to be tired from playing all day than from working all day, right?"

Jackson nods. "You have a point."

He takes a sip from his mug. I tap mine.

"I heard about your wife," I say as I gaze into the bronze liquid.

He lowers his mug. "So Ken told you, did she?"

I nod. "I'm sorry."

He shakes his head. "It's not your fault she died. It was her time to go."

"Well, at least she left someone for you."

"You're right." Jackson smiles. "And I'll forever be grateful."

I, too, smile as I remember him and Maisie playing earlier. She's one lucky girl to have a father who loves her so much.

"You know, she likes you," Jackson tells me.

"Does she?"

"She said you're nice."

I smile wider. "She's a good judge of character then."

"You have no idea. I think she's wiser than some adults I know."

"She does seem like a smart girl."

Jackson nods. "Smart. Independent. Sociable. Kind. Brave."

As he enumerates the qualities of his daughter, his eyes glisten with pride. My chest swells with warmth.

"She can be stubborn, too, though."

I grin. "Can she?"

He looks past the window. "Actually, she reminds me of Trisha sometimes."

My fingers grow still around my mug.

Trisha. I guess it's inevitable for her name to come up when I'm talking to her brother. I just don't understand how Jackson can speak of her so easily when I can't even say her name even after all this time.

"Sorry," he says. "I know you must still miss her. You two were very close, after all."

I set my mug down. "It's not just that. Each time I think of her, it hurts because I can't even remember the last time I was with her."

"What do you mean?"

I hesitate for a moment but decide there's no harm in telling Jackson.

"I... can't remember what happened... the night she..." I pause to swallow the lump in my throat. "That night. I... drowned, too, so apparently something happened to my brain and I can't remember some things."

"I see." Jackson touches his chin. "I'm sorry to hear that."

"I wish I could remember. Maybe then I'd finally be able to move on."

Jackson gets out of his chair and stands next to me. His hand lands on my shoulder.

"I'm sure it will come back to you someday," he says as he squeezes it. "And if not, maybe that's better. Maybe that's what Trisha wants - for you to just remember all the good times you had and not how they ended."

I look at him. "You think?"

He nods. "And you know her. What she wants, she usually gets."

I grin. "Yeah. That sounds like her."

He pats my shoulder. "There. A smile looks better on you."

I look away as I try not to blush.

"I'm sure Trisha would want you to be happy, too," he adds. "She'd only want the best for her best friend."

Jackson's words take me by surprise. Like a wave, they crash against my heart, breaking through its hard shell and seeping in through the cracks. They wash some of the pain and anxiety away.

Are they what I've been longing to hear all this time?

I meet his gaze as I place my hand over his. "Thank you."

Jackson's lips curve into a soft smile. "You're welcome. And if there's anything you need, if you ever need anyone to talk to, you can always come to me."

More words of comfort - but this time, they seem to have a different effect. My pulse quickens. My breath catches as I gaze into those dark pools that seem to glimmer with warmth. I become acutely aware of his hand on my shoulder, his fingers beneath mine.

I pull my hand away and reach for my mug, wishing there was still some steam left to hide my burning cheeks as I lift it to my lips.

Oh, what am I getting all hot and bothered for? He's just acting like a big brother, that's all. He probably misses being one.

I set my mug back down on the desk. "I should get back to work. I need to finish some stuff for Ken."

"You do that." Jackson pats my shoulder again. "But don't work too hard."

I snort. "I've only just started."

"And don't mind Ken too much. She may be tough, but she just wants everything to be successful. She wants you to be successful, too."

I nod. "I know that."

"I think she's really glad that you're her intern. So am I."

Again with the warmth tingling in my cheeks. I ignore it as I fix my eyes on the computer screen and position my fingers on the keyboard.

"I'm grateful for the opportunity, too."

"Well, good night. And drive safely later."

"Good night." I steal a glance as I lift my mug. "Again, thanks for the coffee."

"Welcome."

He walks to the door. I wrap both hands around my mug and press the rim to my lips to keep myself from looking at him. If I do, our eyes might meet again and that smile of his might just send a bolt of electricity down my spine that would speed up my poor heart even more and turn my brain to mush.

Finally, I hear the door close. I put my mug down and let out a breath. Then I rest my hands over the keys once more and start typing.

Back to work, Cathy.

CHAPTER 4

Jackson

She's already here.

A smile forms on my lips as I see Cathy's Toyota parked across from the restaurant just after I get out of my SUV.

I've already dropped Maisie off at a local daycare, which she seems to love, which means that today I'll have more time to work on the new recipe I'm planning to premiere for the restaurant's opening. I have a feeling I'll finally get it perfect today, too.

It's going to be a great day.

I decide to check on Cathy before I head to the kitchen. I open the door to the manager's office, my smile still on my face as I prepare to greet her. As soon as I step inside, though, I notice her lying on the couch.

Cathy?

My heart hammers as I wonder if something bad has happened to her, but as I stand above the couch, I let out a breath of relief.

She's just sleeping, turned to her side. Her eyes are closed. The tendrils of her hair are washed over her cheek. Her grey cardigan is draped over her like a blanket. It only covers the upper part of her body, though, and I can clearly see her legs, clad in black nylon, stretching out past the hem of her sangria-colored dress.

My eyebrows arch. Wait. Isn't that the dress she was wearing yesterday?

I remember because it reminded me of a beet ice cream I once made. I even remember thinking that maybe I should have served it with a few olives because the black and deep red looked so striking and appetizing together. At least, the combination looked good on Cathy.

I look down at her shoes. Sandals. Was she wearing sandals yesterday?

I walk over to her desk. The computer is still on. The mug that she drank coffee from last night is still there, now empty except for a thin layer at the bottom.

I glance at Cathy. Can it be that she didn't go home last night?

Come to think of it, her car is still parked in the same spot.

Just then, the door opens.

"Early today, I see," Ken says as she enters the room with a skip in her step.

She stops, though, when she sees me, and then her eyebrows furrow as she glances at the couch.

"Don't tell me she came here early and went back to sleep."

"No," I answer. "I don't think she went home at all."

Ken's jaw drops. "What the hell?"

Cathy stirs. She brushes the hair out of her face and rubs her eyes as she lies on her back. Then she opens them, and as soon as she sees me, her body jerks into a sitting position. Her cardigan falls to the floor.

"I'm sorry," she mumbles as she picks it up.

She wipes her mouth with the back of her hand, then the corners of her eyes with her fingertips. She starts to comb her hair with her fingers next. When she sees Ken, alarm fills her face.

"Shit. Am I late again? Did I oversleep?"

I fold my arms over my chest as I walk to the couch. "You didn't go home, did you?"

"No," Cathy admits. "It was already late when I finished work."

"What time?" Ken asks curiously. "I thought you were only going to stay an hour."

"I left past eight and she was still here," I say.

"Ten." Cathy scratches the back of her head. "I think."

Ken lifts an eyebrow. "Ten?"

"I thought I might as well finish those spreadsheets you asked me to do," Cathy says.

"All of them?"

Cathy gives a sheepish grin. "After a cup of coffee, I felt like I had enough energy to finish them, so..."

I frown. So it's my fault.

"I guess I could still have gone home, but I was afraid I'd be late again, so I just decided to stay here. It's not... forbidden, is it?"

Forbidden? No. Careless? Yes.

The security cameras haven't been installed yet, and the workers sleep on site. All men. Stocky, brawny men with heavy tools, many of whom have already spent weeks away from their wives.

What on earth was Cathy thinking?

Ken looks at me and sighs. "What am I going to do with her? I don't know whether I should be happy or I should get mad."

I'm mad.

"You should have gone home when I did," I tell Cathy.

"Right." She puts a hand on her neck. "Sorry. It won't happen again."

"No, it won't," I assure her. "Because you'll be staying with me from now on."

Cathy's eyes grow wide. "What?"

"You live more than an hour away. You said it yourself. The house I'm renting is just two blocks away and it has plenty of rooms. You can stay with me."

She stands up and shakes her head. "No. I can't. I..."

"It's not a bad arrangement," Ken speaks. "If you stay with Jackson, you'll never be late. Even if you go home late, it's fine. You think things are busy now? Wait until the restaurant opens."

"But I have an apartment," Cathy reasons.

"Which you didn't go home to last night," I point out. "What good is an apartment if you don't sleep in it? If you're not staying there, it's better that you sleep at my house than here at the office. It's safer."

Ken nods. "Jackson does have a point."

Still, Cathy shakes her head. "Then I'll find another apartment. One that's closer."

"You mean you'd rather pay for an apartment when Jackson is offering you a room for free?" Ken asks her. "Tell me something. The paycheck you're getting at the end of the week - it's your first, isn't it?"

Cathy looks down at her hands as she nods.

"Wouldn't you rather spend that on food? Or new shoes? Or a gift for your mother?"

"Yes, but - "

"Let me give you a word of advice, Cathy." Ken places a hand on her shoulder. "When you're just starting out, there's no shame in accepting all the help you can get. In fact, you need all the help you can get."

"She's right," I second.

Cathy meets my gaze. "I'm just an intern, though."

"So?" I shrug. "You're still on my payroll. Besides, you're not just an intern."

Cathy looks away.

I touch her arm. "Let me help you, Cathy."

"Yes, let him." Ken rests her elbow on Cathy's shoulder and leans on her. "He's got loads of money, so he can afford it."

I say nothing because it's true.

"And if you still feel guilty about not paying rent, you can just watch Maisie during your free time," Ken adds. "I'm sure she'd love that."

My eyebrows go up. A part-time nanny for Maisie and a place close to the restaurant for Cathy. Genius!

I should treat Ken to a beer later on.

Cathy lifts her head to meet my gaze. "Are you sure?"

I nod. "Absolutely. I think it's best for everyone if you stay with me."

Ken nods. "Mm-hmm. If it doesn't work out, you can try something else, but I don't see why you can't give this a try."

For a moment, Cathy falls silent. Then she lets out a deep breath.

"Fine," she gives in. "I'll stay with Jackson."

I give her a smile. "Good answer. You can take half the day off so you can get your things, then later, you can come home with me."

"Half the day off?" Ken's eyebrows arch at me, but then she sighs as she turns to Cathy. "Fine. You heard the boss."

"Thanks," Cathy says.

I pat her shoulder and nod at Ken. "Now, let's all go to work. The day has already started."

And I have a feeling it's going to be even better than I thought.

~

At the end of the day, just as we agreed, I bring Cathy home. Maisie falls asleep in the car as she usually does - if she isn't asleep before she gets inside the car, she falls asleep in the car - so I deposit her in her bed first. Then I give Cathy a tour of the house.

It's a two-story house, not more than five years old. Or so the agent told me. There's nothing grand or stylish about it. I didn't ask for that. All I asked for was a house near the restaurant with a spacious kitchen I can lose myself in and plenty of room for a little girl to run around and not much glass for her to risk running into. Oh, and a spiral staircase. Maisie loves those. Besides, with a spiral staircase, there's less harm if she trips.

I pause at the bottom of that staircase to get another piece of Cathy's luggage before letting her go ahead of me. She doesn't have much - just a backpack, a suitcase, something framed, and a plastic storage box filled to the brim with odds and ends.

She glances over her shoulder. "Are you sure I can stay here?"

"I don't see why not. You're practically family."

That makes her stop on the steps. Her fingers grows still around the railing.

Shit. Did I make her think of Trisha again?

I move a step up. "Besides, this house is too big for just Maisie and me."

Cathy keeps going. "You mean you're the only ones who live here?"

"In this house? Yes." I set her suitcase down on the floor as we reach the top of the stairs. "There's a family living above the detached garage. The man tends to the grounds and his wife and niece clean the house every day."

"I see."

"So you see, there's plenty of room for you," I tell her as I pick the suitcase up again and lead her down a hall. "You can take any guest room you like, and there are plenty of places for you to hide. Unless you come to the kitchen, there's little chance you'll bump into me."

"Hide?" Cathy gives me a puzzled look. "You sound like I'm trying to avoid you."

Isn't she? I can almost swear she hasn't been happy to see me since... well, since she saw me. Except for last night when I brought her coffee, but then she sent me away moments after. Plus I notice she rarely looks into my eyes.

It must be because of Trisha. Like she said, she still misses what she's lost, and I probably remind her of it.

Still, if she wants to deny it, I'll go along.

"I'm just saying if you want to be alone, you know, to think, or just do things by yourself..."

"What things?"

I shrug. "You know, secret girly rituals."

Cathy narrows her eyes at me. "Now you're making me sound naughty."

Am I? Wait. She doesn't think I'm referring to that ritual, does she?

"Just to be clear, I don't have voodoo dolls in that suitcase," she says. "Or a cauldron. Or a broom, for that matter."

So that's the "naughty" stuff she was talking about. Of course. I shouldn't have known her mind isn't as dirty as mine.

Then again, she's twenty-six. Wait. Does that mean...?

"You're not hiding a man in here, are you?" I ask to test my theory.

Cathy sends me a scowl. "You mean like a corpse? Am I a murderer now?"

I chuckle. She sure has a vivid imagination.

"I meant a live one."

She lifts an eyebrow as she points at her suitcase. "In there?"

I shrug. "Who knows? You might have brought your handsome neighbor along."

Her eyebrows furrow. "You're not making any sense."

"I was simply thinking maybe the reason you didn't want to leave your apartment was because you had a handsome neighbor you didn't want to leave behind."

Cathy snorts. "I didn't have a handsome neighbor."

"Someone who lived in the same building, then?"

She shakes her head.

"Across the street? Down the block? There was no one at all who caught your interest?"

"I... wasn't really looking."

"Have you ever looked?" I ask her. "Have you ever been on a date?"

Cathy's eyes narrow. "What's with all this talk of dates and men?"

"I'm just curious if you've ever been with one," I confess. "Didn't you...?"

I almost add "and Trisha" but manage to stop myself.

"...used to drool after boys in movies or sigh over the boys you read about in your books?"

She frowns. "You know, I think I like the old you better."

I chuckle. "You mean the younger one? The puny one? The one you stayed away from because he was so uncool?"

"I wasn't the one who said that, but yeah, the one who didn't care what other people thought and didn't show any interest in anyone else's business."

I lift an eyebrow. Is that what she thought of me?

"I take it that's a no, then."

"What?"

"You've never been with a man," I elaborate.

Cathy sighs. "Fine. No, I haven't been with a man."

So I was right.

"Happy now?"

Am I?

"Now what? Are you going to tell me I haven't lived?" she asks. "That I'm missing out on what could be a valuable experience?"

"I'm not - "

"You know what? Maybe now that I've got a job, or an internship at least, I should move on to getting a date. That way, no one will pester me about it."

"I wasn't - "

"Maybe I should bring him here." Cathy touches her chin as she considers the notion. "And hide him in one of those secret places you mentioned."

I frown as my fingers tighten around the handle of her suitcase.

The very thought of it makes me want to hurl something against the wall, the way I throw the pot when I taste something disgusting in my kitchen.

"I didn't mean - "

"I'm just kidding." Cathy waves a hand. "I'd never do such a thing. Not when I'm living in someone else's house and there's a little girl who lives here."

But she would otherwise?

"Besides, it's not like I have time for a man now," she adds. "Like what Ken said, things are going to get busier. And I don't think anyone's interested anyway."

I'm curious as to why she thinks that. Has she always thought of herself as plain and boring? Did anyone make her think that? Well, I don't. Even now, as I glance at Cathy, I find myself admiring the way wisps of her hair fall over her cheeks. A little messy, maybe, but in my years of cooking and plating up dishes, I've learned that something messy can still be beautiful and satisfying. I see the honey in her eyes, which grow wide as a painting in the hallway catches her attention. I see the quiet grace and strength with which she holds her slender shoulders as she grips the straps of her backpack. I can only imagine what invisible burden she carries on them. True, much of her remains a mystery even to me. She's always had a wall around herself. That fact only makes me more intrigued, however, just like when a dish under a cloche sends the wheels in my head turning or a dome of tempered chocolate makes me lick my lips. I can't wait to lift the cloche or crack the dome to see what surprises await on the plate.

Plain and boring? No way.

I don't tell her that, though. I've noticed compliments make her uncomfortable. I keep my silence until we reach the hall where the guest rooms are located and I set her things down.

"Pick a door," I tell her.

"Okay."

I watch Cathy as she peeks through each of the three doors. After opening the third one, she remains at the doorway.

"I like this one," she says as she taps the silver knob.

"Door number three it is."

I grab her things and bring them inside the room. She's chosen the one with the four poster bed, the cerulean curtains and the ivory dresser in the corner. Is that why she chose this room? Something tells me the rocking chair between the window and the bookshelf has more to do with it.

"Good choice," I say.

"Yup. It's not bad. Not bad at all."

As Cathy takes in the room, she shrugs off her backpack. I wince as it hits the lamp on the bedside table. She notices it in time and manages to keep it from falling, but the weight of the backpack on her arm messes with her balance and she stumbles. I catch her.

"Whoa." I place an arm around her waist while using my other arm to put her bag on the floor. "Are you alright?"

She nods. "I'm fine."

She tucks a strand of hair behind her ear as she straightens herself up. The gesture draws my attention to the smooth skin of her neck and to the scar at the base, almost an inch long. I don't think that was there before.

I reach out to touch it. "Your scar. Where did you - ?"

"Don't." Cathy places her hand over it as she steps away.

I step back. Okay. No touching.

"I think I'm alright now," she tells me. "I just have to unpack my stuff."

In other words, she's sending me away. Again.

"Okay." I back up towards the door. "If you need anything, you know what to do."

She nods. "Thanks again."

"No problem."

I walk out of the room and close the door. Afterwards, I run my fingers through my hair.

I should just leave Cathy alone, give her some space. After losing Trisha, she's probably scared to let anyone get close to her again. Who am I to tell her not to be? I felt the same after Evelyn died. I still haven't had a woman since. I haven't even brought one home except for Maisie's nannies.

Until now. Now, I have an intern at my restaurant, an old friend of Trisha's living with me.

A woman.

As I recall the feel of Cathy's body against mine when I kept her from falling, a surge of heat goes down my spine. I gaze at the taut palm of my hand as I feel it tingle.

Maybe I didn't think this through, after all.

I curl my fingers to form a fist and let it fall to my side. Well, it's too late now. I should just leave her alone like I said I would.

I pull a deep breath into my lungs.

And maybe take a long, cold shower.

~

I've just come out of the shower when I hear Maisie crying.

I grip the damp towel around my neck and run to her bedroom next door in my boxers. With each leap of my heart against my ribcage, worry swirls through my veins.

Did she have another nightmare? Did she fall off the bed and hurt herself?

When I get there, I find Cathy already there. Of course. She must have heard Maisie, too.

She's sitting on the bed, Maisie on her lap with her head snuggled against Cathy's chest. Cathy rocks her back and forth as she strokes her hair and hums a lullaby.

Maisie's sobs are already beginning to fade. Her shoulders stop trembling. Moments later, she grows still and silent. Her small fingers let go of Cathy's sleeve. Her arm drops to her side.

Cathy continues to rock her back and forth. As she lifts her head, our eyes meet. She holds a finger to her lips. I nod and let out a deep breath.

It seems like there was no need for me to worry about Maisie after all. She probably just had a nightmare. Now, she's back asleep in Cathy's arms.

Suddenly, she makes a sound, something between a whimper and a groan. Afterwards, her lips start smacking together like a fish's. Then they stop moving. Their corners twitch up into a smile.

I smile in turn. It seems like she's going to be alright now.

"Thank you," I whisper to Cathy.

She just nods.

I walk back to my room, relieved and glad. I guess it was a good decision to let Cathy stay here, after all.

CHAPTER 5

Cathy

I close my eyes as I breathe in the fresh morning air, painted with the scent of grass still heavy with beads of dew and the needles of the pine tree standing at the edge of the lawn. Soft sunlight warms my cheeks. I stretch my arms as I let out a yawn.

Finally, it's my day off. Today, I was able to sleep in, even if it was for just half an hour. Today, I can finally rest my weary muscles and battered mind. Today, I can finally take a stroll through this garden that I've been admiring from my bedroom window.

I start to follow the paved path. After a few steps, I glance at the house.

I still find it hard to believe that I live here now. Such a big house. My room alone is more than half the size of the apartment I used to live in.

I was reluctant to move in at first. Anyone would be if asked so suddenly, especially if it's moving in with your boss and his daughter. Even if I've met Jackson before and he considers me family, he's still practically a stranger. Plus, he's a man. Thoroughly so. And he's single. I couldn't just agree to live with him. I mean, what would people think?

Besides, there's still the matter of Trisha - the matter which made me think twice about taking the internship at the restaurant in the first place. Each time I look at Jackson, I can't help but think of her. They have the same mahogany eyes, after all. Do I really want to live with a man who reminds me of the best friend and the memories I've lost? And what about Trisha's warning for me to stay away from Jackson?

In the end, though, I had to agree with Ken and Jackson that it was the best thing to do. I needed to be closer to the restaurant and I was going to lose my apartment anyway. And Ken's right. Now that I'm not paying for a place to stay, I can use my money for other things, even start saving.

Yes, things were awkward in the beginning. I can still remember the way Jackson pressed my body against his when I nearly fell. I can still remember how he looked when he walked into Maisie's bedroom wearing just his boxers, his skin still glistening from the shower. After that, things settled down, though. Like he said, unless I go to the kitchen, I don't bump into him. Sometimes we go to work together. In the evenings, when Maisie comes to my room, he sometimes drops by to check on her or to bring her to bed. Other than that, we don't really see each other much, so I don't have a chance to feel uncomfortable.

So far, moving in here has been a good decision.

"Cathy!"

I turn around at the sound of Maisie's voice and footsteps. She's running towards me in her pink pajamas. I bend down and spread my arms so I can catch her.

"Good morning, sweetheart." I give her a squeeze.

As I bury my face in her hair, I breathe in the scent of her strawberry-scented shampoo.

"Did you sleep well?"

Maisie nods as she pulls away.

I brush the wisps of hair off her forehead. "No nightmares?"

She shakes her head.

"Good."

She hasn't had one since the night I first stayed here. I was so worried when I heard her screaming and crying that I ran to her as fast as I could. Thankfully, she calmed down shortly after I held her in my arms, though I still don't know what she dreamed of. What gives a child nightmares?

"Daddy said you keep the nightmares away," Maisie tells me.

I give her a puzzled look. "Did he now?"

I don't know why Jackson said that, but I guess I should consider it a compliment.

Maisie nods. "He also said you and I can play today."

"Really?"

"That's why she woke up so early," Jackson says as he walks out of the house. "Last night, I told her that you didn't have work today and she got so excited to spend time with you."

I look into Maisie's eyes. "Did you now?"

She nods even more enthusiastically.

"I hope you don't mind," Jackson adds.

I shake my head as I glance at him. "It is part of our agreement, after all."

"It was Ken who said that," he answers. "I offered you a place to stay because I wanted to. I don't want you to feel like you have to do anything you don't want to."

"It's okay," I assure him as I touch Maisie's cheek. "After all, who wouldn't want to spend time with the most adorable little girl in the world?"

Maisie chuckles.

She's worked like a charm for me, actually. Ever since I've been around her, I've been feeling less lonely, less haunted. It's as if the shadow of death had been hanging over me like a rain cloud and Maisie is the sunshine of life. It's amazing what the innocence and wonder of a child can do.

"So it's okay for me to leave her with you?" Jackson asks. "Because I've got some stuff to do today."

Of course he does. He's even busier than I am. It's no surprise he doesn't get a day off.

"Sure," I tell him. "I'll watch Maisie."

She throws her arms up in the air as she starts jumping up and down. "Yay!"

"And I'm sure we'll have lots of fun together," I add as I touch her little nose.

"What are we going to do?" she asks curiously.

"Oh, lots of things." I lower my voice to a whisper. "Lots of girly things."

She giggles.

Jackson scratches the back of his head. "Why do I have a feeling I'm going to regret having the two of you teamed up together?"

"Oh, shush." I wave a hand at him. "We're good girls. Aren't we, Maisie?"

She nods. "We're going to do good girl stuff."

Jackson cocks his head. "Oh, is that so?"

"Secret good girl stuff," I add with a grin.

Jackson lets out a breath. "Well, in that case, I'm not needed here anymore."

"Nope." Maisie shakes her head. "Because you're not a girl."

He frowns.

"Don't worry," I tell him as I put my hands on Maisie's shoulders. "We'll be fine. You just... do what you have to do."

"Okay. The two of you have fun."

"We will," Maisie replies. She grabs my hands and places them around her neck.

Jackson waves before going back into the house. As soon as he's gone, Maisie turns around to face me. A big smile lights up her small, round face.

"Now we can do girl stuff," she says.

"Right." I pat her head. "The question is, what are we going to do first?"

She shrugs.

I touch my chin. "Let's see..."

~

"There." I meet Maisie's gaze in the mirror of her dresser after I finish drying her hair. "You look and smell like a princess again."

She giggles.

We've spent the whole day doing one fun thing after another. First it was making pancakes for breakfast, then playing with dolls, then coloring. After we had sandwiches for lunch, which we ate in the garden, I read her some fairy tales. Then we played dress-up. I let her try on my heels and some of my clothes. I even let her try on my make-up, which maybe wasn't the best idea because she ended up looking like a clown and then I had to give her a bath. Still, we had fun.

"Do you think Daddy will like the pictures we took?" Maisie asks.

We did take a lot of snapshots on my phone.

"I'm sure he will. He'll probably laugh at some, like that picture of you with lipstick all over."

Maisie laughs.

I, too, grin as I recall the red streaks that covered almost half her face. But then I sigh as I remember what's left of my lipstick - not much.

"I guess I'll need to buy a new one."

She turns her head to look at me. "You think Daddy will buy me a lipstick?"

I narrow my eyes at her. "No. And you shouldn't ask your daddy to buy you one."

"Why not?"

Why indeed?

"Well, because lipsticks aren't toys. I might have let you use mine, but that doesn't mean you should play with one. Lipsticks are special. They're like a girl's secret weapon. You put them on and you feel better. You feel like you can do anything, face anyone."

Maisie's eyebrows go up. "Really?"

"There are hundreds to choose from, in many different colors."

"Even purple?"

"Yes, all different shades of purple."

"And blue."

"I think so, though no one really wears blue lipstick."

"Why not?"

That seems to be her favorite question.

"Well, because blue makes you... look like an alien."

She laughs.

"But hey, you can wear whatever color you want," I tell her. "Whatever you think looks good on you or makes you feel good. That's why you should pick your own lipstick, and that's why you should wait until you're old enough to get your own."

Maisie nods. "I understand."

I smile. Well, that explanation sounded better than I thought.

I grab the comb and start combing her hair.

"Did I ever tell you that you have pretty hair?" I ask as the cinnamon strands flow through the teeth of the comb.

She just shrugs.

It's better than mine. Soft. Silky. Shiny. Obedient. Often, I feel like my hair has a life of its own, which is why I'm rarely fond of it. Maisie's looks like it could star in a shampoo commercial.

Just like Trisha's.

That last thought comes out of nowhere, making me pause.

Why? Why do I always remember her even though I can't remember what happened to her?

"When did you get your own lipstick?" Maisie asks suddenly.

So she's still thinking about lipstick, huh? Well, I'm grateful for the distraction.

"Let me see. I think I bought my first lipstick when I was in college."

"College?"

"It's the school you go to where you learn to become... whatever you want to be, whether it's a doctor or a lawyer or a manager or a businessman. I think I was around twenty-two."

Maisie starts to count on her fingers.

I grin. "But my mom got me one for my seventeenth birthday. I tried one of her lipsticks, too, when I was about your age."

Maisie looks up. "Really?"

"I think it's something all little girls do. There was also a time I tried her lipstick with..."

Trisha. I almost say her name.

My mind just keeps going back to her, doesn't it?

"With who?" Maisie asks me curiously.

I pause. Should I tell her about Trisha? Well, she is her aunt.

"With a friend," I decide to say. "My best friend."

I can't keep avoiding talking about her forever, after all. And young as she is, somehow, Maisie seems to be the perfect person to talk to her about. Or maybe that's why. Maybe it's because Maisie's a child and so this conversation doesn't feel real.

"Another girl?"

"Yes," I say as I keep combing her hair. "Just like you and me. She was pretty, just like you. And amazing. She could do all sorts of things."

"What things?"

"Anything she wanted. She could play baseball and soccer. She could dance. She could do impersonations."

"What's im...per...?"

"Oh, it means she could sound like famous people," I explain. "She could make everyone laugh. She was a clown, but she could also be serious. When she talked, everyone listened."

"She sounds perfect," Maisie says.

I smile at my reflection. "She was."

Strange. I know Maisie never knew Trisha. I know she's just a child. Still, I find myself talking about Trisha like it's the most natural thing to do. And it feels... good.

"Can I meet her?" Maisie asks.

The question makes my chest tighten a bit. Still, I stroke her cheek as I smile.

"I wish you could, sweetheart, but some people just... well, they've gone somewhere else, somewhere we can't reach them."

"Like my mom?"

My chest tightens even more. Maybe I shouldn't have started talking to her about Trisha after all. It's too late now, though.

"Yes, like your mom," I answer. "They're somewhere far away where we can't see them."

"But Daddy says my mom watches over me," Maisie says.

I squeeze her shoulder. "I'm sure she does. You can't see her, but I'm sure she's always watching over you."

"But she can't touch me?" Maisie asks. "She can't play with me?"

I shake my head slowly. "I'm sorry, sweetheart."

She frowns as her face drops. My heart sinks.

I lift her chin. "But hey, you've got a great daddy who loves you so much. And now, you've got me."

"Are you going to be my new mommy?" she asks.

The question takes me by surprise. I decide not to take it seriously.

"No, sweetheart. But I can be your new friend."

Her eyebrows furrow. "You're already my friend."

"Really?" I plant a kiss on the top of her head. "Then I feel like the luckiest person in the world."

Finally, her smile returns. As always, it lightens my heart.

That's it. That's the way it should be.

"Can we keep playing until Daddy comes home?" Maisie asks me.

I brush my fingers against her cheek. "Sure."

Anything to keep that smile on her face.

"What do you want to play next?"

~

"It sounds like the two of you had a lot of fun," Jackson says as he takes the pork out of the oven.

The aroma of herbs and perfectly cooked meat escapes into the kitchen and makes my mouth water.

As soon as he arrived home, Maisie fired away like a loose cannon and bombarded him with her report of the day's activities while showing him the photos we took. That must have used up the last store of her energy, because when she was done, she fell asleep. It was up to me to give Jackson the rest of the details as he cooked dinner, which I've just finished doing. I've told him just about everything, except for the conversation Maisie and I had about Trisha and the fact that she almost choked on a grape during lunch, both of which I find unnecessary to disclose.

"We did," I tell him after swallowing. "It's mostly thanks to your daughter, though. She's up for anything, and her smiles and laughter are just contagious."

"That they are," Jackson agrees.

I lean on the counter. "You've done a good job raising her."

"Have I?" He stirs the gravy in a saucepan. "She's barely five. I don't think she's raised yet. Besides, I haven't done anything. She's mostly been in the care of nannies and daycare personnel."

I frown at the way he's putting himself down.

"But you do your best to spend time with her," I point out. "You give her everything she needs. You tuck her into bed."

He lifts a spoon to his lips. "Some people think that's not enough."

I hoist myself onto a stool. "Well, screw them. You know, I've learned these past few years that people like to play God. They'll wonder about you, they'll come up with their own theories and pronounce their judgments, which usually end the same - you're not good enough. But who cares? They don't know what you're going through. They'll never understand, so their judgment isn't good enough either."

Jackson looks at me. "You've grown wiser."

"Yeah, I guess." I shrug. "Some people grow up to be more buff and some grow up to be wiser."

His eyes narrow. "Are you making fun of me?"

"No. I'm just stating a fact. I mean, you are more buff."

I gesture at his arms and he glances at them, too.

Heck, that's an understatement.

"You mean I am buff, period," Jackson corrects me.

I chuckle. "Yeah. That's what I meant."

He grins.

"You know, I am curious," I tell him. "About how you... ended up this way. Is there a story there, or was it just some kind of growth spurt, like second puberty?"

"Second puberty?" He laughs, then turns serious. "Actually, I took something."

My eyebrows arch. I wasn't expecting that. "What?"

"Some kind of new serum, something like the one Captain America took."

Well, that explains the heroic transformation from puny to killer booty. But wait. Is he serious?

Suddenly, he grins. "I'm just messing with you. Of course there's no such thing."

I frown. Now he's making fun of me.

"There is a story, though. Want to hear it? This pork still needs some time to rest."

"Yeah, sure."

"It actually goes hand in hand with my journey to become a chef," Jackson says. "And it started after... well, shortly after the last time I saw you."

He means after Trisha died.

"My mom got sick and didn't have anyone to take care of her, so I did. I dropped out of college."

That explains why he's not in front of a computer in an office or in a laboratory in Switzerland trying to figure out how to make the world a better place on a molecular level. I always thought he'd end up as one of those two.

"While doing that, I worked part-time, and I learned how to cook. I think I started gaining weight around then. Then she died and I was all alone, so I buried my sorrows in food."

I frown as I feel a pang of pity. At least I had my mother and Hal to help me deal with grief. Jackson didn't really have anyone.

"As you know, when you eat a lot, you put on a lot of pounds. I wasn't just eating, though. I was trying out different kinds of food. I was doing research on food, making my own experiments. You know, cooking is a science. It requires precision and a lot of adjustments to achieve perfection."

So he applied his love and knowledge of science to food.

"I don't doubt that."

"Do you know I never went to cooking school?" Jackson asks me.

I shake my head. "No."

I just assumed he had.

"I'm mostly self-taught. Anyway, one day while I was at a restaurant, trying to study the dishes I'd been served and trying to pair different flavors, a retired chef approached me. He became my mentor, you know, taught me all the details, the finer stuff. I was a cook. He made me a chef."

I nod. "Sounds impressive."

"He was also the one who told me to get fit. He told me I had to understand that while people want to be fed, they don't want to be fattened up. If I was going to open my own restaurant, I had to convince my customers that I was feeding them, not fattening them up. And the best way to convince them was for me to get fit myself."

"Makes sense."

The best way to give an example is to be an example, right?

"I went to the gym and started a rigorous workout program. I started to eat healthy. Actually, I got some tips from my nutritionist, too, which helped me make my food healthier just in time for the opening of my first restaurant. And that's pretty much it. I got this body, liked it and kept it ever since."

"So basically, you got depressed and got fat, then started exercising and eating healthy, which is how you got fit," I sum it up. "Cliche."

He lifts a finger. "But with a great story."

I smile. Well, I guess it is.

"Well, it suits you," I blurt out. "This body, I mean."

"Yeah." Jackson glances down. "I've noticed you've been staring at me."

Blood rushes to my cheeks and I sit up. "Have not."

He laughs. "Just messing with you."

I frown.

He turns his back to me. "I think the pork's ready. Here. Why don't you try it?"

He walks over to me with a slice of pork and a bowl of gravy.

"Wow," I say as I take the pork from the tip of his fork. "I can't believe I'm eating food cooked by a Michelin-starred chef."

Since becoming an intern at Jackson's restaurant, I've done my research. I've found out that he has nine restaurants across the globe and a total of five Michelin stars. Totally awesome.

"I have made you dinner before, remember?" he says.

"Nothing this special."

Just stir-fries, salads, pasta.

"It's just roast pork," he points out.

"Roast pork prepared by a Michelin-starred chef. Not too many people get to eat that."

Jackson shrugs. "Well, I wanted to make something nice for you as my way of thanking you for taking care of Maisie today. And doing such a great job of it, too."

"It was my pleasure."

I dip the slice of pork into the gravy, making sure to coat it generously. Then I put the piece inside my mouth. As the flavor explodes on my tongue, I close my eyes. The meat is tender, melting in my mouth, and perfectly seasoned. The skin cracks beneath my teeth and shatters, its taste and texture sending chills down my spine. And that's just the pork. The gravy has hints of beef stock, mushrooms, wine and herbs. Its rich flavor complements the pork perfectly, its smoothness highlighting the crispness of the crackling.

A moan escapes my throat.

If this were a concert, everything would be in perfect harmony inside my mouth, every note hit with utter sublimity.

Divine.

When I open my eyes, I have a compliment ready for the chef, but that vanishes as I meet Jackson's gaze. His eyes are narrowed, studying me intently. And they're smoldering like the glowing metal inside the oven.

Surely, that's not the way someone looks at his little sister.

My heart stops. This time, something more intense travels down my spine.

Why is he looking at me like that? And why, why can't I look away?

With his gaze still holding mine, his hand goes to my face. His thumb lands on the corner of my mouth. My heart begins to race. My feet would like to go with it, but they seem firmly planted on the floor. I can't move a muscle. I can barely breathe as my eyes focus on Jackson's face so close to mine, on his parted lips.

He's not going to kiss me, is he?

Suddenly, he steps back. He brings his thumb between his lips and licks it. The gesture causes my pulse to spike even more.

"It's good," Jackson says. "The gravy's good."

My eyebrows furrow as I try to make sense of what just happened. So he was just wiping the gravy from my face? But why do it so... sensually? Is he teasing me?

Frustration washes over me, made worse by the fact that I don't even fully understand why I'm feeling it. If he's trying to mess with me again, this time, he's succeeded. I feel an utter mess, every cell in my body out of place.

I frown. "Actually, I don't like the taste."

Jackson's eyebrows arch.

"And I think I'm not that hungry after all. I'm going to my room."

With that, I turn on my heel and walk out of the kitchen.

"Cathy," he calls after me.

I ignore him. Trisha was right. I should stay away from her brother.

CHAPTER 6

Jackson

I should have stayed away.

I set down my cup of coffee and slap my forehead as I remember how Cathy stomped out of my kitchen last night. She didn't say much to me this morning either. And all because I couldn't control myself.

How could I when she had on the most exquisite expression when she ate that piece of pork? When she made the most delightful sound, which went straight to my groin? I could have sworn she was having an orgasm.

God, I wanted to give her one.

I wanted to kiss her lips made shiny by the fat and juices off the pork. I wanted to lick the gravy from the corner of her mouth. Hell, I wanted to pin her against the counter and devour her.

Cathy may have been surprised, but she was willing. I could tell from the look in her eyes.

Still, I managed to hold back. But it was too late. Cathy had already seen all the things I wanted to do and she ran away in fear.

Or did she? Is that why she's angry at me? Because I scared her? Because I did something I wasn't supposed to?

At any rate, I should stay away from her for now, give her time to cool down. Or maybe I should give myself time to cool down.

"Tell me, is that look because you're having trouble coming up with a new recipe, or is it because you've finally had your heart broken?"

I turn my head to look at the man who's just interrupted my thoughts, the man I've been waiting to meet at this cafe.

"Simon." I get out of my seat and offer him my hand. "Thanks for meeting me."

He shakes it firmly. "Thank you for asking me to meet you. I must say I was surprised, because I hadn't heard from you in years."

Right. The last time we saw each other was back in college when we were roommates, just before I dropped out. He's gained some weight since then, but he still has that cleft chin. He seems to be wearing the same rimless eyeglasses, too, or at least a similar pair.

"I've been busy," I tell him as I take my seat.

"I know." He pulls out a chair. "I haven't heard from you, but that doesn't mean I haven't heard about you. My wife is actually a big fan of yours. A chef groupie, I think that's the term. She follows your Instagram and buys your books and all that."

Chef groupie. I've heard it before.

"Well, tell her I'm grateful for her support."

As long as they follow my career and not me, that's fine.

"I would if we still talked," Simon says. "As it is, our marriage is on the rocks."

"I'm sorry to hear that."

He shrugs. "It happens. How about you? I heard you're a widower. Any plans on getting married again?"

Strangely, the thought of Cathy is the first that comes to mind. I dismiss it.

"I'm not - "

"Don't." Simon points a finger at me. "Marriage sucks. I swear if I get out of this one, I'll never do it again."

Okay. I don't remember him being this bitter before. He did used to complain a bit, but it was mostly about the guys in the other rooms being noisy, and the amount of homework. Overall, he was a nice guy. He was as devoted to his studies as I was. He never talked about relationships, in fact. I don't think he had a girlfriend back then.

Then again, I can't say I really knew him. I was only his roommate for a year. He's from a rich family, so he could have stayed in his own bachelor pad. Instead, he decided to live in the dorm just for the experience, for a dose of reality. I resented that at first. I actually thought his father paid for him to get into the university. But then I figured out how smart he was. And nice. In spite of his background, we got along.

That's why I decided to contact him a few days ago.

"Let's get down to business, shall we?" I suggest.

"Right." Simon takes out his laptop and puts it on the table. "As you said in your email, you wanted me to come up with a program that would give your new restaurant a touch of innovation."

"Yes." I nod. "We're near Silicon Valley, after all. It would be nice if the restaurant could reflect that, even just a bit. Timeless food, old-fashioned setting, but modern service."

"I understand. Well, I've come up with a few ideas."

For the next hour, I listen to Simon explain them, making my own comments every now and then in between sips of coffee. He has good ones to share, just as I expected from a high-ranking IT executive.

When we're finished, I shake his hand again. "Thank you. I was right to ask you to handle this."

He closes his laptop. "I'll do my best to incorporate your suggestions and requests and see what I can come up with."

"I look forward to seeing it."

He puts his laptop in his bag. "Oh, by the way, I never did offer my condolences, not just for the loss of your wife but for your sister, the one who died when we were in college."

So Simon heard about her, too, huh?

Strange. Trisha seems to be coming up a lot lately.

I nod. "Thanks. And I hope your marriage still works out."

He snorts. "No hope for me, I'm afraid. For you, however, it's a different issue. Trust me, don't ever let a woman think she has a hold of you or she'll never let you forget it. They're more twisted and selfish than they let on."

I simply give another nod as Simon walks away. I don't agree, though. Evelyn was wonderful, the most selfless woman I've ever known. And Cathy? She has a heart of gold. I know she's still hurting, but even after all she's been through, she's still trying to be strong, trying to move on in her own way. She may have erected thick walls around herself, but she still cares about others.

I let out a deep breath as I tap my empty cup. Maybe I should apologize and make up with her later.

~

I find Cathy and Maisie lying on the grass in the garden.

"What's this?" I ask as I stand above them. "Are you making grass angels on the lawn?"

"No, Daddy," Maisie answers. "We're looking at clouds."

"I see." I look up at the sky.

"And now, we're playing tag." Maisie jumps to her feet and touches Cathy's arm. "Tag. You're it."

Then she runs off.

Cathy lets out a sigh as she sits up. As she does, I notice a pair of leaves embedded in her hair. They're sticking out on either side of her head. I'm about to take them out, but she turns her head.

"What?" she snaps.

"Nothing." I take a step back and quickly hide my arm behind me.

I don't want her to think I'm trying to do anything else suspicious to her.

She stands up and shakes the dirt from her jeans. "Your daughter is sneaky. I wonder where she gets that from."

I frown. "I take it you're still mad at me?"

"Yes," she admits.

At least she's talking to me.

"I'm sorry," I tell her. "What I did was childish and inconsiderate and..."

I pause as a breeze blows, making the leaves on her head stand up. They look like ears, and I struggle to keep a straight face.

"...and disrespectful."

"You think?"

"I shouldn't have made... fun of you."

Shit. She looks so cute and silly at the same time that I don't know how much longer I can keep my laughter at bay.

Cathy seems to have noticed my problem. Her gaze narrows as she crosses her arms over her chest.

"Wow. And I'm supposed to believe you're sorry when you're making fun of me right now?"

"I'm not."

"Yeah, right. You're not serious at all. You're just - "

Suddenly, Maisie bursts out laughing from a few feet away. Her hands grip her stomach.

Cathy's eyebrows crease. "What? What's funny?"

Maisie keeps laughing. "Cathy has... bunny ears."

I can't hold it any longer. My shoulders shake as I explode into laughter as well.

Cathy frowns as she places her hands on her head. Within seconds, she finds the leaves and takes them off.

"I see." She looks at me. "You couldn't have just told me they were there?"

"I tried to," I tell her as I try to stop laughing. "But I just thought it was more important that I apologize."

She places her hands on her hips. "Right."

Uh-oh. Have I made her angrier?

"Besides," I add. "You looked cute."

"Cute," Maisie repeats.

"Cute, huh?" She turns to Maisie. "You know what? I think I just thought of a new game. Let's call it 'Tickle Daddy'."

What?

"Yay!" Maisie cheers as she runs towards me. "Tickle Daddy!"

I run off. No way.

We run in circles around the garden. After a minute, though, I stop so she can catch me before she starts crying in frustration. I sit on the grass and laugh as she tickles my ribs. She laughs louder as I tickle her neck.

As I glance at Cathy, I see her laughing as well.

"Oh, you think it's funny, do you?" I get up and run towards her.

"No!" She lets out a girlish squeal as she runs off.

"Go, Daddy!" Maisie cheers.

Eventually, I catch Cathy. I grip her waist and tickle her sides. She laughs out loud as she tries to swat my hands away.

"Stop!" she shouts between squeals and giggles.

She falls down on the ground. I keep going, not just because I'm intent on having my little revenge, but because I'm loving the sound of her laughter. I stop, though, when she grips my arms. I don't want her crying in frustration either.

Only then do I realize that I'm kneeling on top of her. Cathy realizes it, too, and her cheeks turn red beneath my gaze. Her eyes grow wide.

She lets my arms go and opens her mouth, but before she can say anything, I hear another voice.

"Well, well, well. What do we have here?"

A voice I didn't expect or want to hear right now. Betty's.

Fuck.

"We weren't doing anything," I tell Betty for what seems like the hundredth time since we started talking in the parlor.

What is she even doing here?

"Really?" She lifts her cup of tea to her lips. "You were on top of her. Out there in the garden. In plain sight of my granddaughter."

"With our clothes on," I add. "We were just playing."

What? Did she think I'd have sex in front of my daughter?

"So you weren't doing anything." Betty sets down her cup.

"We were playing a game with Maisie," I explain. "That's why she was there."

"And did she know of this game you were playing? And who was this woman you were playing with, anyway, hmm? Is she the new nanny?"

"She's an intern at my restaurant," I answer.

"I see. But she's living here?"

I pause a moment before answering. "Yes."

I'd lie, but I know Betty will find out the truth anyway. In fact, she may already know it.

"With you and Maisie?"

"Yes."

"On the same floor?"

I frown, because I know what she's getting at. "Cathy and I –"

"Oh, her name is Cathy?" Betty asks me. "How old is she?"

"Twenty... six," I answer after a quick calculation. "She's not as young as you think."

"So you think it's okay for you to play with her? To fuck her?"

My jaw clenches and I throw her a warning glance. "Betty..."

"So Maisie doesn't have a nanny? I haven't seen one."

"No," I confess. "I fired the last one because she wasn't doing her job properly."

"Were any of them?"

"I haven't had time to get a new one."

Betty frowns.

"In the meantime, Maisie is going to daycare."

"Daycare?" Betty's eyes grow wide with horror. "So she's at one of those germ-infested facilities in the hands of inept strangers? Jackson, have you lost your mind?"

"They're not inept," I argue. "They know what they're doing, and Maisie likes them."

"Maisie likes everyone."

That I can't argue with.

"It's not every day," I say in an effort to ease her displeasure. "Some days, I have Maisie with me at the restaurant."

"Where she could easily grab a knife and chop off her finger," Betty says sourly.

Of course she wouldn't approve of that, either.

"And during weekends, she's here at home with Cathy. Cathy watches over her."

"So she babysits and gets paid with sex?" Betty asks.

I narrow my eyes at her as my patience inches dangerously close to its limit. I don't care what she thinks of me. I already know I'll never live up to her expectations, not after I let Evelyn die. But I'm not going to let her talk shit about Cathy when she doesn't know a thing about her.

"Watch your words, Betty. You may be my mother-in-law, but I - "

"Oh, I don't think I'm your mother-in-law any longer," she cuts me off. "I'm not Evelyn's mother anymore now that she's not here. You don't have to think of me that way. But I am Maisie's grandmother, and there's nothing you can do about that. And I will not tolerate my granddaughter living in a house with a stranger when she could be living with me."

"Maisie's not living with you," I say adamantly. "We've been over this before."

A million times.

"Well, she's definitely not living here while you bring random women from your restaurant over to play with."

"I haven't brought any other women over," I tell her.

"So Cathy's the first to have caught your fancy? Even so, she's a stranger."

"She's not. She's an old friend."

"Is she, now?"

Of course that's not good enough for Betty.

"And how long is she staying? Until you find a new friend?"

I stay silent because I'm still trying to come up with the answer.

Think, Jackson. If I don't say something that will satisfy her, something that will get me out of this argument, I'll lose. She won't leave until she takes Maisie with her, and I'll be damned before that happens.

"Fine," I say. "I'll tell you the truth."

Betty's eyebrows arch.

"Cathy isn't a friend and she's not some random woman," I say. "She's my fiancee."

Betty's eyes grow wide. "What?"

It's the best I can come up with.

"Cathy is my fiancee, which means she won't be going away anytime soon. When I marry her, she'll be Maisie's new mother."

Betty snorts.

"They adore each other, which you would have noticed if you weren't too busy focusing on other details," I add.

She doesn't seem to have heard that. "So you finally admit that the two of you are fucking in this house?"

"Never in the same room with Maisie," I tell her.

Still, she shakes her head.

"My point is, you don't have to worry about Maisie being with Cathy. Cathy loves her and I trust Cathy completely."

"Well, I don't," Betty says. "I don't even believe you."

Of course not.

"Fine." I stand up. "I'll call her and you can ask her."

"No." She stands up as well. "I'll talk to her."

I frown. What? Did she notice that I was lying and suspect that I would tell Cathy to do the same? Which is exactly what I was going to do, of course.

Fuck. Why does Maisie's grandmother have to be so clever? But of course she is. She was raised by a politician and a college professor. I think that's also why she thinks she has every right to meddle with my affairs, apart from the fact that she's Evelyn's mother.

Betty leaves the room. I follow her. She throws a questioning glance over her shoulder.

"I don't want you scaring her," I explain. "Besides, this is my house."

She can't prohibit me from going wherever I want.

"Fine, then. Lead the way."

I lead the way upstairs and find both Cathy and Maisie in Maisie's bedroom. I gesture for Cathy to come out of the room.

"This won't take long," I tell Maisie before closing the door.

"Cathy, I don't believe we've been introduced," Betty says as soon as all three of us are in the hallway. "I'm Betty, Maisie's grandmother, the mother of Jackson's former wife."

Cathy nods. "It's a pleasure to meet you."

"And Jackson tells me you're his fiancee."

Cathy grows still. Her wide eyes stray over to me.

I grab her hand. "I know you wanted to keep this a secret, honey, but I've decided to tell Betty. She is Maisie's grandmother, after all. Please don't get mad at me. It's for the best, I think."

I give her hand a squeeze, hoping that that will help convey my hidden message and convince her to go along with this crazy idea I've come up with.

"So it's true, then?" Betty asks her.

I give her hand another squeeze.

"Y-yes," Cathy finally answers. "We... we're engaged."

Betty touches her chin. "I see."

She glances at Cathy's hand.

"Where's your ring?"

Shit.

"I..." Cathy starts.

"We haven't told anyone about the engagement yet," I explain as I place my arm around Cathy's shoulder. "It only happened recently. Just last week."

"Oh." Betty looks into Cathy's eyes.

I feel her tremble.

"Why do you look so scared?" Betty asks as she notices Cathy's fear.

Shit.

"I... Well, I'm sorry, but I've never been engaged before," Cathy answers as she seems to regain her composure. "And I wasn't ready for this."

Betty's eyes narrow. "Not ready for the engagement?"

I glance sideways at Cathy.

"Not ready to meet you," she elaborates as she squares her shoulders. "I know Jackson's mother passed away, so I didn't think I would have to get anyone's approval."

"She doesn't need approval," I say as I draw Betty's gaze. "She's my fiancee, and that's that."

"And what about Maisie?" Betty asks. "Does she know about this? Have you asked her if she's okay with this?"

"We haven't told her yet," I answer. "But..."

Suddenly, the door opens. Maisie rushes out and goes straight to Cathy, wrapping her arms around Cathy's waist.

"Don't leave," she begs.

Cathy touches her cheek. "Oh, sweetheart."

Maisie looks at her grandmother as she hugs Cathy tight. "Don't make Cathy leave, Grandma."

I lift an eyebrow. Has she been listening the whole time?

"She's my friend," Maisie adds. "I want her to stay here."

I look at Betty. "You were asking?"

For a moment, she stays silent. Then she sighs.

"Fine. Do as you wish. I better not hear of Maisie being neglected, though, just because there's a woman in your life."

"I would never dream of it," I assure her.

"And she better not be seeing things a child shouldn't see."

"Agreed."

Betty turns to Cathy. "And I better not hear her say you're hurting her in any way, or I swear to God I'll - "

"I'd never think of hurting her," Cathy promises. "She's the sweetest child I've ever known."

Betty draws a deep breath. Then she turns to Maisie.

"I'll see you again soon, darling."

Maisie nods.

Betty walks off, head still held high. I follow her.

"I know where the door is, and don't worry, I'm leaving," she says after a few steps.

"I wasn't - "

"But that doesn't mean I'm okay with this." Betty turns around. "This discussion is not yet over."

"This discussion is unnecessary," I tell her.

She snorts and turns on her heel. I stop following her, simply watching her leave.

Oh, why did she have to come here today? Why did she have to see me and Cathy like that? And why couldn't she just believe that Cathy's presence here isn't bad for Maisie? Why can't she just trust me to do what's best for her?

I let out a sigh. What's done is done now, though. There's no stopping this wheel that I've started turning, at least not anytime soon.

As I turn around, I see Cathy still standing in the hallway, her arms crossed over her chest. As our eyes meet, she frowns. With that look, she's almost as scary as Betty.

Great. I'd just gotten back in her good graces and now I'm out again. And this time, I have a feeling she won't forgive me so easily.

CHAPTER 7

Cathy

"What on earth were you thinking?" I ask Jackson as I pace my bedroom.

With each step, my heart races. My thoughts tumble in somersaults.

I've been simmering ever since Betty left. I wanted to talk to Jackson right away, but Maisie was there so I did my best to hold my tongue and my temper. Now that she's asleep in her room, though, I can finally let my thoughts and feelings out. I can finally unleash all this confusion and frustration that have been gnawing at me from inside.

"I'm sorry that I put you in such a terrible position," Jackson says.

My eyebrows arch. "Terrible position?"

Sitting with your legs pinned under you for more than five minutes - that's a terrible position. What Jackson did? I felt like I'd been dangled over the edge of a cliff.

"But to answer your question, I was thinking that it was best for everyone."

"You asked me to lie for you." I beat my hand against my chest as I stop in front of him. "And to the most terrifying woman I've ever met."

For a moment there, I thought she was going to eat me alive.

"I know."

"Tell me how that's best for everyone?"

"I didn't have a choice, Cathy." Jackson lifts his head and looks into my eyes. "Betty saw us."

"She saw nothing," I tell him. "We weren't doing anything. We were just playing with Maisie."

"She knows you live here. If I hadn't said we were engaged, she would have threatened to take Maisie away from me unless I threw you out. And trust me, Betty doesn't make threats lightly. If she says she'll do it, she'll do it."

I don't doubt that, not after being on the receiving end of her icy gaze.

"I wasn't going to let you get thrown out when I was the one who invited you to stay here," Jackson goes on. "And I sure as hell wasn't going to let Betty have my daughter."

That I understand. What I don't understand is why anyone would want to take a child away from a great father. I know Betty is Maisie's grandmother, but surely she must know that a child should be with its parent.

"Why would Betty want to get Maisie?" I ask. "Can't she see that Maisie's happy here with you?"

"She sees only what she wants to see," Jackson answers. "Like you said, some people are determined to see the worst in you, or to see only your failures. For her, I'll never be good enough."

"But you are. And others can see that. There's no way a court would allow her to take Maisie from you."

"Do you think I want this to go to court?"

The hurt look in Jackson's eyes makes my chest tighten.

Of course he doesn't. If I were in his position, I wouldn't either. No parent should have to go to court just to keep their own child.

I look down at my hands. "You should have just told her I was leaving, then. I don't belong here anyway."

"Do you still think that even after spending time with Maisie? After hearing how much she adores you, how she can't bear to see you go? Do you really want to leave her?"

"Of course not, but if it's either her or me..."

"It's not," Jackson raises his voice a notch. "Neither of you is leaving this house."

I sigh. Has he always been this stubborn?

"But now Betty thinks we're engaged," I tell him.

"And as long as she believes it, we'll be fine."

My eyebrows go up. "Are you saying that lying to her isn't enough? Are you saying we have to pretend we are engaged as well?"

Jackson clasps his hands in front of his face. "Exactly. We'll have to act like we're engaged from now on."

I shake my head in disbelief. How can he say that so calmly?

"No." My fists clench at my sides as I bow my head. "I can't do this."

"Do you hate me so much that you can't stand the thought of even pretending to be engaged to me?"

"It's not that," I answer. "I don't like fooling other people."

"You think I do?" Jackson asks me.

I say nothing.

He stands up. "I don't like this, either, Cathy. Like I said, I don't have a choice. But you do."

He walks over to me.

"You can walk away from all this, but it will be a clean break. You'll lose your internship. You'll never see Maisie again. Or me."

I frown at the thought of that.

"Or you can go along with this. You can pretend to be my fiancee for just a few months."

"And after that?" I ask curiously.

"We'll pretend to break it off. Maisie and I will leave. We have to leave eventually anyway. We're only here because I'm opening a restaurant."

I'd never thought of that, but now that Jackson has mentioned it, it does make sense. Of course he'd want to put up more restaurants, and of course he'll have to be wherever they are. Why did I think he'd stay here forever?

"You can stay here and keep working at the restaurant," Jackson goes on. "I'll hire you as a management trainee."

A trainee? Not just an intern?

"That means that once you're done with training, you'll be helping Ken manage the restaurant. And maybe someday, you'll manage it on your own. I'll be leaving it in your hands."

So I'm guaranteed a job.

"And you can keep staying here at the house. After Maisie and I leave, we can keep renting it as a staff house. You can have the other employees stay with you so you'll all be close to the restaurant."

Not just a job but permanent lodging, too? It sounds too good to be true.

"Of course, Maisie and I will still visit once in a while," Jackson adds. "Or you can come see us. If other people wonder about it, we'll just say we're still friends even if we're no longer engaged."

I nod. "It seems like you have everything figured out."

"I just thought of all that right now, actually," Jackson confesses. "So, what will it be?"

I pause to weigh my options. If I refuse to go along with the fake engagement, I'll lose my internship and I won't have a place to stay. I might have to go back home empty-handed. And I'll never see Maisie again. That will break her heart. On the other hand, if I decide to play along, I'll get a job and a place to stay for the foreseeable future. Heck, I'll have a future. Sure, I'll have to part ways with Maisie eventually, but that was already in the cards anyway, and at least I can still see her again.

And Jackson.

"Well?" he asks me.

I let out a deep breath as I make up my mind. "Fine. I'll be your pretend fiancee."

Right now, it seems like the better thing to do.

Jackson smiles. "I'm glad to hear it."

"But remember, it's only pretend." I lift a finger. "When we're here at the house, we'll act as if nothing has changed."

"Of course," Jackson answers. "We don't even have to stay in the same room or anything."

Stay in the same room? That never even crossed my mind.

"And even if we're outside, you're not to hold my hand or... kiss me."

I suppress a blush at that last thought.

"Not even if Betty's watching? She might not be convinced of our act unless we do it well."

He has a point. Even so...

"Not unless it's absolutely necessary," I concede.

Jackson nods. "Okay. Any other conditions?"

I touch my chin as I pause to think.

"Well, it's not a condition, but I was thinking we should talk about what to tell other people, especially about how we met and got engaged."

"That's easy," Jackson says. "We'll just say we used to be in a relationship. When we met, we realized we still had feelings for each other and we decided to rekindle the old flames. We realized we were meant for each other and got engaged."

It does seem plausible. I guess he really has thought of everything, huh?

"Sounds good?"

I nod. "Yeah."

"We'll just keep things vague whenever other people ask us something. We won't go into details. That way, it will be easier to maintain the lie."

Maintain the lie. I suppose I have to get used to that.

"Do we have a deal, then?" Jackson offers me his hand.

I stare at it for a moment as I feel a final jab of hesitation prompted by my conscience. I ignore it, though, as I swallow the lump in my throat. I've already told myself this is the right thing to do.

It's all for a good cause. For Maisie and for me.

I square my shoulders and grip Jackson's hand. "Deal."

We shake hands. Jackson smiles.

"Good. Now, there's only one thing left to do."

I give him a puzzled look. "What's that?"

Jackson gives me a wide grin. "Why, get a ring for my new fiancee, of course."

~

I stare at the diamond ring on my finger as I sit at my desk. The princess cut gem glistens in the sunlight. The white gold band gleams.

I'm not used to it yet. Last night, it nearly got wet in the shower because I forgot to take it off. Earlier, when I was combing my hair, I did forget it was there, and so I ended up getting my hair tangled in it.

I bring the ring closer to my face. It doesn't feel real, more like something out of a fantasy. Just like my engagement to Jackson. Well, our engagement really isn't real. But this ring is. Even to my untrained eye, the diamond looks genuine. It's heavy, too. And the band feels like solid gold. Jackson wouldn't tell me how much it cost, but I'm pretty sure it's worth at least five thousand dollars.

Is it really alright for me to wear this?

"Would you look at that?" Ken whistles as she approaches my desk and sees the ring. "You could probably feed a state with that ring."

My eyebrows arch. "I could?"

So it's more expensive than I thought.

I touch the diamond. What a waste.

"I had a feeling it was coming," Ken adds. "But boy, the two of you sure didn't waste any time, huh?"

I feel even more puzzled. "What do you mean it was coming?"

Ken rests her elbow on my desk. "You know, you and Jackson. Why else would he ask you to move into his house?"

My eyes narrow at her. "If you're saying Jackson is in love with me..."

"I saw the way he was looking at you the day you arrived," Ken says. "Like he wanted you. And what a rich, gorgeous man like that wants, he gets."

I shake my head. "You're mistaken. This engagement isn't -
"

"I know, I know." Ken chuckles as she straightens up. "I was just teasing you. Jackson told me everything."

He did?

"I've met Betty before, so I understand. That woman even scares the shit out of me sometimes."

"I was afraid she was going to turn me to stone with her gaze or something."

"Like Medusa? That's not a bad comparison. I think of her more like the evil queen from Snow White, though. The one who says 'Bring me her heart', that kind of thing."

Come to think of it, she could easily be cast in that role.

"Do you know why she doesn't like Jackson?" I ask curiously.

If Jackson tells Ken everything, maybe she knows about that, too.

"Sweet Cathy, no woman likes the man her daughter marries," Ken answers. "It's just much, much worse in Betty's case. She's got a lot of hate in her."

"She seems to care a great deal for Maisie, though," I say.

"Of course she does. The only thing she's capable of loving is her own blood."

"So she's always wanted to get Maisie?"

"Had her eye on her since the dawn of time. Maybe it's because she lost her daughter so she wants a new one. Or maybe she just wants whatever she can't have. Some people are like that. Or maybe she just can't stand to see others happy because she's damned miserable. But hey, it's none of my business."

I look down at my hand. I guess it is my business, though. If not for Betty's desire to get Maisie, if not for her meddling, I wouldn't have to pretend to be engaged.

"Hey." Ken puts a hand on my shoulder. "Don't let her get to you."

I sigh. "That's easier said than done."

"Don't try to kiss her ass or anything. She hates that. But don't try to provoke her either."

"I think my mere existence provokes her."

"Just let her know you're your own person. Stand your ground. Be yourself."

"That's a little hard to do when I'm pretending to be someone else."

"And whatever you do, don't show her that face," Ken says.

"What face?"

"The one that looks like she's already defeated you."

I sit back. "I don't even want to fight her."

"But that's the deal, isn't it? Fight her and get a job."

So Jackson told her about that, too.

"Hey, just because you're Jackson's fake fiancee doesn't mean I'm not going to drive you like a slave."

I nod. "I know that. I didn't expect any less."

"In fact, now that I know you'll be taking over this place one day, I'm going to be a little harder on you."

I sit up. "Bring it on."

Ken smiles and pats my shoulder. "Now, that's the Cathy I know."

I smile in turn.

"The Cathy Jackson can't stay away from," Ken mutters.

I frown. "You're still going on about that?"

"What? You think a man will ask a woman to be his fake fiancee if he's not remotely interested in her?"

I don't know the answer. I've never been a fake fiancee, or known anyone who was. Is Ken suggesting that Jackson has real feelings for me? That's ridiculous.

"You think..."

"Whoa. Look at the time." Ken looks at her watch. "Time for us to start working, future Mrs. Holloway."

I sigh. I guess she's just teasing me again. Best to let it slide.

I stand up and hold my hand above my eyebrow. "Cathy Jeffries, reporting for duty."

~

Ken does remind me of a drill sergeant sometimes, I think as I walk to the van to get more of the pots and pans we bought.

She wasn't kidding when she said she'd be harder on me. My muscles are already sore.

I stretch my arms. Maybe I should start doing yoga.

Just as I'm approaching the van, I stop. There's a woman standing a few feet away on the sidewalk. Red strands peek out of the blue baseball cap she's wearing. A black backpack hangs from her shoulders and a DSLR camera sits in her hands. She lifts it and snaps a photo.

My eyebrows arch. Wait. Did she just take a photo of the restaurant?

I walk towards her. "Excuse me."

She lowers her camera and grows still.

"Are you a reporter?"

"No," she answers.

"A professional photographer?"

She shrugs. "I guess that's one way of putting it."

"I don't mean to be rude, but I don't think you're supposed to take pictures here. The restaurant isn't finished yet and - "

"So this is Jackson Holloway's new restaurant?" she asks with eyes wide.

Shit.

"He did say something about putting up his tenth restaurant somewhere in the Bay Area. I bet it's going to look a bit like his restaurant in Cape Town. It looks like it has the same windows. And those pieces of wood. They look like they form the letter M. Must be a tribute to his daughter, Maisie."

The fact that she knows Maisie sets off an alarm inside my head. What is she? Some kind of paparazzo? At any rate, I get the feeling I should make her leave.

"You should go," I tell her as I step forward. "You're not supposed to be here."

"Is Chef Jackson here?" she asks as if she hasn't heard my question.

"You should go," I repeat. "Please?"

She falls silent as she studies me. Then her eyes grow wide as they fall on my hand.

"Oh my God. You're her, aren't you? You're Chef Jackson's new manager who he got recently engaged to?"

What? How does she know that?

I hide my hand behind me before she can take a picture of it. Her camera flashes in front of my face, though.

"Hey." I put a hand on her camera. "Who told you that?"

"Don't touch my camera." She wrenches it away.

"Sorry." I lift my hand. "I..."

Why am I apologizing when she was the one taking my picture without asking my permission?

"Who told you about the..."

"About the engagement? It's on the site."

"Site?" What site?

"The one for all Chef Jackson's groupies."

Groupies?

She rolls her eyes. "God, you don't know we exist, do you? You don't have any idea how amazing Jackson Holloway is. You don't deserve him."

I frown at the insult. "Well, I don't know you. And you don't know me, so you have no right to - "

"You're not even as nice as Evelyn," the woman says.

Evelyn?

"She tried to get along with us. She didn't mind sharing Chef Jackson."

I have no idea what she's talking about.

"You're not worthy to take her place," the woman adds.

Her place?

Now I get it. She's talking about Jackson's first wife. I didn't even know her name was Evelyn.

"He's not going to marry you anyway," the woman tells me. "He's married to food now. He's only experimenting with you now, like he does with his dishes, but he'll throw you away eventually. Everything spoils."

My jaw clenches. Now she's gone too far.

"I don't know who you are, but if you're not going to leave right now, I'm going to call the cops," I threaten her.

"You wouldn't."

"Try me." I hold my chin up. "Or don't. Like I said, you don't know me."

For a moment, she just stands there with her lips curled like some dog about to attack. Then she turns and bolts.

I let out a sigh of relief as I touch my nape.

Well, that was crazy. She was crazy. What did she call herself again? A chef groupie?

I guess I'll have to ask Jackson about that.

CHAPTER 8

Jackson

"Yup. That's what they call themselves," I tell Cathy as I set a bowl of ice cream in front of her. "Chef groupies. They're fans of chefs in general or one particular chef. They follow their social media accounts, buy their books, try to replicate their recipes, go to their restaurants."

"And insult their fiancees?" Cathy suggests.

I frown as I sit beside her. Cathy hasn't told me exactly what the groupie said, but I can tell it offended her and I can't help but feel a little guilty. I should have known this could happen. I should have warned her.

"I know I'm not your real fiancee," Cathy goes on. "But they think I am. How do they even know?"

I shrug.

"She said it was on their site. I tried to look for it, but I can't find it."

"I can give you the link and the password," I offer. "They sent one to me."

Cathy sighs. "I just don't know how they know."

I say nothing as I eat my ice cream. She slips a spoonful into her mouth and then turns to me with the spoon still between her lips. She pulls it out.

"You don't think Betty told them, do you?"

"That's possible," I say. "Like I said, she's capable of many things. I wouldn't be surprised if she's pretending to be one of my groupies on that site. She might even be an administrator."

Cathy frowns. "But why would she tell them?"

"Because she knew this would happen," I answer. "She probably wanted them to scare you off or at least cause you some trouble. Maybe it's a test. Maybe she wants to see what kind of woman you really are."

"Well, I don't like it." Cathy puts down her spoon. "I don't like being tested or being insulted. I don't like the world meddling in my affairs."

"I know." I place my hand over hers. "I don't like it either. I didn't ask to be a celebrity or to have groupies. I mean, I'm okay with the fact that they buy my books and go to my restaurants, but I don't like it when they cross the line and try to get personal."

Cathy looks at me. "So they've caused you trouble before?"

"One of them tried to get a lock of my hair once when she came to my restaurant and took a picture with me." I touch my head. "That hurt."

Cathy frowns.

"And some of them send me messages, asking me to come to their house and cook for them or saying stuff like they want to eat me all up."

Cathy grimaces. "That's... disgusting. How do you deal with stuff like that?"

"I don't. I just ignore them."

Cathy lets out a sigh. "I guess I'll have to do that, too."

I pat her hand. "You'll get used to it."

"I'm not sure I want to." She picks up her spoon. "Dealing with Betty is hard enough. Now, I have to deal with the whole world."

I chuckle. "I'm pretty sure I don't have that many fans."

"But your fans sure are crazy."

"Aren't they all? I thought that's why they're called fans. Fanatics."

"Well, they hate me," Cathy pouts as she sticks her spoon into her bowl. "They love you and they hate me."

"Well, I don't care."

I touch her hand once more. She turns her head and meets my gaze. I hold hers.

"It doesn't matter what they think. Didn't you say that? Didn't you say their judgment isn't good enough?" I squeeze her hand. "You are my fiancee."

"Your fake fiancee," Cathy corrects me.

"Who's a real stunner," I tease.

Just as I expected, she blushes. Hell, something must be wrong with me, but I just can't help but think she's hotter when her cheeks are all aflame like that.

She pulls her hand away. "I'm being serious here."

"Too serious," I tell her. "You should be in a lighter mood when you're eating ice cream, especially ice cream as good as this."

I eat another spoonful of my berries and vanilla concoction. Cathy does the same.

"It is good," she agrees. "Not too sweet. And the texture is just... exquisite."

She takes another spoonful and finally smiles.

"Well done, Chef."

I, too, smile as I pretend to tip a hat. "I'm honored."

That's why I became a chef - to bring comfort and joy to others through food, to help them forget their worries for a little while. It's not easy, but every smile from every diner makes every bead of sweat worth it.

Cathy eats the rest of her ice cream in silence. When she's done, she grabs a table napkin and wipes her lips. She keeps it in between her fingers as she puts her hand down.

"You know what bothers me the most?" she asks me softly.

"What?"

"The fact that those groupies seem to know more about you than I do," she answers. "Here I am living with you, eating with you, working with you, being your fake fiancee and all, and yet, I still don't know anything about you."

"That's not true," I tell her. "You knew me while I was growing up, before I became a chef. You know me better than they do."

"Maybe. But they know about your wife and I don't." Cathy's shoulders sink as she breathes out a sigh. "I didn't even know her name was Evelyn."

My eyebrows crease. "I didn't tell you?"

She shakes her head. "Now, I know it's none of my business, but I - "

"It's okay." I place my hand on her lap. "I guess you have a right to know."

"Do I? I'm not your real fiancee, after all."

"But you are living with me and taking care of Maisie," I say. "And I think it's better if you know, what with Betty being on your case and all. Besides, I think Evelyn would want you to know. I think she'd like you, actually. I think the two of you would get along if she was still around."

"She seems like a very nice person."

"She was," I confirm.

I fall silent as I think of Evelyn. Cathy says nothing. She looks like she's waiting expectantly for me to tell her more. And I intend to. But before that...

"You know what?" I get out of my chair. "I think we need more ice cream."

~

"So you and Evelyn met each other when you were in Thailand?" Cathy asks before licking the spoon in her hand.

"Yes." I set mine down and grab my glass of water to take a sip. "She was working for a nonprofit organization that caters to the needs of families in third-world countries and I was opening up my third restaurant. One time, she reserved a table for ten and brought a poor family in to eat my food. I was immediately touched by her generosity, her devotion to her cause. I thought I was already trying to make the world a better place, but she seemed to be doing it better."

"She sounds like a saint."

"I think to the people she was helping, she was, especially the children. They really looked up to her." I set down my glass. "Anyway, I told her she didn't have to pay for the meal. She insisted on paying at first. She was kind, but she had a stubborn streak in her. Or maybe it was just pride. Whatever the case, I didn't let up and she eventually gave in. Then we started talking about some kind of partnership. I was making money there, after all, so I wanted to help the locals as much as I could. I wanted to give back to the community."

"It sounds like she was able to recruit you to her cause."

"I think we had the same cause. We both wanted to make people happy, make their lives a little less hard. Cooking food was a great way to accomplish that."

"I believe it is." Cathy sets her spoon down in the middle of her empty bowl. "See. Just that bowl of ice cream has made me happy."

"Want another?" I ask her.

"No, thanks." She touches her stomach. "Like you said, people want to eat but they don't want to put on the pounds."

"I don't think a few pounds would hurt you," I tell her. "Besides, Ken gives you a workout every day."

"That she does," Cathy agrees with a grin. "But I think I've had enough ice cream just the same."

I chuckle. "If you say so."

"So what happened next?" she asks curiously.

Where was I? Right.

"We started dating. She started her own organization which focused more on improving people's lives through food. Then we moved back here to the US. Her family lives in New York."

"Betty?"

"And Andy, her father, who's a stockbroker. She has a brother and a sister, too. She's from a rich family, but I had already guessed that. I think if I wasn't already a Michelin-starred chef, her parents would never have approved of our relationship. Not that Evelyn and I wouldn't have gone through with it anyway. As it was, they were thrilled."

"Betty was thrilled?" Cathy gives me a look of disbelief.

"Well, she didn't disapprove of me, at least. I remember her bringing her friends to my restaurant in New York once and telling them how glad she was that her son-in-law was a chef."

"So you lived in New York?"

"For a while. That's where Evelyn and I got married. But you know me, I had to open more restaurants, so I had to go from place to place. The more restaurants and stars I got, the busier I became. My marriage to Evelyn started suffering from it. No matter how kind and patient a woman is, she has limits, after all."

"Of course," Cathy agrees. "Everyone gets tired of always giving."

"I actually thought we'd get divorced," I continue. "But then she got pregnant and everything changed. I realized I had to take care of my family."

"I guess a baby can save a marriage."

I nod. "It was like Evelyn and I were back at the start. Everything was exciting again. We couldn't bear to be apart. But just when I thought everything was going to be alright, Evelyn found out she was sick."

I frown as I remember that day. I'll never forget it. I'll never forget how she cried as she told me about her condition and then how she gave a big smile afterwards when she told me what she was going to do about it.

"She could have been treated, but not while she was pregnant. She would have had to get rid of the baby, and Evelyn couldn't do that. She said she couldn't live if it meant someone innocent had to die."

Cathy gasps softly. I can tell she's reliving the emotions I felt that day - the pain, the anger at how cruel everything was and how helpless I felt.

"I told her she was innocent, too, but she wouldn't hear it. I had no choice but to respect her decision. I hated it. I hated the fact that she was dying each day while our baby grew inside her. I hated the fact that I couldn't do anything to save her. All I could do was try to make her happy and hope that after the baby was born, it wouldn't be too late for Evelyn to keep living. But my hope was useless." My hands clench into fists on my lap. "It was too late. Evelyn started getting the treatment, but it wasn't doing much for her. Childbirth had taken too much of her strength. She died weeks after Maisie was born."

Cathy places her hand over mine. "I'm so sorry. I'm sorry about what happened to her and I'm sorry you had to relive it by telling me."

I shake my head. "It's not like I'll ever forget it."

Sure, I've managed to move on. It doesn't hurt so much to think of Evelyn anymore. But I'll remember her as long as I live.

"Betty isn't ever going to let me forget it," I add.

Cathy frowns. "Does she blame you?"

I nod. "She thinks I could have talked Evelyn into getting rid of the baby, into living."

"She didn't know about Evelyn's condition?"

"No. Evelyn didn't want anyone else to know. And that's one more thing Betty resents me for. She thinks I should have told her."

"I see."

I reach for my glass of water as I run out of things to say. To my surprise, she squeezes my hand. When I meet her gaze, I see the sadness on her face.

She's not going to cry, is she?

"It's not your fault Evelyn died," Cathy tells me as she looks into my eyes. "It was no one's fault, but it was her choice."

"I know." I look away. "But I still can't help but think maybe she made that choice because of me. Maybe she wanted to have a baby so badly because I made her feel so alone, because I'd let our marriage fall apart."

"Don't think that." Cathy places her hand on my cheek and turns my face to hers. "Whatever Evelyn's reasons, it was her choice. And you supported her. I know that must have been very hard for you, but things were a hundred times harder for her. She had the toughest choice to make of all - choosing between being with the man she loved and saving the child she might never get to see grow up. She needed your support, and you gave it to her. You tried to make her happy. I'm sure she had no regrets in the end. She wouldn't want you to have any, either."

I say nothing as I gaze into Cathy's eyes. I thought she was on the brink of tears because she felt sad about what happened to Evelyn, but now I realize those tears are for me. My throat tightens.

"You deserve to be happy, Jackson. Evelyn would want you to be."

As she gives me a soft smile, the fog of sadness in her eyes thins. It's still there, but I can also see other things now - hope, concern and something that sends warmth flooding into my chest.

I said she had a hard shell around her heart, but I had one, too, and now it seems like that shell is melting away.

I place my hand over hers. I suddenly have an urge to plant a kiss in her palm, to place my own hand on her cheek and bring her face close to mine.

I want to taste more of that warmth Cathy's offering, the warmth that's made me feel alive again.

The ringing of my phone shatters the moment. Cathy's hand slips away, her eyes breaking contact with mine. I mutter a curse as I get my phone out of my pocket. I feel like saying another when I see Betty's name on the screen.

"I should go," Cathy mumbles as she gets off her stool. "I have to get some rest or I won't survive Ken's workout tomorrow."

I nod. "Good night."

"Good night."

I watch Cathy walk out of the kitchen, my heart heavy. Somehow, I can't help feeling like I've just missed out on an incredible opportunity.

After she leaves, I let out a sigh and hold my phone to my ear. "What is it, Betty?"

This better be good, though I already have a feeling it isn't.

"Must you really sound so annoyed to get a call from me?" Betty asks.

I draw a breath and make an effort to sound more calm. "What is it?"

"Is Cathy with you?"

"Not right now, no."

Not anymore.

"Good, because I wanted to talk about her," Betty says.

I shake my head. "There's nothing we need to discuss about her, Betty."

"But there is. I asked someone to look into Cathy's background."

I roll my eyes. Of course she did.

"Do you know that she has amnesia?" Betty asks.

"She can't remember a few things. I know."

"Or that she got so depressed after she nearly drowned that she stopped going to school?"

"Of course she was depressed. And it's not because she nearly drowned. It's because her best friend did drown. My sister."

"Oh." Betty sounds surprised.

So Cathy's file didn't say that, did it?

"I know what you're doing, Betty, and I'm telling you now: Stop it."

"I won't. My granddaughter's welfare, her future, her life are at stake here. I won't have her living with a woman who's mentally unstable."

Yet she wants Maisie to live with her? That almost makes me laugh.

"Just stop it, Betty," I tell her. "I mean it."

I hang up. As I finish what's left of my ice cream, now mostly a puddle, I curse the fact that Evelyn left me her mother. God, she's the most difficult woman I know.

That's not all Evelyn's left me, though. She also left me Maisie, my greatest treasure. And memories. Memories to give me strength.

Don't be afraid to find happiness, Jackson. I can almost hear those final words from her ringing in my ear, words that I thought I'd forgotten.

You deserve to be happy. Cathy's words echo inside my head as well.

My lips curve into a smile as I remember that look in her eyes as she told me those words.

Who knows? With her help, I just might be.

CHAPTER 9

Cathy

"You look happy," I tell Maisie as I glimpse her smiling face in the backseat through the rearview mirror.

"I had fun today," she says. "I made a castle out of pink clay."

"Did you now?" I try to catch her gaze. "I wish I had seen it. I'm sure it was enchanting."

"What's enchanting?"

"Magical."

"Hmm. It was okay."

I grin.

"Will you read me a story again later?" Maisie asks.

"Sure, sweetheart."

Her face lights up with an even wider smile. "Thank you."

Then she turns her attention out the window. I grip the wheel and focus my eyes on the road.

Maisie really is such a sweet little girl. It's a pity she never knew her mother.

Ever since I heard about Evelyn a few days ago, I've been seeing Maisie in a different light. I hug her a little tighter before tucking her into bed at night, knowing that she could easily have not been born. I'm even more determined to take care of her, even more watchful of her when we play in the garden, even more careful when feeding her grapes, because I'm aware of the sacrifice that was made for her to exist. One day, Maisie will find out about it, and I hope that when that day comes, she won't feel a shred of guilt but instead feel more special. Until then, as long as she's under my care, I'll treat her like a precious gem and give her all the love a mother could give. I owe it to Evelyn.

And it's not just Maisie. It's Jackson, too. I know now why he dotes on his daughter. I'm grateful for it. I'm glad he didn't choose to be cold towards her because she reminds him of what he's lost but instead embraced her because she's a living reminder of what's left behind. It has made me think I shouldn't blame Jackson for reminding me of Trisha.

I know now why he insisted on this false engagement, why he didn't want to send me away. He wants to protect me like he was unable to protect Evelyn. He doesn't want to lose me to have his daughter by his side. He already lost his wife to have Maisie. He wants to keep us both by his side.

He's usually smiling, but now I know the pain he's endured through the years, ever since I last saw him. I feel like I know him better now. And having suffered myself, I have even more respect for how he's managed to move on. Admiration, even. Maybe a bit of envy. And a heightened concern. I don't want him to suffer anymore, especially not alone.

I want to stay by his side.

That last thought takes me by surprise. I shake my head. What am I thinking? I'm his fake fiancee, nothing more.

Do I want more?

My thoughts come to an end as I reach the house. As I pull into the driveway, I notice a silver Subaru sedan parked near some bushes. I recognize the make and the license plate and my eyes grow wide.

No way.

As soon as I park the car, I hear a familiar voice calling my name.

"Cathy!"

"Mom?" I throw her a puzzled look.

What is she doing here?

I wait until she's given me a hug to ask her questions.

"What's with the surprise visit?" I hide my left hand behind my back so she won't see the diamond ring. I try to take it off but it won't budge. "Shouldn't you be with the other kids?"

"You'll always be my kid." She tucks a loose strand of hair behind my ear. "I wanted to see you. I've been missing those nighttime conversations we used to have."

"I'm not avoiding you on purpose, Mom," I tell her as I slip my hand into my pocket.

I make a mental note to go to the bathroom in a bit so I can use some soap to take the ring off and hide it somewhere.

"I've just been busy with work."

"I know." She touches my cheek. "You've finally grown up, and I always thought you would, but now I can't help but wish you were a child again."

"Mom..."

"And of course I wanted to personally congratulate you on getting a job. Tell me all about it. You said it's a management internship?"

"Actually, I'm a management trainee now," I update her. "That means I'm hired for the job as a manager but still in training. When I'm done with training, I'll manage the restaurant."

"That's wonderful."

I glance at her car. "Um, how did you know where I live now?"

"I went to your old apartment and Mrs. Garland gave me your new address." She puts a hand on her hip. "Frankly, I'm disappointed that you didn't tell me you moved out."

Right. I didn't tell her about that. I was going to, but I was afraid she'd come over if she knew. Well, she came over anyway.

"At least, I was," she says as she glances at the house. "Now that I see what an amazing place you moved into, I feel better. How much are you paying to stay here, though? Are you staying with someone?"

I don't get to answer her question because I hear Maisie's voice from inside the car. My eyes grow wide as I realize she's still strapped into her car seat.

Didn't I say I'd take better care of her?

I run to the backseat.

"I'm sorry, sweetheart," I tell Maisie as I bring her out of the car.

"It's okay." She glances at my mother. "Hello."

"Well, hello there." My mother puts her hands on her knees and smiles. "What's your name?"

Maisie walks towards her. "Maisie. What's your name?"

My Mom chuckles. "Nina. I'm Cathy's mommy."

Maisie looks at me. "She's your mommy?"

I nod. "Yes."

Maisie turns back to my mother. "How old are you?"

My Mom touches Maisie's cheek. "Oh, darling, one never asks a mother that question. It's a secret."

Maisie looks confused but doesn't press the issue.

"Are you looking after this little girl?" my mom asks me. "Don't tell me you've adopted now, too."

"No." I shake my head. "I didn't adopt her. She's - "

"Cathy lives with me and my dad," Maisie blurts out.

My mother's eyes grow wide. My jaw drops. Oh shit.

My Mom straightens up and looks at me. "Cathy?"

"It's not what you think, Mom," I explain. "It's true. I live here with Maisie and her dad. Her dad owns the restaurant and he invited me to stay here at his house."

"I see." She puts a hand on her hip. "Is that why you didn't tell me you moved out of your old apartment? Because you're living with a man now?"

"Mom..."

"Cathy, let's go inside," Maisie interrupts.

I glance at the house. I see Mrs. Henderson, the housekeeper, through the window.

I pinch Maisie's cheek lightly. "Why don't you go inside, hmm? Ask Mrs. Henderson to help you look for that stuffed bunny you said you couldn't find this morning."

"Okay." Maisie runs off into the house.

I watch her until she's through the door and then peek through the window to make sure Mrs. Henderson has her.

"That little girl treats you like her mother," my mom observes out loud.

"That's because she doesn't have one," I answer. "Her mother died shortly after giving birth to her."

"Poor thing." My mom clicks her tongue as she glances at the house. Then she turns to me. "So that means the man you're staying with is a widower. That's a relief, at least. I was afraid you were staying with a married man."

"What?"

"Or a divorced man."

"No."

"I'm still not sure I like the idea of you living with a man and his child at their home, though. It just doesn't seem right, Cathy."

"Well, he's not just any man," I tell my mother. "You know him, actually."

"I do?"

"Jackson Holloway," I give her the name.

She clasps a hand over her mouth as she gasps. "You mean... T... Trisha's...?"

"Her older brother, yes. He's a chef now. He owns a lot of restaurants."

Her hand slides down to her chest. "Oh, who'd have thought?"

"I know. I never expected it, either."

"But is it okay with you?" she asks me. "I mean with him being... her brother and all."

"You mean doesn't it bother me to live with a person who reminds me of... Trisha? It did at first, but not anymore. It's not his fault he reminds me of her or that she's gone."

"Of course not." She takes my hands in hers. "I just meant that you've been trying hard to move on and now..."

She stops suddenly, then her gaze drops to my hands, particularly to my left.

Oh, shit.

I pull my hand away. It's too late, though. She's already seen the ring.

"Is that...?"

I step back. "It's nothing, Mom."

She narrows her eyes at me suspiciously. "Cathy Josephine Jeffries, are you engaged?"

I let out a sigh. I guess I have to explain everything to her now.

"It's not - "

"You're engaged to Jackson?" She takes my left hand. "Why, this ring is beautiful."

"It is," I agree.

"The diamond is real, isn't it?"

"Yes, but - "

"Oh, I'm so happy for you." She squeezes my hands. "I was so worried that you'd never get to live your own life, that you'd dwell in the past forever, but look at you. You have a future. You have your whole life ahead of you."

How am I supposed to tell her the truth after hearing all that?

I squeeze her hands in turn. "You don't have to worry about me anymore, Mom."

"There I was wondering if you'd ever get a boyfriend or even ever go on a date and here you are, engaged."

She looks genuinely happy for me and I don't have the heart to break hers, not after I've caused her so much sadness and worry.

I shrug. "Yes. Here I am."

"I'm disappointed you didn't tell me about it, though." She crosses her arms over her chest. "Why didn't you tell me?"

I rub the back of my head. "I... wanted to tell you in person, but I'm so busy with the restaurant opening that I didn't have time to go home."

"Then it's a good thing I've come." She touches my cheek. "I knew it. I knew there was a voice telling me to come see you."

I give her a smile.

She hooks her arm around mine and leads me into the house. "Now, you must tell me everything. Tell me how this wonderful thing happened. And of course, I must meet your fiance. Tell me, has he grown handsome?"

"You won't believe your eyes, Mom."

At least that isn't a lie.

She chuckles. "Well, I'd like to tell him a few things."

"He's not home yet," I tell her.

"Then I'll wait. In the meantime, you can tell me about how you got engaged, about when you plan to get married. Oh, you must let me help you pick your wedding gown. How was your reunion with Jackson? Was it love at first sight? Did you...?"

I let out a deep breath as I stop listening to her questions. It's not like I can answer them all at once anyway, or even remember them all.

Thank goodness it's my day off tomorrow, because I have a feeling this is going to be a long night.

~

"Your mother left already?" Jackson asks me in the morning as I enter the kitchen.

"Yes," I answer.

I pull out a stool and sit at the counter resting my face on my hands.

Finally, my interrogation is over.

Jackson sets a cup of coffee in front of me. "You look relieved."

"Not really." I place both hands around it and inhale the steam. "I don't know how I'm supposed to tell her now that the engagement isn't real."

"You don't have to." He leans on the counter in front of me. "You can just tell her when the engagement has been broken off."

The thought brings a frown to my face, though I don't know what makes me sadder - the fact that breaking off the engagement will break my mother's heart or the fact that her heart may not be all that gets broken.

"At least she was happy for us," Jackson says. "Unlike Betty."

"Right." I grin. "But of course, she isn't like Betty."

They're as different as night and day.

"Did you hear what Maisie said? She said your mother makes a better grandma."

My eyebrows arch. "She did?"

Jackson nods.

"Well, I don't blame her. I think the same thing."

"Same here," he says. "Your mother's still as kind as ever. She hasn't changed much, actually. She still looks... young."

I lift my cup to my lips. "Do you know your daughter asked her how old she was? She didn't like that."

Jackson chuckles. "What did Nina say?"

"She said that one never asks a mother that question." I take a sip of coffee and set down my cup. "I was actually afraid then that she would ask Maisie about her mother. I'm glad she didn't."

"It would have been fine," Jackson says. "I don't think it really bothers her."

Doesn't it? When Maisie was talking about her mother last weekend, it sounded like she wished she was still around. But of course she does. Who wouldn't? Or maybe she just wants a mother.

"I've been meaning to thank you, by the way." Jackson places his hand over mine.

My pulse quickens.

"For listening to me tell you about Evelyn," he says as he looks into my eyes. "I haven't really spoken about her to anyone since she passed away."

It feels like I might drown in those dark pools. I hold my breath.

"And for all the things you said. They... gave me strength."

I suddenly become aware of the warmth of his hand. My palm starts to tingle. His burning gaze lights a fire in my cheeks and in my chest. A lump forms in my throat.

I swallow. "I'm sure you don't need me to give you strength. You've managed to move on all on your own. You..."

I pause as I try to pull my hand away. He holds it fast.

My heart stops.

"Just the same, I'm grateful," Jackson tells me, his voice sounding a tad deeper. "I'm glad I saw you again, Cathy."

My breath catches. What is this? Is he playing some game with me again? He looks serious, though.

"Cathy!" Maisie suddenly bursts into the kitchen in her blue pajamas. "Daddy!"

At once, Jackson lets go of my hand. He goes around the corner to give her a hug.

"Good morning, sweetheart." He lifts her in his arms. "Slept well?"

Maisie nods. "Because Cathy told me lots of stories."

I smile. I don't know how I still managed to tell her bedtime stories after answering my mom's questions, but I did.

"Maybe you should ask your daddy to read you stories next time," I suggest.

"Will you?" Maisie asks him hopefully.

"Sure." Jackson plants a kiss on the top of her head. "Why not?"

Maisie grins. "That's my favorite question."

Jackson and I laugh.

Maisie gets out of Jackson's arms and runs to me. She tugs my shirt.

"Come, Cathy. I want to show you something," she says.

"Okay. But maybe after I'm done with my coffee?"

I lift my mug.

She shakes her head. "I want you to see it now."

"Maisie," Jackson warns.

"No, it's fine." I get off my stool. "I'll just bring my coffee."

I hold it in one hand and grab Maisie's hand with the other. "Let's go."

Jackson says nothing as Maisie leads me out of the kitchen. When I glance back, though, I notice a frown on his face.

Why does he look like he's just been robbed?

CHAPTER 10

Jackson

I check the last security camera in the corner of the restaurant's dining area, then walk to the middle of the room to assess the work that's been done.

The interior is finished now. The walls, floors and ceiling have been repainted, the new light fixtures installed, the windows replaced. All that's left is for the furniture to be brought in, particularly the dining tables and chairs, and for the interior decorator I've hired to work her magic and give the room a cozy, almost romantic ambience.

Everything is slowly falling into place.

At least, it is in the restaurant. At home, nothing has changed. I haven't made any progress with Cathy. I've barely been able to get her alone. Each time I try, I get a phone call or she remembers something she has to do or more often than not, Maisie barges in just like she did yesterday morning. Frankly, it's getting frustrating.

"Wow," Cathy's voice breaks into my thoughts as she enters the room. "This place is starting to look fantastic."

I throw her a puzzled look. "What are you doing here? Isn't it your day off?"

"Ken called and told me the wines were being delivered today," she says. "She asked me to handle it, so here I am."

Here she is.

"I was going to take Maisie to daycare since I don't know how long this will take, but Mrs. Henderson and Alice offered to take care of her. I hope you don't mind."

I shake my head. "They seem to be taken with her, too."

Cathy shrugs. "Who isn't?"

At any rate, that means that Cathy and I are alone. Well, there are still some workers around, but they're all outside. In here, it's just Cathy and me.

I'm about to take a step closer to her when I hear a truck pull into the driveway.

"That must be the wines," Cathy says as she heads to the door. "They're early."

"They are," I say sourly.

Oh well. I guess I'll just have to wait for another opportunity.

Cathy stops at the doorway and glances at me. "Can you help me?"

"Sure." I put on a smile. "Let's bring in those wines for my restaurant."

~

Merlot. Shiraz. Pinot Noir. Cabernet Sauvignon. Riesling. Chardonnay. Rose.

I grin in approval as I look at the varieties of wine displayed in the crates and boxes spread out on the floor. There's one from every prominent region - France, Italy, Spain, Australia, Chile, and of course, here in California. I'm sure there's one to complement every dish I've created and to suit every diner's taste perfectly.

"Isn't this too much wine?" Cathy asks as she types something on the tablet she's holding.

"What do you mean? We're going to have a lot of diners, so we need a lot of wine."

"I just don't understand why you need wine to enjoy food. Won't the wine actually keep you from enjoying the food? I mean, will you still be able to taste it if you're drunk?"

I lift an eyebrow. "You've never had wine, have you?"

She shakes her head. "Nope. Never found it necessary, either."

"Well, now it is." I approach her. "How will you know which wine goes with what if a diner asks you unless you try them? How will you know which pairings are good and which are not?"

She gives me a puzzled look. "Surely that's someone else's job."

"But isn't it also your job to know everyone's job?" I ask her. "If you don't know what the staff is supposed to do, how can you make sure they're doing it?"

Cathy frowns because I'm right.

"Besides, you'll be managing this restaurant in the future," I add. "Shouldn't you know everything there is to know about it?"

"So what are you saying? That I should taste all the wines here?"

"Exactly." I take the tablet from her hand. "I'll cook some food, we'll open a few bottles, and we can have a wine tasting party. It will be a celebration of the fact that you're now a permanent employee here, too. How does that sound?"

Cathy shrugs. "Fine. If you say I have to do it, then I'll do it."

"Good."

She lifts a finger. "Just try not to get me drunk, okay? I don't want Maisie to see me swaying up the stairs, barely able to open my eyes."

I nod. I don't want her to get drunk either. If she does, I won't be able to do anything, which will defeat the purpose of this little exercise.

"Okay."

~

I did try.

I opened six bottles, but I poured only a little of each. I made sure Cathy drank the wine with food and that she drank water in between. But it was no use.

Right now, her eyes are already halfway closed. She looks like she might either fall off her chair or fall asleep at the table. And she's been talking. A lot. Some of the same things over and over, others that don't make any sense at all.

She's drunk, alright.

I let out a sigh. This is what I get for inviting someone who's never tasted wine before to a wine tasting.

So much for wanting to move things along. I guess I'll have to move her, though. I'll have to carry her home.

I walk over to her. "Come on. Let's go home."

"We're going home already?" Cathy asks in a slurred voice as she looks up at me.

"Yes." I grab her by her arm. "I think you've had more than enough."

"More than enough what?"

I pull her to her feet and place her arm around my shoulder. "Wine. Besides, Maisie's waiting."

"Maisie," Cathy mumbles.

"You do remember Maisie, don't you?" I ask her.

She nods. "Poor girl. To think that her mother died so that she could live. You think she'll be fine when she finds out?"

I frown. I'm not really looking forward to telling her, actually, though I know I'll have to someday. Not soon.

"I hope so," I answer.

"Well, she is strong. Still, to think that she never knew her mother. And she was so wonderful, too."

I say nothing as I lead her to the door. I'm more dragging her, though, since she can barely stand.

"Come on, Cathy."

"And poor you."

To my surprise, Cathy turns and puts her arms around me. I grip her waist to keep her from falling.

"Cathy..."

"It must have been so hard for you," she whispers against my chest as she squeezes me tight. "Watching the woman you loved die. And to think you couldn't tell anyone. You must have felt so alone."

I don't pay her words any heed because I know she's drunk. She won't remember all this rambling tomorrow. I find it harder to ignore the tender mounds of flesh pressing against my chest. And the scent of her hair. What's that? Orange with a hint of vanilla?

Already, I can feel my body reacting. Flames burst beneath my skin. Excitement buzzes through my veins.

This isn't good.

"Cathy..."

I'm about to push her away when her arms fall to her sides. I feel her grow limp against me and she starts to slide off my chest.

"Cathy!"

I manage to catch her as she falls, but the clip holding her hair in place clatters to the floor. I put her down gently so I can pick it up. I gaze down at her peaceful face and frown.

"Oh, what am I going to do with you?"

I put her clip in my pocket and brace myself to carry her like I do Maisie when she's fallen asleep. Suddenly, though, her eyes open halfway. Golden irises peek from beneath her eyelids and hold mine captive.

"Are you going to kiss me?" she asks softly.

I frown. "No."

Don't tempt me.

"Why not? I thought you wanted to kiss me."

My eyebrows furrow. Is that the alcohol talking? Or has she noticed what's been going on inside my head?

At any rate, I can't let her persuade me. Not now.

"You're drunk," I tell her as I take her arm. "Let's get you home."

"Are you going to turn me away again?" Cathy asks.

What?

"You're always like that, teasing me, leaving me hanging."

What is she talking about? Wait. Does that mean she wanted me to...?

Cathy sits up shakily. She looks into my eyes.

"Kiss me."

I swallow the lump in my throat. "No. I don't - "

"You don't want to?"

"It's not that." Hell, I've been wanting to kiss her for so long. "But now isn't - "

The rest of my sentence dwindles off as Cathy wraps her arms around my neck and presses her lips to mine. Clumsily. And yet it sends heat all the way to my groin. My cock throbs.

Oh, damn it to hell.

I place my hands on her cheeks and kiss her back. I slip my tongue between her lips and taste wine.

She's under the spell of wine. I'm under the spell of her.

I push my tongue in further, letting it rub against hers. Cathy moans.

I know she may not remember this tomorrow. I know she may even get mad at me and not forgive me. But right now, she's the one asking this of me. She's the one wanting. And I've waited far too long.

There's a limit to how much temptation a man can take, to the extent a man can rein in his desires. I've reached mine.

I slide one of my hands down to her neck and then to her back. I caress her spine and feel the fastenings of her bra.

I move my mouth to her ear as I slip my hands beneath her shirt. I trace the lobe with the tip of my tongue while my fingers work to release the hooks of her bra. Cathy gasps. Once they are undone, I bring my hands to the front to touch her breasts. She shivers.

I plant my mouth on Cathy's neck and caress the soft skin there with my lips and my tongue as I rub her breasts. Cathy's fingers grip my hair and she throws her head back. Her stiff nipples poke my palms.

I press my thumbs against the pebble-like nubs. I circle them and flick them until Cathy starts moaning and trembling. My cock turns hard as rock inside my boxers.

I want to savor this. I want to savor her. But I'm out of patience. Already, my mind is slipping away. My senses, my instincts are taking over.

I'm sorry, Cathy, but I can't hold back any longer.

I lay her down on the floor and take off her pants, then her underwear. I have them down to her knees when Cathy lifts her arm. Her hand touches my cheek.

"Jackson," she whispers my name as I meet her gaze.

I try to decipher it. Is she trying to tell me something? Is she asking me for something? At any rate, she doesn't seem like she wants me to stop, which is good, because I'm not sure I can at this point.

I claim her lips again. She whimpers. As I keep her mouth busy, I slip my hand between her legs. I find the damp folds of her skin and caress them.

I know I'm at my limit but I also know she's a virgin. She admitted as much. I have to try to be gentle. I don't want to hurt her.

I slip one finger in. It slides in all the way. No resistance. She's soaking wet inside. And burning hot. It feels as if my finger might melt away.

The knowledge that my mere kisses and quick touches have made her this way sends a roar of triumph and desire through my chest. A groan rumbles low in my throat.

I made her this way. Just me.

I move my finger in and out a few times before slipping in another. This time, Cathy pulls her mouth away from mine to let out a gasp. Her head falls to the side.

I plant a kiss on her cheek and lick her ear as I move my fingers slowly inside her. It's a tight fit. She's clamping down on my digits.

"Relax," I whisper in her ear. "Trust me."

I feel her start to draw deep breaths. Gradually, the sheath around my fingers loosens. I reach in deeply. Cathy moans. She shivers beneath me.

I lift her shirt and take one of her plump breasts inside my mouth as I move my fingers in and out slowly. Cathy lets out a soft cry. I drag my tongue across her nipple as I part my fingers to form the shape of a scissor so I can stretch her. Then I begin to thrust them into her faster.

Cathy's body continues to tremble. When I withdraw my fingers, she lets out a whimper.

I hurry to unfasten my belt and unzip my pants. I take my aching cock out of my boxers, the cotton now stained. I kneel between Cathy's legs and position the tip at her opening.

"I'm going in."

I make the announcement in a hoarse whisper just a moment before I start to push my cock inside her. She lets out a loud gasp. As I continue pushing, her hands grip my arms. Cries spill past her lips.

I clench my jaw and grit my teeth as I resist the urge to just thrust into the depths of her while her velvety skin clings to me. My cock drowns in her heat and throbs.

It seems an eternity until I'm even halfway inside her. I can't wait any longer. I grip her thighs and push the rest of my cock in with one thrust before I start jerking my hips. I lift my head and close my eyes as I savor the sensation of my cock rubbing against her, inside her, of our bodies melting into one.

When I open my eyes and gaze at Cathy's face, the exquisite sight makes my cock swell even more inside her. Her cheeks are even redder now than before. Her eyelids are still halfway open, her irises dilated beneath them, seemingly glowing. Beads of sweat dot her forehead. Strands of golden hair stick to her cheeks. Her mouth is gaping open and I can hear sweet sounds coming from her throat.

I force my hips still as I decide to bring her pleasure first. She may not remember this tomorrow, but I still want her body to experience it.

And I want to see Cathy in the throes of ecstasy.

I reach down just an inch above where our bodies are connected and find her nub. I stroke it with my thumb and her lips purse. Her eyelids fall shut. Her features twist in rapture.

Beautiful.

My cock quivers inside her but I make it wait as I focus on Cathy's pleasure. With each swipe of my thumb, she seems to be inching closer and closer to its peak. Finally, her back arches. I stop stroking her and watch in fascination as Cathy unravels beneath me. She lets out a loud cry as she grips my shoulders. Her nails dig into my skin through cotton and she tightens around me.

Fuck.

My muscle clenches as I wait for some of the tightness to fade. As soon as I can, I start moving again. I'm close as well. Hell, I've been close from the beginning.

I manage a few thrusts before I feel a burning heat in my balls.

"Coming!"

I bury myself inside her as it bursts. My cock jerks wildly in its sheath as all my pent up desire and frustration spill out. Grunts escape my lips.

After a few moments of catching my breath, I pull my spent cock out. Cathy's arms fall to her side. She can barely keep her eyes open as she looks at me.

I bend over to plant a kiss on her forehead. After I move away, I find her eyes shut. Her lips curve into a smile. Seconds later, I hear her even breathing.

Seems like now that she's gotten what she wanted, she's finally given in to the alcohol and fallen asleep. Or maybe it's just the exhaustion of sex.

Whatever the reason, I have to get her home. I fix my clothes and then hers. Then I carry her in my arms like a bride. As I bring her to the car, I hear her snore softly.

I sigh.

Really, what am I going to do with you?

CHAPTER 11

Cathy

What did I do?

I try to recall the answer to the question as I sit on my bed with my head between my hands. I feel like if I take my hands off, my head might split apart. And that's not the only discomfort I've been feeling since I woke up to bright sunlight seeping through the curtains.

My stomach feels uneasy. My back hurts. My panties feel weird, and when I look, I find them reversed - the wider part facing the front and the thinner part giving me a wedgie - as well as wet and sticky. I feel sore between my legs as well, like I've been riding a horse for hours.

What the hell happened?

I draw a deep breath and try to dispel the fog of panic in my brain so I can think through the pain.

Think, Cathy. What were you doing yesterday?

I remember Ken calling about the wines. I remember going to the restaurant and finding Jackson there. Right, he was there. Then I remember trying to make my inventory of the wines and then confessing that I'd never drunk any, after which Jackson suggested a wine tasting party. And I remember the party, or at least some of it. I don't remember the names of the wines I tried, or which was best with what - I'll have to ask Jackson again - but I do remember slowly starting to feel fuzzy. I remember talking, though I can't recall exactly what I said.

And I remember Jackson telling me we had to go home to Maisie.

I touch my chin. What happened after that?

Let's see. I don't remember walking to the car, but I do remember Jackson helping me walk and I remember lying down on the floor. What the hell was I doing on the floor? Did I fall? Then I remember Jackson above me.

On top of me.

I peek beneath my pants. Wait a second. Does that mean we...?

I hold the thought as my stomach churns. I rush to the bathroom, making it to the toilet before I spew out most of the wine I drank.

I grimace. Why did I let Jackson convince me to drink wine? It's disgusting. And the smell is just...

Ugh. I'm never drinking wine again.

When my stomach has finally settled, I wash my face, change my clothes and go back to bed. I rest my head against the pillow and stare at the ceiling.

Did I really have sex with Jackson?

I can't remember the details, but just imagining it makes me blush. I place another pillow on top of my face.

How on earth could I have been so careless and stupid?

I'm still trying to get rid of my embarrassment when I hear the door open. I lift the pillow off my face and see Jackson enter the room carrying a tray.

"Oh, you're awake. That's good. I've brought you a bowl of meatball soup, which is supposedly good for hangovers, a pain reliever and a glass of apple juice. It's better if you take them."

He sets the tray down on the table in the corner.

As I glance at the table, my eyes go past the alarm clock. Wait. What time is...?

Another wave of panic washes over me as I realize it's already almost nine. And it's Monday. What the hell? I'm late for work.

I sit up and swing my legs out of bed but find myself unable to stand because of my headache.

Shit.

"Ken is so going to kill me," I mutter.

"No, she won't," Jackson tells me as he turns around. "I've already called her and told her you're not going to work today because you're not feeling well. I figured you'd have a hangover."

"And whose fault is that, hmm?" I glare at him. "Who was the one who told me to drink wine?"

"I told you to taste the wine," he reminds me. "You were the one who asked for full glasses."

"You also told me you wouldn't get me drunk."

"Well, I shouldn't have. I realize now that you can't stop someone from getting drunk. That is entirely up to them."

I frown. "So you're saying it's my fault I got drunk?"

Jackson doesn't answer that question. Instead, he grabs the glass of juice from the tray and brings it to me.

"Here. Drink this."

I look at him. "Are you going to say it's also my fault we had sex?"

Jackson grows still.

"Well?"

His face grows somber as he sets the glass down on the bedside table. "If you're asking me if you were the one who initiated it, yes you did."

My eyes grow wide. No way.

"Why would I do such a thing?"

"Because you were drunk, and when you're drunk, you tend to be more honest with yourself and more willing to act on your desires."

I give him a puzzled look. "You're saying I've been wanting to have sex with you."

"Haven't you?" Jackson asks me.

I look away. True, there have been times when the look in his eyes made me feel hot, when a brush of his fingers made my heart stop. I've looked at him and wondered how it would feel to have a man's body next to mine. And fine, maybe I've wondered how sex with Jackson would be like.

Does that mean I've been wanting to have sex with him?

"You should have said no," I tell Jackson. "You should have pushed me away."

"I tried."

"Not hard enough."

"Maybe," he admits. "I haven't had a woman since Evelyn died, so my self-control is a little rusty."

The confession takes me by surprise. I'm the first woman he's been with since his wife died?

Still, I frown. "You promised me that nothing would change because of our 'engagement'. We're just supposed to be... a fake couple. We're really a boss and an employee. Or friends. Nothing more."

"So it's my fault that I indulged you?"

"I didn't want you to!" I raise my voice then bow my head as I shake it. "I wasn't expecting you to. I thought you saw me as a little sister. Didn't you say I was practically family?"

"Because you work for me," Jackson says. "I treat everyone who works in my restaurants as part of my family."

Oh. So that's what he meant.

"And for the record, I never saw you as a little sister."

My eyebrows go up. What?

"But you're right," he goes on. "It's all my fault. I'm your boss. I shouldn't have told you to drink. And I'm older than you. I'm the experienced one. I was the sober one, the one who was supposed to be thinking clearly. But I didn't. I let my emotions and my senses carry me away. I gave in to desire."

I fall silent. I should be glad he's taking the blame. Instead, the pain in his voice is just making me feel more guilty.

"But my biggest mistake is that I thought you'd grown up. Clearly, I was wrong about that."

Jackson leaves the room. I lie back on the bed and put the pillow back over my face, my head hurting even more than before.

Now what have I done?

~

By noon, I decide I'm tired of doing nothing all day.

Besides, I feel better. Thanks to the pain reliever Jackson brought me, a few more hours of sleep and a shower, my headache is nearly all gone. After throwing up one more time and then eating the soup he made for me, my stomach feels more settled. My back doesn't hurt anymore, either, and I'm no longer sore. Or sticky. I am feeling guilty for being mean to Jackson when he came to my room to take care of me, but physically I've just about made a full recovery, so I see no reason why I should stay at home.

I change into some work clothes and head to the front door. I find myself unable to go through, though, because someone is standing right in front of it, seemingly about to ring the doorbell.

Someone who makes me wish I could crawl right back into bed.

"Betty." I greet her with the best fake smile I can muster.

"Cathy," she says my name plainly with just a twitch of a grin.

What is she doing here? Isn't she supposed to be back in New York?

"If you're looking for Jackson and Maisie, they're not here," I tell her. "Jackson is - "

"Working, I know," Betty finishes. "And Maisie is at daycare. I came to see you."

My eyebrows furrow. "Me?"

"Yes." She barges into the house, hitting my shoulder. "You didn't go to work today. Why?"

My eyes grow wide. How on earth did she know that? Has she been spying on me?

And so what if I didn't go in? Is that a crime?

"I'm about to go in, actually," I say.

"But you didn't this morning," Betty says. "Why?"

Why does she want to know?

"I'm sorry, but I have to go in now," I answer.

In other words, it's none of her business. Betty doesn't take the hint, though.

"Are you not feeling well?" she asks me.

I draw a deep breath as I try to rein in my temper. "I - "

She places her hand against my neck. "You don't seem to have a fever."

She steps back and takes a look at me.

"And you're not sniffling. You don't seem to have a cold."

"I don't."

"What is it, then? A stomachache?"

Really, it's none of her business.

"I - "

"You're not pregnant, are you?" Betty blurts out.

The question makes me pause, not just because of how rude it sounds but because it makes me wonder about something for the first time today.

When you have sex, you get pregnant, right? Judging from the sticky stuff I found between my legs, Jackson didn't use any protection. What? Did I tell him not to? At any rate, he didn't. Could I be pregnant?

"No," I answer Betty as confidently as I can.

I can't be pregnant. I only just had my period. Besides, surely, it's too cruel for me to get pregnant the first time I have sex. Does that even happen to anyone?

Betty narrows her eyes at me. "You're sure?"

I narrow my eyes in turn because my patience has run out. "Sure. Now, can you please let me...?"

"Good," she cuts me off. "Then it's not too late."

I give her a puzzled look. "Not too late for what?"

"For you to break off the engagement," Betty says as she heads off to the living room. "That's what I've come to talk to you about today, whether you went to work or not. I was going to postpone it if you looked anywhere near the brink of death, but you don't, so I'll proceed."

I frown. Does this woman only ever think of herself? Something tells me yes.

I don't really want to follow her into the living room, but I seem to have no choice. I can't leave her here.

I go after her. "If it's the engagement you want to talk about, Betty, you'll have to talk to Jackson. He was the one who proposed, after all."

"And you were the one who said yes," she points out as she makes herself comfortable on the couch. "Don't act like some victim here."

"I'm not. I - "

"You have the power to break off the engagement if you so choose, and I'm here to convince you to choose so, to use that power."

I sigh. "I know you don't approve of our engagement..."

"Of course not," Betty confirms without a shred of hesitation. "How could I approve of someone like you becoming a stepmother to my granddaughter? You're practically a child yourself."

Another insult.

"I'm twenty-six, Betty," I tell her as I place my hands on the back of a chair.

"Yet you've only just finished college," she points out. "You're only an intern."

"I'm a management trainee now," I correct her.

"Which you've only been for what? Three days?"

A bit more than that, but this time, I don't bother to say so.

"Regardless, this is your first time working, isn't it?" Betty asks.

"I don't see how that is important," I tell her.

"Ah, but it is. It means you don't know much about life yet. Like I said, you're still practically a child."

I frown but find myself unable to argue with her on the matter. She does have a point. I've just barely started living my own life. Besides, didn't Jackson himself say that I hadn't grown up?

"Maybe that's why Jackson is still in love with you," Betty goes on. "Because you haven't changed. Maybe to him, you're still this little girl he needs to protect."

So Betty knows about that, too, does she?

"Men like that, you know. They like protecting someone or even feeling like they are. It makes them feel like... well, men."

She turns her head towards me to meet my gaze.

"And you, you look like the kind of girl who likes to be protected."

My temper rises, but I try to keep it at bay. "If you're saying I want to feel safe, I won't deny it. Who doesn't? But if you're saying that's the only reason I'm with Jackson - "

"Why are you with him, then?" Betty gets off the couch to face me. "Is it for his money? Because he's so successful now?"

My trembling hands clench at my sides. How dare she?

"Or is it because you can't let go of Trisha?"

I grow still at the sound of her name.

"Is that why you're clinging to Jackson? Because by having him by your side, you still feel like you have - "

"Enough!" I snap at her.

She can insult me all she wants, but I'm not going to let her drag Trisha into this.

"Are you saying you love him, then?" Betty asks me as she looks into my eyes.

Again, I freeze.

"Are you saying you're not just physically attracted to this Jackson who looks very different from the one you used to have a crush on? That you don't just feel obliged to love him because you think he loves you?"

I don't answer. I don't know the answer.

I know I'm supposed to say yes. That's what a real fiancee is supposed to say. But I can't. I can't make up an answer when the question feels too real.

Am I just physically attracted to Jackson? But if that's the case, doesn't that mean all I want from him is sex? If so, why would I get mad at him for having sex with me?

Why do I want to stay by his side, then? Because of Maisie? Because I want to help him take care of her? Am I just trying to repay his kindness, or is it something else entirely?

Betty snorts. "Just as I thought, you don't love him."

I glare at her. "And you think you're an expert in love, do you?"

Betty's eyes grow wide.

Right. I can throw insults, too.

"You think that loving your granddaughter means having her all to yourself," I go on. "Do you think that taking Maisie away from her father will make her happy?"

Betty's jaw clenches. Now I've made her mad. Well, that means we're on the same playing field now.

"Are you presuming to know what's right for my granddaughter when you're not related to her in any way, when you're only using her father for your own selfish needs?"

I hold my chin high. "You think it's none of my business. Maybe you're right. Well, now you know how it feels to have someone meddle in your business the way you've been meddling in mine."

The veins on Betty's forehead look like they're on the verge of popping.

"Why, you little bitch!"

"Says the woman who came here just to insult me. Hasn't anyone taught you that if you can't say anything kind, you shouldn't say anything?"

Did she think that she'd win by trying to make me feel like dirt? All she's accomplished is to show me just how despicable she can be.

Betty doesn't answer. Her eyes glare at me. Well, she can glare all she wants, but I'm not going to turn into stone.

"Just go," I tell her calmly as I gesture to the front door.

For a moment, she just stands there, still glaring, seething. Then she draws a deep breath, grabs her purse and walks out of the room. Moments later, I hear the front door opening and slamming shut.

I sink into a chair and touch my forehead.

God, Maisie's grandmother is such a pain to deal with. It's almost worse than the hangover I was feeling earlier.

I let out a sigh as I look at the ceiling then close my eyes. Betty is just so exhausting.

I think of going back to bed, of taking the rest of the day off as well. Instead, I sit up. I've shown Betty that she can't squash me so easily. I'm not letting her stop me from doing what I have to do.

Besides, Jackson might have told Ken I'm not going to work because I'm not feeling well, but I'm sure she's still pissed I'm not there.

I stand up and walk to the front door.

~

"Well, well, well." Ken puts her hands on her hips as soon as she sees me. "Look who came back from the brink of death."

"I'm sorry I didn't come in this morning," I say as I pull the chair out of my desk. "I feel better now."

She leans on my desk. "Do you mean that the alcohol has worn off now or that you and Jackson have made up?"

I look at her with arched eyebrows. "What?"

Did Jackson tell her what happened?

"No, he didn't tell me anything," Ken answers my silent question. "But it doesn't take a genius to put two and two together. There were some open bottles of wine lying around when I got here. Only you and Jackson were here yesterday. You weren't feeling well and he seemed pissed. So yeah, I think you had your own little party, got drunk, had sex, and both regret it now that you're sober."

Her unbelievably accurate assessment leaves me in awe.

"Wow," I say when I've recovered my speech. "That... that was..."

"All true?"

I narrow my eyes at her. "Are you sure you're not psychic?"

"No, just really good at reading people and situations," Ken answers. "Which you need to be to be a good manager."

I nod. Of course.

She pulls a chair close to my desk and sits on it. "So? Tell me all the details. You owe me that much for not coming in this morning."

I sigh, then start telling her everything. It doesn't seem like I have much of a choice anyway.

When I'm done, Ken says nothing. She simply scratches her chin.

"Well?" I ask her. "What do you think?"

"That you're not as smart as I thought you were," she says.

I frown. She really doesn't mince words. Even so, I don't feel as insulted as I did when I was talking to Betty this morning. Maybe that's because I know Ken's telling the truth.

I was stupid.

"I don't care what Jackson told you," Ken tells me. "You shouldn't have drunk with him. The first time you drink should either be alone or with someone you trust completely. Drinking with someone who's attracted to you or who you're attracted to? Bad idea. Worse when it's both."

I look at her curiously. "Do you really think Jackson is attracted to me?"

Well, he did say he doesn't see me as a little sister. Correction. He never saw me as a little sister.

"Darling, the two of you had sex. I think that's proof of mutual attraction, don't you?"

I blush at the memory, or at least the thought of us... of Jackson's body against mine, of his...

Oh, stop thinking about it, Cathy.

"But I was wrong," Ken says. "Jackson's not pissed because he regrets it. On the contrary, he seems to have enjoyed it, which is why he's pissed that you regret it."

I scratch my head. "It did seem that way."

Ken shrugs. "Well, it's no wonder you regret having sex with Jackson if you were drunk, especially if it was your first time. I almost feel sorry for you for not remembering everything."

"That's not what I - "

"But you did agree to it. You said you even started it."

"Jackson said that," I correct her.

"And I see no reason for him to lie," Ken says. "Nor do I see that man pouncing on someone who doesn't want him."

I say nothing. I didn't say he did any such thing. I know he wouldn't. Is that how I made him feel?

"You made him an offer, one you now wish you hadn't made, but you did and he couldn't resist. You can hardly blame him for that. It's like blaming your dentist for fixing your tooth when you asked him to because you ate a load of candy that you shouldn't have."

I frown at the analogy. Isn't that going a tad too far?

"Anyway, my point is, stop the blame. What's done is done. Deal with it. That's the difference between children and adults - kids cry over spilled milk and adults wipe it off the floor."

My frown deepens. That's the third time I've been called a child today. Am I really so immature?

Ken pats my shoulder. "If you can't deal with the consequences, just pretend it never happened. Act like it. But don't get stuck in the past and don't sulk over something you haven't tried doing anything about."

She's right, of course. I've done something stupid, but I can't let myself keep acting stupid. I have to deal with it. I'm an adult, after all.

The question is: How?

I'm about to ask Ken for suggestions when her phone rings. She answers it.

"Hello."

I look away and try not to listen as she takes the call, but I can't help but arch my eyebrows when I hear Maisie's name.

Maisie? Does that mean she's talking to Jackson?

I look at Ken's face, alarmed when I see worry written all over it. Something bad has happened. I just know it.

"Alright," Ken says. "I'll tell you if we see her. In the meantime, try to stay calm."

She hangs up the phone.

If we see her? What does she mean?

"What's going on, Ken?" I ask her, unable to rein in my curiosity any longer.

Ken lets out a deep breath. "Maisie's missing."

I feel the blood drain from my face.

What?

CHAPTER 12

Jackson

I can't believe I lost Maisie.

I picked her up early from daycare because I had some free time and I wanted to spend it with her, especially since I didn't get to spend time with her yesterday. I was going to cheer her up with some ice cream, too, because she looked a little upset this morning from not being able to see Cathy.

As soon as I picked her up, though, Maisie started begging me to go to the park. It was just around the block from the daycare facility, so I thought, why not? I watched her as she ran around and went down the slide over and over.

I was pushing her on the swings when my phone rang. Looking back now, maybe I shouldn't have answered it, but I did. It was a supplier. I remember Maisie telling me to keep pushing her, but I couldn't. I could barely make conversation with the caller. The kids on the playground were just too noisy and I could hardly hear a thing. I told her to go and play and that I'd push her on the swing again when I was done with my call. I saw her go to the slide and I started walking away until it was quiet enough to talk. I was reluctant to leave her, but I didn't seem to have a choice. Besides, I trusted her.

She's a smart kid, I told myself. She wouldn't go anywhere with anyone.

But minutes later, when I was done with the phone call, which took longer than I thought it would, there was no sign of her.

Maisie was gone.

I called and called for her, up to a point that the other parents started to stare at me and worry. Only one of them offered to help me, though. We both searched around the playground, but it was no use. We couldn't find Maisie.

I went back to the daycare. She wasn't there. Some members of the staff offered to help look around. When we still couldn't find her, I called Ken. I knew there was precious little chance Maisie would be at the restaurant, of course. She'd have had to take a cab and tell the driver the address, which I'm not even sure she remembers. Still, I had to ask Ken, or at least inform her of the situation. I would have called Cathy, too, but I wasn't sure if she was feeling better yet.

Now, I'm at the police station, reporting the incident. Ever since I started talking to this cop, I've been feeling embarrassed, guilty. I have a feeling that inside his head, this officer is thinking what a lousy parent I am, and I can't disagree with him.

I am a lousy parent for having lost my only child. If something bad happens to her - and there are a hundred possibilities - or if she's never found, a possibility that's growing by the second, I will never forgive myself.

I clasp my hands in front of me as I try to keep them from shaking.

Oh, what have I done?

"We'll do our best to find her, Mr. Holloway," the officer promises.

"Please do everything you can," I beg him. "I don't know what you need to do, and I don't care how much money you need. Spare no expense. I can pay for everything. Just do whatever it takes."

"We will do everything we can," he assures me. "Please wait in the lobby."

I do as he says and drop myself on one end of the couch. I can't rest easy, though.

Will they really do everything they can? And will that be enough to find my little girl?

I bury my face in my hands.

I'm sorry, Evelyn. Please keep our little girl safe. Help her come back to me.

Please.

Suddenly, my phone rings. I frown as I see Betty's name on the screen. I didn't inform her about Maisie being missing, but I have a feeling she already knows.

I hold the phone against my ear. "Betty?"

"Is it true that Maisie is missing? Is it true that - ?"

"Not now, Betty," I cut her off. "I'll let you know if anything happens."

She starts to protest, but I hang up. I can't deal with her. Not right now. All I can think about now is finding Maisie.

Please let her be safe.

My phone rings again. With a sigh, I answer the call. "Betty..."

"It's me, Cathy."

I perk up at the sound of her voice.

"I'm sorry," I tell her. "I thought you were - "

"I found her," Cathy says. "I found Maisie."

~

"Maisie!" I run to my little girl as soon as I get out of the car.

I wrap my arms tightly around her and close my eyes as I savor the smell of her, the softness of her hair against my face, the warmth of her small body. I thought I'd lost her. I thought I'd never hold my baby girl in my arms again.

"I'm so glad you're safe."

I bury my hand in her hair and press her head against my shoulder. When I open my eyes, I see Cathy standing a few feet away. She looks better than she did when I left her this morning. A soft smile lights up her face.

I carry Maisie in my arms as I stand up.

"Where did you find her?" I ask Cathy.

"In the playground," she answers.

"The playground? But I looked and looked and..."

"Did you look inside those shells near the sand pit?" Cathy asks me.

She glances behind her at the shells, which seem to form some kind of cave or tent.

"No," I confess.

I thought the shells were just part of the decoration in the park, some eco-friendly art project. I didn't think a little girl would fit in there, much less go in there, but it seems Maisie did.

"I remembered that once when Maisie and I drove by the playground after I picked her up from daycare, I saw those shells and remarked that they looked like a mermaid castle," Cathy says. "When I saw them now, I immediately remembered that the last story I read to Maisie was 'The Little Mermaid'. I looked just in case she might be there, and there she was."

I look at Maisie and touch her cheek. "Were you in there the whole time? Didn't you hear me calling your name? I was so worried."

Maisie looks away without answering me.

"She seemed upset," Cathy tells me. "Or maybe she just didn't come out because she was pretending that she was a mermaid and you were a shark."

I have a feeling, though, that she was hiding from me because I yelled at her. I didn't mean to, but I must have because it was noisy. And then, even though she must have heard me calling, she must have ignored me because she was mad at me for sending her away.

I wrap my arms tightly around Maisie once more. "I'm sorry, sweetheart. I didn't mean to yell at you or send you away. I promise it won't happen again."

"Mm-hmm," I hear her answer.

I look into her eyes. "Do you forgive me? Do you forgive Daddy?"

Maisie nods. "I'm sorry, too, Daddy."

I brush her hair away as I give her a sweet smile. "I love you."

"I love you, too."

This time, she wraps her arms around my neck. I give her a squeeze as I whisper in her ear.

"I promise I'll never let you out of my sight again."

Maisie chuckles. "That's impossible, Daddy."

I, too, laugh. "You're right. It's impossible."

I touch her cheek.

"But I promise I'll take better care of you. I'll never let you get lost again."

She shrugs. "I wasn't lost."

I don't argue with her. I just plant a kiss on her forehead, then look at Cathy.

"Let's go home."

~

"She must be exhausted after that little... adventure," Cathy says as I pull the covers up to Maisie's chin.

Already, she's sound asleep. Her eyelids flutter. It's hard to believe that just minutes ago, she was singing at the top of her lungs in the car, having cheered up after we all went for ice cream.

I look at Maisie's peaceful face and smile. I'm just glad that she's back in her bed, that she's safe.

I'm going to make sure she stays that way.

I plant a kiss on her forehead before turning off the bedside lamp so that the spinning nightlight in the corner is all that illuminates the room. I walk quietly to the doorway where Cathy is waiting. I step out of the room and she closes the door behind her. The knob gives a soft click as she lets it go.

"Do you think she'll be alright?" I ask Cathy as we walk down the hall.

She nods. "She was already alright after those two ice cream cones."

I grin.

"Children are lucky," Cathy adds. "They get over their worries easily. Besides, I don't think Maisie was that worried.

She was safe in that shell, in her own world. It's strange, isn't it? When you're a child, imagination keeps you safe and happy. I guess that's what innocence means. When you grow up, imagination only causes fear and anxiety."

"I'm just glad she's safe," I say. "I don't know what I would have done if anything happened to her."

She shakes her head. "It wasn't your fault."

"Betty thinks so. She had a lot of bad things to say about my... capabilities as a father. If I hadn't hung up, I'm sure I would have heard more."

"Doesn't she always have bad things to say?"

"But this time, she's not entirely wrong," I answer. "I did fail to watch Maisie. She was right beside me and I sent her away. I was careless and irresponsible."

"You didn't send Maisie away," Cathy points out. "You told her to go and play. Most parents do that."

"Well, most parents don't take their eyes off their kids. I did."

"That's not true and you know it. Parents are humans, too. They make mistakes. They're allowed to. It's not a crime."

I shake my head. "And what if someone else had found Maisie? What if she got hurt? Would it still not be a crime?"

Cathy sighs. "And here I thought adults were supposed to wipe the milk off the floor."

I throw her a puzzled look. "What?"

"Maisie is safe, okay?" Cathy tells me. "That's what matters most here. As for what you did or didn't do, it's done. If you insist you've done something wrong, fine. But it's done. There's no use sulking over it. All you can do is be more careful next time. That's what grown-ups do, right? Admit their mistakes and learn from them."

I pause because I realize she's not just talking about what I did. She's talking about what happened yesterday, too.

I stop walking. "Cathy."

"Yes?" She stops and turns to me.

"Thank you for finding Maisie."

She shakes her head. "I was worried about her, too. You know how much she means to me."

"And I'm sorry," I add. "For the things I said this morning."

I draw a deep breath.

"And for yesterday, for - "

"You didn't do anything wrong," Cathy cuts me off. "I was the one who drank too much wine. I... seduced you."

My eyebrows arch at the confession.

She looks away with blushing cheeks. "What I'm saying is, I asked for it. I agreed to it. I'm... just as guilty as you. So you're right, it was immature of me and unfair to blame it all on you."

"But you still think it's a crime?" I ask her. "You still regret it?"

Cathy tucks a strand of hair behind her ear. "Well, I can't say I enjoyed it. I mean, I barely remember it. I would have wanted to, what with it being my first time and all."

Is that why she feels bad?

I grab her hand. "We can do it again, while you're sober. This time, you'll remember it. And you'll enjoy it."

I'll make sure she does.

Cathy pulls her hand away and tucks it inside her elbow as she crosses her arms over her chest. "Jackson, I... I don't know if we should. We're not a real couple, remember?"

"We could be," I tell her. "You know how I feel about you."

I told her I didn't see her as a little sister, and I mean it.

She touches the side of her neck. "But I don't know how I... feel about you. I'm... not even sure if I'm ready to feel anything other than pain and loneliness and..."

I take her hand once more. "You told me I deserve to be happy. The same applies to you. Trisha would want you to be happy, too."

"I know that, but..." She sighs as she fails to find the words to express how she feels.

"But you can't help but feel guilty, feel like it's wrong for you to be alive and happy when she's not?" I guess her thoughts.

The look Cathy gives me tells me I'm right.

"It's just not right," she says. "We said we'd do everything together. We said we'd never leave each other behind."

"But she's..."

"Dead, I know." Cathy's voice cracks. "Even so, I still hate doing things without her."

"Of course you do. You were her best friend, after all."

Cathy shakes her head. "I don't want to leave her behind."

"You won't," I tell her. "Not if you say goodbye."

Cathy gives me a confused look. I squeeze her hand.

"You never got to say goodbye, did you?"

CHAPTER 13

Cathy

I trace the letters on top of the marble tombstone, cold against my touch. I can tell it used to be ivory, but it's now greyish brown from dirt and age. Moss grows in the cracks along the sides.

Trisha Holloway. 1992-2008.

I wasn't able to attend her funeral because I was still in the hospital. When I got out, I didn't have the heart to visit her grave. And then we moved and I never returned.

Until now.

I place the bouquet of white lilies in my hand on top of Trisha's grave.

"I'm sorry, Trish," I say. "I should have come here sooner."

"Who's Trish?" Maisie asks behind me.

"Like I said earlier, Trish or Trisha is your aunt," Jackson explains to her as he places his arm around her shoulder.

"She was my best friend," I add as I get up on my feet. I brush the dirt off my knees. "Remember the friend I told you about?"

"The one you tried lipstick with?" Maisie asks.

I smile. "That's right."

"Lipstick?" Jackson's eyebrows crease. "I didn't know about that. But I do know that Trisha and Cathy got into a lot of trouble together."

"Trouble?" I snort. "You must be thinking of someone else. Trisha and I were well behaved."

Jackson ignores me and turns to Maisie. "Do you know that one time they went into my room without permission and stole my science experiment?"

"We borrowed it," I correct him. I remember returning it afterwards.

"And more than once, they ate my ice cream," Jackson adds.

"Not my idea," I say in my defense.

"Hear that, Trisha?" Jackson talks in a louder voice. "Cathy says it was all you."

I frown.

"What's that?" He holds his hand against his ear as if listening to someone, then he turns to me with a grin. "She says it's okay. She knows it was always her who had the crazy ideas, but she's grateful you went along just the same. That's why you were her best friend."

My eyes grow wide. I know there's no way Trisha just spoke to Jackson. I mean, she's gone. And yet, I can't help but think those words really sound like her.

I glance around. Is she here?

"She's a little annoyed that I've brought you here," Jackson goes on.

My eyebrows arch. Trisha doesn't want me here?

"Because she told me to stay away from you."

Oh. That.

"But I'm sorry, Trisha." Jackson steps closer to the tombstone. "I couldn't stay away. I can't. I can promise you this, though. I'm not going to hurt her. I'm going to be her new best friend."

I smile at that. I hold my hand over my heart as my chest swells with warmth.

"But I'm her new best friend," Maisie argues.

I chuckle.

Jackson kneels in front of her. "You're right, sweetheart. You're her new best friend. I think your Aunt Trisha would like that, too."

Again, he cups his ear with his hand.

"What's that?" He places his hands on Maisie's shoulders. "See, she says she would. She says you and Cathy should have lots of fun together."

Maisie looks up. "We will, Aunt Trisha."

I wrap my hand around the quivering lump in my throat as I look at her. So innocent and yet so earnest. I run to her and wrap my arms around her tight.

"Oh, sweetheart."

"That means I'll have to be better than a best friend," Jackson says.

I glance at him. It's an offer, I know. I still don't know how to reply to it, though.

"Come." Jackson touches Maisie's arm. "Why don't we leave Cathy alone? I'm sure there are some things she wants to tell Aunt Trisha. Let's let them talk alone, okay?"

"Okay." Maisie takes her father's hand.

Jackson gives me a nod.

I glance at the tombstone. Talk to Trisha?

"Go on," Jackson urges me. "She's waiting."

Slowly, I turn and walk to her grave. Behind me, I hear leaves crunching beneath Jackson and Maisie's footsteps as they walk away.

I kneel and feel the cold, hard earth beneath my knees. A breeze blows. It sweeps the loose strands of hair off my face.

As I close my eyes, I suddenly remember Trisha doing that - brushing hair from my cheeks.

"You shouldn't hide such a pretty face, you know," she tells me.

I frown. "It's not like I'm doing it on purpose. You know my hair is stubborn."

"Unlike the rest of you, you mean. Maybe we should exchange hair."

"I'd love to have yours."

"Would you like to exchange brains, too? I wish I could get my homework done faster."

I don't answer.

She laughs. "Just kidding. I like me the way I am. And I like you the way you are. Most of all, I like us the way we are - the very best of friends. Forever."

"Forever," I whisper as I open my eyes.

Tears brim in them as I stare at Trisha's tombstone. I place my hand on the marble.

"I'm sorry, Trisha." My voice trembles under the weight of my emotions. "I'm sorry that I can't remember what happened that night, that I can't remember the last things you said to me. I'm sorry I couldn't come to your funeral and I'm sorry that I haven't come here until now. I've kept you waiting, and that's terrible. I know you hate to be kept waiting."

I wait for an answer but hear none. Still, I get the feeling she's listening.

"I miss you." Tears streak down my cheeks. "I miss everything about you. I miss everything we had. I miss everything we were supposed to have. Didn't we say we'd grow up together, grow old together? Didn't we say we'd do everything together?"

I rest on the back of my legs and place my hands on my lap.

"Sometimes I wonder why I'm the one who got left behind. It doesn't make sense. You're stronger than I am. If I was the one who died, you would have been able to find a new best friend in months. You would have been able to move on and be happy. And I'd be happy just watching over you. Why? Why did it have to be you?"

But you're the better one of us. Words Trisha said to me once before echo in my ears. You'll get farther than me. I know it.

Farther? I nearly laugh. I haven't gotten anywhere at all. I've been stuck in the past for so long.

So get yourself unstuck, I almost hear her say. You're not glue, are you?

I grin. Right. That's what she'd say. If she's been watching me all this time, she's probably mad at me for not doing anything, for being so boring, for not having the courage to move on. All because I've been afraid to leave her behind.

But what if I'm actually the one holding her back? She's already left me. She's gone. She's in a better place now, or at least she should be. What if she can't go because I won't let her?

Because she's too worried about me to leave my side? She's always been worried about me, after all.

I look up. "Am I holding you back? Are you stuck here because I'm stuck?"

No answer. I don't need to hear one, though. I know now what I have to do.

All these years, there's been a fog shrouding my head, a wall surrounding my heart, a shadow hanging over me. I've kept telling myself Trisha's death caused them and that they'll never disappear, but the truth is that I'm the one who made them. I can cast them aside. I've just been afraid. I've been afraid to let go of the pain, of the past, because if I did, then what would I have left? I didn't want to let Trisha go because I had no one.

Now, I realize how selfish I've been. And how foolish. I can't keep hanging on to Trisha. I can't keep using her as an excuse not to live my life. If anything, I should live my life for her, not die with her. I survived, so I should live enough for the both of us. It's what she'd do if she was the one who got left behind. It's what she'd want me to do.

"All this time, I haven't been listening to you, have I? What a best friend I am."

I thought I was, but in truth, I've only been listening to the voice of pain, of fear. How can that be Trisha? She's not in pain anymore. She has nothing to fear. She's never been afraid.

Well, that stops now.

I clasp both hands over my heart, close my eyes and draw a deep breath.

"You can go now, Trish. You don't have to keep watching over me. I'll be fine. I won't waste my life anymore. I won't dwell in the past anymore. I'll live my own life. I'll live enough for us both. I'll never forget you. Your words will always stay in my heart and you will always be my best friend. But I'm... letting you go." I pause as my voice cracks. "You've taught me... enough about life. The memories of our friendship will give me strength to move on. So you can leave me behind now. I'll be fine. Someday, maybe, you and I will see each other again and we can pick up where we left off. I'll tell you so many things and I'll listen to everything you have to say. But until then, it's okay for us to part. You can go."

I wipe my tears and slowly open my eyes. I can almost see Trisha standing there, just a few feet away, in her favorite outfit - a hanging pink blouse over a tight-fitting grey long-sleeved shirt and faded jeans held by a sparkly white belt. Her hair flows past her shoulders and silver hoops hang from her ears.

"Goodbye, Trish," I tell her as I place my hand over the charm bracelet on my wrist, the bracelet she gave me for my eleventh birthday to match hers.

The charms of her own bracelet jingle as she lifts her hand. The dimples on her cheek show as she gives me the sweetest smile.

Goodbye, Cathy.

I close my eyes again as I feel another breeze blow, this a bit warmer than the last. When I open them again, she's gone.

Trisha's gone.

This time, though, I no longer feel empty or lonely. I don't feel pain or fear. Only peace.

I've made my peace.

My lips curve into a smile. "Thank you, Trish."

I get off the ground and blow my nose as I walk to the car where Jackson and Maisie are waiting. I slip into the passenger seat.

"Well?" Jackson asks me. "Were you able to say goodbye?"

I nod. "I feel better now."

"You look better."

"Did she say goodbye?" Maisie asks from the backseat.

I turn my head and give her a smile. "Actually, she did."

Jackson smiles. "I knew she'd talk to you."

"And she told me I could give you this." I take off my charm bracelet and lean over the backseat to hand it to Maisie. "Because you're my new best friend."

"Wow." Her face lights up as she takes a closer look at the charms.

She tries to put the bracelet on, but it's too big.

"Maybe someday you can wear it," I tell her. "Someday when you're old enough to wear lipstick. For now, keep it."

Maisie nods. "Okay."

Jackson turns his head to look at her. "What do you say when someone gives you something, Maisie?"

"Thank you," she says.

I reach out to touch her cheek. "You're welcome."

Jackson puts on his seatbelt. "Shall we go home? I was thinking we'd celebrate."

I lift an eyebrow. "Celebrate?"

"Yeah. Celebrate Trisha. I mean, we've mourned for her for so long, you especially. Don't you think we should celebrate her instead?"

I nod. "I think she'd like that."

"I can cook her favorite dish," Jackson says. "The problem is, I don't know which one it is."

I put on my seatbelt and give him a smile. "I do."

~

"Those garlic butter Parmesan chicken wings were amazing," I remark to Jackson as we take a stroll in the garden after dinner, me with a cup of hot chocolate and him with a bottle of beer.

I can still taste the sweetness of the toasted garlic. The creaminess of the butter lingers on my tongue, which still feels slightly burned from when I ate that first piece of chicken just moments after it got out of the deep fryer. I couldn't help it. It just looked so delectable. And it was. That chicken was just perfectly cooked, the meat juicy and so tender I could rip it off the bone and the skin crispy to the bite. And the addition of the Parmesan was just perfect. There was just enough of it to tie the whole dish together.

"If you're going to keep making that face, I'm going to kiss you," Jackson threatens.

I turn to him with a look of surprise. "What?"

"Nothing." He tips his bottle of beer over his mouth and takes a gulp.

I tuck a few loose strands of hair behind my ear. "Seriously, though, the wings were great. I think I ate more than twenty of them."

"I think you ate twice that many."

I scowl. "I did not."

Jackson chuckles.

"Maisie ate a lot, too," I say. "She said it was her new favorite food."

"Yeah. I was surprised. I guess she has the same taste as Trisha."

I smile at the mention of her name. Weird. Not so long ago, I'd freeze each time I heard it. It feels nice that I don't anymore.

"Maybe you should put it on the menu," I tell Jackson. "I know it's too simple, but - "

"No, not at all," he says. "Besides, isn't simple food the best of all?"

"But I thought you were all into that complicated stuff. What was that? Atomical gastronomy?"

"Molecular gastronomy," he corrects me. "Just a fancy name for using science to make food look and taste better. But that doesn't mean my food isn't simple anymore. Actually, my food is simple. Deceptively simple. You see the dish and you think you know it because it looks and smells familiar, and then you eat it and you can tell a lot of work was done to elevate its taste and texture."

"So it's not simple at all."

Jackson grins. "But there are some dishes that I don't tweak much. I don't need to. Maybe I can keep the flavors the same but just think of serving the chicken in a more elegant way for the restaurant."

"You mean so people can eat it in a non-messy way?" I touch my chin. "That sounds interesting. And maybe we can call the dish Trisha's Wings because calling it Garlic Butter Parmesan Wings just sounds like too much of a mouthful."

"Thinking like a manager now, are you?" Jackson teases me. "But you're right. That sounds great."

"Now it will really be her dish."

I smile before bringing my cup of hot chocolate to my lips.

"I can't believe I didn't know that was her favorite," Jackson says. "I thought it was beef and broccoli casserole or sticky ribs or pizza."

"She always got the garlic butter wings when we ate at the diner," I tell him. "And then she'd grab the bottle of Parmesan and pour it on them. Sometimes the waiter would give us this evil eye."

Jackson chuckles.

"Sometimes she'd eat it with pasta, sometimes with salad, sometimes even with bread. It was weird."

"Well, there's an idea I might be able to use."

My eyes grow wide. "Chicken wings and bread?"

He doesn't answer, but I can tell the wheels inside his head are already turning as he takes another gulp of his beer. I take another sip of hot cocoa as well.

"Then again, I'm not surprised you knew her better than I did," Jackson tells me. "You spent more time with her. Besides, she liked you more."

"Only because she couldn't really find things to talk about with you," I say. "But once you went to college, she did visit you, didn't she?"

"Yeah. We started having more things in common. She started asking me for advice."

"See. She loved you."

"But the two of you were the peas in a pod," he says.

I can't argue with that.

"I know, though I still sometimes wonder how that happened since the two of us didn't really have much in common."

"What do you mean?"

"We're exact opposites, actually. She's stylish. You know, she used to layer her clothes and she knew exactly how to do them."

"Not exactly. She'd stress about that and try different combinations until she found the right outfit."

I shrug. "I just pick whatever fits my mood or whatever is on top of the pile. Boring, right?"

"No," Jackson answers. "You were never boring."

I look away as I suppress a blush.

"And she was always ready for anything. She was the daring one. I was the shy one. She was athletic, outdoorsy. I was bookish. I preferred the cozy indoors. Still do. She liked horror movies. I hated them. I liked classical music. She hated it. She was artsy. She could draw. Her penmanship was much better than mine."

Jackson grins. "I bet yours isn't as bad as mine."

"Strangely, as adventurous she was, she liked guys who were, well, neat and pretty, like the princes in the movies. Me? I liked the villains sometimes, or the rugged ones with the big..."

"Arms?" Jackson asks. "Chests?"

I stop as I find myself staring at his body. I quickly tear my gaze away, drowning my embarrassment in hot cocoa.

"No wonder you never paid any attention to me," he says.

I frown. "I..."

"It's fine. I'm not proud of what I was either." He touches the back of his head. "I was a loser."

"No, you weren't."

"Yes, I was," he insists. "Isn't that why you couldn't bear to look at me?"

"No fair. I was..."

"I'm just kidding." Jackson chuckles.

He stands in front of me and looks into my eyes.

"I, on the other hand, couldn't keep my eyes off you."

The intensity of his gaze takes my breath away. The affection I see in it makes my heart flutter. The desire sets my skin on fire. A tingle of heat goes down my spine.

I swallow. "So you're saying you... you liked me even then."

Jackson's fingers brush against my cheek. "I loved you even then."

His choice of word makes my pulse quicken. My heart soars, taking my soul with it. I feel like my feet might suddenly float above the ground, too, like I'm a hot air balloon brought to life with a spark, a flame that burns brightly inside my chest.

Jackson loves me.

He said I knew how he felt, but he hasn't really said it plainly until now. Now that he has, it feels more real and yet at the same time more magical.

I snort as I regain my composure. "How could you? I was young and foolish and my hair was always a mess. Well, I still am young and foolish and..."

"I don't know," he interrupts me. "I just know that while other people compared you and Trisha all the time because you were always side by side, for me, it was only you I saw. My eyes were always only on you."

"But of course. It would be so wrong if they were on your sister."

"I think she knew. That's why she told me to stay away from you."

"And me to stay away from you."

"Yet here we are. In the end, we couldn't stay away, maybe because we're meant to be together." Jackson strokes my cheek. "And you know what? I think Trisha's happy we are."

I nod. "I think so, too."

I know she'd want me to find a man who loves me. I know she can tell Jackson does.

I still can't believe it, though.

Jackson loves me.

I see the love in his eyes before they close as he brings his face closer to mine. I close my eyes as well and hold my breath. His lips, softer than I expected and cold from his beer, brush against mine. His hand slides down to my chin and grasps it gently as his lips press down.

I feel my whole body blush with heat and excitement. A shiver goes down my spine.

So this is the magic of a kiss.

I nearly drop my cup. Instead, I grip it in my trembling hands as I lean forward and kiss Jackson back.

A breeze blows. It cools my heated cheeks and sends strands of hair over my face.

I pull away to tuck them behind my ear. As I open my eyes, I find Jackson staring back at me, the desire in his gaze stronger now.

I can see the plea in them. No, an invitation. An offer. One I can't refuse.

I draw a deep breath and swallow the lump in my throat. "Shall we go inside?"

~

As soon as we're inside my bedroom, Jackson's mouth seals mine once more, robbing me of breath.

He locks the door and pushes me against it. His hand cradles my jaw as his lips crash over mine again and again. I grip the front of his shirt as I try to keep up.

When the tip of Jackson's tongue brushes against mine, I shiver. His tongue rubs mine and coaxes it into a dance, pushing back and then pulling away. When I stick my tongue past my lips, he sucks on the tip. When I retreat, he licks my lips and the roof of my mouth before letting his tongue slide above mine. The friction sends a jolt of electricity down my body all the way to the back of my knees. A moan escapes my throat.

I wrap my arms around his neck and try to mimic his actions. His hand goes to the back of my head. He tugs on the ponytail and my hair cascades past my shoulders.

Jackson's hands take turns caressing my hair and rubbing my shoulders. I move my hands as well, sliding them to his shoulders and down to his broad chest before bringing them up again behind his neck. My fingers tug at his hair.

Then one of his arms goes around me and pulls me against him. My breasts collide with hard muscle and swell and ache. Their peaks tingle with need.

When I pull my mouth away to catch my breath, Jackson's tongue caresses my ear instead. It tickles and makes me gasp, but at the same time it feels... exhilarating. My heart hammers in my chest. My knees grow weak and I grip Jackson's shoulders.

His fingers travel down my spine. His hand rests against my lower back as he pulls my earlobe gently between his teeth. Then he grips a piece of my ass and squeezes it as he grinds his body against mine. I feel his erection against my hip.

The knowledge of it drags a moan from my throat. A fresh fever washes over me. As Jackson's tongue grazes over the patch of skin beneath my ear, my pulse races. Desire sparks a fire between my legs.

Is this how it feels... to want a man?

I place my hand on Jackson's cheek and look into my eyes. The thirst I see in them takes my breath away. I wonder if he sees the same in mine.

I part my lips and pull his to mine. I revel in the taste of him - the beer and something far more interesting and intoxicating. His hand moves from my shoulder to the side of my breast. My hand slips between our bodies to search for the bulge that has caused my pulse to throb.

When my fingers wrap around it, the rod of flesh throbs against my palm as well. I start to stroke it and Jackson hisses, but then he grabs my wrist.

"No," he tells me as he holds my gaze. "Last time, it was about me. This time, it's your turn."

I don't know exactly what he means, but I don't protest. He takes my hand and leads me to the bed. When he's standing next to it, he turns to face me. His lips keep mine busy as he unbuttons my blouse.

One by one, the buttons come off. Then Jackson breaks the kiss. He slides the blouse down my shoulders, down my arms. It gets caught on my wrists and I pull it off.

It's barely touched the floor when his fingers start to work again, this time on the button of my jeans. It pops. The zipper goes down. I push it off myself, past my knees and down to my ankles. I remember that I'm still wearing my shoes and I sit on the edge of the bed to undo the laces. I kick them off and Jackson pulls my jeans off my feet.

As soon as they're gone, he's on top of me, kissing me again. I don't even have a moment to become embarrassed by the fact that I'm nearly naked in front of a man. It may not be the first time, but it feels like it. I can feel my skin burning from my cheeks to the soles of my feet.

Jackson's hands slip between my skin and the sheets. His fingers unfasten the hooks of my bra and I feel it loosen. He breaks the kiss and I hold my breath as his thumbs slip beneath the garment.

They caress my skin as they move to the front. When they brush against the sides of my bare breasts, I let out a soft gasp.

He captures my lips again as he traces the curves of my breasts. When his palms close over them, I feel them swell.

Jackson's lips form a grin against my own. I pull away to give him a curious look.

"What?"

How can he be laughing when he's touching my breasts?

"I'm sorry," he says. "I was just thinking how your breasts have turned out to be so... incredible."

He gives them a firm squeeze.

"I mean, considering how... flat they were before."

I frown. "Are you saying you were staring at my breasts even then? You were creepy, after all."

Jackson chuckles. "I was a boy. Now, I'm a man."

To prove his point, he lets his erection brush against my knee. I feel it throb even through layers of fabric.

"And you're a woman."

He pushes my bra up and takes one of my breasts inside his mouth. His hot tongue wriggles against my sensitive skin. I tremble. My head falls to one side and a moan spills past my lips.

Jackson pulls his mouth away and blows on my nipple. The cool air tickles my heated skin. The tip of his tongue circles my stiff nipple. His thumb does the same to the other. They rub the peaks of my breasts. My eyes fall shut under the weight of the pleasure. My fingers grip the sheets as heat spreads over my belly and gathers between my legs. I feel something warm leak into my panties.

Jackson's mouth switches to my other breast. His curled lips tug at my nipple as his fingers twist the other one gently. I tremble even more.

"Jackson," I gasp out his name in impatience.

It's not that I don't like what he's doing. It's just that I want... something else.

He lifts his head to meet my gaze. "What?"

"Touch me," I whisper.

Jackson's eyebrows crease. "But I am..."

He stops talking, his gaze following my hand as I dip it between my legs.

He grins. "Yes, ma'am."

He plants a kiss on the soft curve of my belly before pulling my panties all the way off my ankles. Then he settles between my legs.

I feel him staring at my sex and I cover it with both hands.

"Don't stare," I tell him. "It's rude."

"Not when you're staring in admiration."

"Are you going to tell me that this part of me has turned out to be incredible, too? What? Were you peeking while I was changing in Trisha's room or when I was taking a shower at your house?"

"Of course not," Jackson answers. "But it makes me happy to know that no other man has ever seen this part of you. Just me."

He takes my hands and kisses them, then pushes them aside to plant another kiss, this one right on top of my curls. Then his gaze holds mine as he moves his head lower. I feel his fingers spread the folds of my skin wide.

I prop myself on my elbows. "Jackson, what are you - ?"

I lose my voice and my breath - maybe even my mind - as I feel Jackson's tongue brush against a part of me I never expected a man's tongue to be on. Yes, I've read about oral sex.

But I was always hesitant to try it. I told myself I wouldn't if I didn't have to.

I'm still reluctant to have it done to me, but as Jackson licks me over and over, my reluctance fades. His tongue slips inside me and I admit defeat. My head crashes down on the bed. My arms fall at my sides and my fingernails rake the sheets.

What is this sensation?

Suddenly, Jackson's tongue brushes against my sensitive nub. I let out a loud gasp.

"Jackson!"

I put my hands on his head and try to push him away as the sensation proves too much. I feel like I'm melting. I feel like I might explode. With each swipe of that tongue, my mind goes crazy. My body goes wild.

Jackson doesn't stop, though. His hands hold my quivering thighs in place. His tongue prods me over and over.

I grip his hair as my head thrashes from side to side. The heels of my feet rise off the floor. My toes curl. I bite down on my lower lip to hold back my cries.

When he pauses, I finally catch my breath, but the reprieve is momentary. Jackson presses my pleasure button again, this time with his thumb while his tongue slips in and out of me.

The double assault makes my back arch. My body trembles all over and my moans spill out freely into the air.

In just moments, the intense pleasure causes me to snap. I let out a cry as the top of my head digs into the mattress. My eyes seem to roll back in their sockets. My mind goes blank.

When I feel the bed beneath me again, I stare at the ceiling and take a few seconds to catch my breath. My legs hang limply over the edge of the bed. Vaguely, I feel my hands at my sides. When did I let Jackson go?

I see his face again as he climbs onto the bed. And not just his face. He's not wearing his shirt, so my eyes linger on his bare chest, which has just a small patch of hair, and on his ripped stomach.

"How was it?" Jackson asks me.

I don't answer at once for three reasons - one, because I'm still out of breath; two, because I'm too busy admiring the sight in front of me; and three, because I don't know how to describe what I've just been through.

"Just tell me if it was good or bad," Jackson says as he brushes a wisp of hair off my cheek. "Although I think I know the answer."

I frown. "If you know the answer, why ask?"

He chuckles. "If you still have enough energy to be mad at me, I guess you still have enough to go on."

My eyebrows furrow. Go on?

As he lifts me in his arms and positions me in the middle of the bed, I feel his erection against my leg and realize what he means.

I've had my fill of pleasure, but he hasn't had his. I start to wonder what I should do, but then he kneels between my legs. He pulls down his zipper and reaches inside his boxers to take out his cock. I find myself gaping as I see its size and its glistening tip.

That's... going inside me?

Then again, it already did. Once. I take some comfort from that fact as I draw a deep breath.

Jackson pushes a finger deep inside of me. My breath leaves me in a hiss.

"Relax," he tells me as he pushes in another finger.

I don't know how. Still, I tell myself to calm down.

"Does it hurt?" Jackson asks.

"No," I answer.

I know it's tight where his fingers are, and it feels a little weird to have something down there, but there's no pain.

Jackson withdraws his fingers. After a few seconds, I feel a wet, firm knob of flesh prodding between my legs.

"Here I come."

He pushes the tip in slowly and I gasp as I feel myself getting stretched. I purse my lips and hold my breath as he keeps pushing, filling me little by little.

"Are you alright?" Jackson asks me.

I open my mouth, about to complain about how big he is, about the tinge of discomfort I'm feeling, but then I see the look on his face. I see the beads of sweat on his forehead. I see the tension in his jaw. In his eyes, I can see smoldering desire, but it's tempered by concern.

He's holding back. He's doing it for me.

The thought fills me with warmth and courage.

"Don't worry about me," I tell him with a smile. "I've done this before, remember?"

Jackson grins. "But I thought you didn't."

"I'll be fine," I assure him. "It's your turn now, remember?"

He shakes his head. "It's our turn."

He bends over to kiss me tenderly and whatever fears I have left evaporate. I place one arm around him. My other hand strokes his hair.

With his lips still on mine, Jackson continues to move, a little faster this time. With a few jerks of his hips, he fills me to the brim. Afterwards, he lifts his head and pauses to catch his breath. I just stare at him, taking a moment to savor the feel of him deep inside me, of our bodies connected as one.

When he throbs inside me, ripples of heat flow through my veins. I give him a squeeze.

"Aren't you going to move?" I ask him with a grin.

Jackson chuckles, then moves off me and grips my thighs.

"You asked for it."

He starts out slowly, so slowly that I almost feel like he's teasing me. I'm about to tell him to speed up when he does just that. He starts pounding into me. His cock rubs against other pleasure buttons which I never knew existed but which send fresh swirls of heat through my chest and my belly.

I close my eyes and grip Jackson's shoulders as I surrender to this new wave of pleasure, somehow not as sharp as earlier but still good, maybe even better. This thrill isn't like an assault on the senses. It's gentle, like a song lulling me into the depths of an abyss, urging me to fall over.

Jackson moves even faster. Beneath me, I hear the bed creak. Above me, I hear him panting in between grunts. I can feel his balls slapping against my skin. I feel myself getting wetter and hotter around him.

"Cathy," he says my name in what seems like agony. "I'm co..."

I don't hear the rest because I finally fall into the abyss. As Jackson's hips jerk sporadically, I move my own. When he buries himself deep inside me, I cling to him with trembling arms. As he grunts, I let out soft cries. As his cock spills, I feel floodgates break open inside me as well, my heat mingling with his.

For a moment, we stay still, gasping for air in the silence. Then Jackson bends over to press a kiss to my forehead and pulls his cock out of me.

Only then do I open the eyes I've squeezed shut. I see Jackson tucking his cock back into his boxers and zipping up his pants. He leaves the button undone, though. As for me, I'm too tired to put my clothes back on. I can't even put my bra back on, so I just slip it off my arms and toss it aside.

Jackson glances at my breasts, then narrows his eyes at me. "Are you tempting me again?"

"No," I answer weakly.

He sighs. "At least move under the covers. You'll catch a cold."

I do that with his help, then pull the covers up to my chin. Jackson lies down beside me.

I turn my head to look at him. "Thank you."

He meets my gaze. "For what?"

"For bringing me to Trisha's grave," I say. "For helping me say goodbye. For helping me realize that I should be living for her instead of letting myself die with her."

Jackson shakes his head and grasps my chin. "I only did what I think she would have wanted me to do. And I only wanted you to be happy, or at least, feel less lonely."

I take his hand. "Well, I don't feel so lonely anymore."

He smiles. "I'm glad to hear it."

He plants a kiss on my hand, then strokes my cheek. "You should sleep now. You've got work tomorrow."

"Don't you?" I ask him.

"Yes. We both have lots of work to do this week. After all, it's almost time for the restaurant to open."

He's right. In just a few days, the restaurant will have its opening.

"I guess things are going to get even more hectic," I say.

"They are," Jackson agrees. "Are you ready?"

I look into his eyes. With the love I see in them, I feel like I can have the strength to do anything.

"I am."

CHAPTER 14

Jackson

I'd expected a huge crowd on opening day, but I wasn't ready for this.

It's about four in the afternoon and the line of diners extends from the front door to the corner of the block. It's been like that since the restaurant opened its doors at eleven. I can recognize some of them - food writers and groupies who weren't able to make a reservation because the limited slots were already filled up a month ago.

Who would have thought this restaurant tucked away in a quiet neighborhood would be just as popular as the one I have in the heart of Manhattan? If this continues for the next hour, we'll have to cut off the line or we'll be serving until midnight.

It's crazy, I know, but as I gaze across the fully occupied dining area, I can't help but feel a sense of joy and pride.

I know that it's hectic in the kitchen. I've been in and out of it all day. The air is filled with the rumble of pots constantly boiling on the stoves, of knives clashing on the chopping boards, of oil spattering in pans, of plates clattering, of water running from the faucets, of doors to ovens and chillers opening and closing, of feet shuffling, of my executive chef shouting for dishes to be sent out on time. It's utter chaos. It usually is on opening day.

Here in the dining area, though, I can see that the diners are enjoying themselves. Most of them are relaxed, soaking up the atmosphere that I've put a lot of effort into making cozy. Some of them are laughing out loud, some chattering, some enjoying their meals in silence, sipping their wine every now and then. I can tell from their clean plates and the looks on their faces that they're satisfied, and that gives me a sense of accomplishment unlike any other.

This is why I love being a chef.

Whether they're celebrities, food critics, food writers or just ordinary people looking for a meal, they all love food and I love giving them the best I can, even if it's just to see them pat their full tummies with satisfied smiles.

One of the diners leaves her table and walks over to me. "The food was amazing, Chef Jackson."

As she takes off her sunglasses, I realize she's a popular actress, one who I admired back in my teens. My eyebrows arch in surprise. I try not to get all star-struck, though. It's not like this is the first time I've had a celebrity at my restaurant.

I give her a warm smile. "I'm glad you think so, Ms. Dawson."

"And the restaurant is lovely. I had a great time." Her ruby lips curve into a smile. "I'll surely come again."

"Thank you for your kind words. Please do come again." I place my hand over my chest and give a slight bow. "We'll be just as honored to have you."

She puts her sunglasses back on, as well as her wide-brimmed hat, and walks out into the parking lot with her assistant and her bodyguard in tow. As soon as she's gone, the waiters rush in to clean up the empty table, collecting the used plates and replacing the tablecloth, utensils, glasses and napkins with new ones. Within minutes, a new group of diners is ushered in, their menus handed out.

Just like that, the cycle begins all over again.

Cathy walks over to me. "Was that...?"

"Felicia Dawson?" I supply. "Yes, it was."

She lets out a whistle. "Wow. That's the fourth celebrity I've seen today."

Is it? I haven't been counting.

She puts a hand on her hip. "You don't seem fazed at all."

I shrug. "Should I be?"

Cathy grins. "Of course not. You're a celebrity, too, after all. I mean, look at this crowd."

She turns to face the dining area and then glances at the door.

"The diners just keep coming."

"About that, we may have to cut off the line soon," I tell her.

"You mean turn away diners?" Cathy asks.

I nod. "As much as I hate to do it, we have to or we'll never close."

She lets out a breath. "Right. There doesn't seem to be any end to them."

I can tell from the look on her face that she's not looking forward to the task, though. I understand. Those who are turned away will surely be displeased, and some will put up a fuss. Still, sometimes, you just can't please everyone no matter how hard you try. I've learned that after serving food for nearly seven years. As a manager, Cathy should learn it, too.

"You're doing great, by the way." I give her a pat on the shoulder to encourage her.

I know she's tired. There are more than a few strands of hair out of place, and I've seen her sigh a few times. But all day long, she's put a smile on her face and kept on going.

She puts on another smile for me now, and I, too, feel encouraged.

"Thanks. I admit I was a bit overwhelmed at the beginning, but I think I've got the hang of it now."

I nod. "Sure looks like you do."

Cathy shrugs. "It's all thanks to Ken's training."

I shake my head. "Partly, but not all, I think."

Yes, Ken's training might have prepared her for the pressure and taught her the basics, but she's the one pulling herself together, trying to keep her head above water. And she's handled everything well so far.

"You were already amazing to begin with. That's why Ken took you under her wing."

Cathy lifts an eyebrow. "You think?"

I smile. "I know it."

Just then, I hear a throat clearing. I turn my head and see Simon behind me.

"Hey." I shake his hand and pull him closer to give him a pat on the shoulder. "I'm glad you could make it."

"I almost didn't," he says. "Do you know that I had to park my car three blocks away and walk all the way here? I nearly turned around halfway."

"I know. We're working on it."

"Then again, it's no surprise there's no parking given how long the line is outside." Simon lets out a breath. "I sure am glad I don't have to wait in it."

"Yeah, I'll have a table prepared for you," I tell him. "It's the least I can do for someone who helped me put up the restaurant."

He snorts. "I only did some stuff for your computers."

I pat his arm. "Come now. Don't be modest. It's not like you."

He chuckles, then turns serious as he glances at Cathy.

"I'm sorry. I'm not interrupting something, am I?"

"Not at all," I answer. "Though it's my pleasure to introduce you to the manager of this restaurant and my..."

I pause. Cathy is my girlfriend for real, right? Even though I haven't formally asked her to be, and she hasn't actually told me she loves me.

"Fiancee," I finish.

That's what people think of her, anyway.

"Fiancee?" Simon's eyebrows go up. "No wonder she's got that big ring on her finger and that gleam in her eye."

He nudges my arm with his elbow as he studies Cathy with his gaze. "You're a lucky man, Jackson."

I'd probably punch any other man ogling Cathy like that, but I decide to give Simon a pass.

"Yes, I am," I agree.

"I'm Cathy." Cathy offers Simon her hand. "Cathy Jeffries."

He shakes it. "Cathy?"

"And this is Simon Hessler." I place my hand on his shoulder. "He used to be my roommate in college, and he was the one who designed that brilliant program we're using to track orders."

"Really?" Cathy looks impressed.

Simon, on the other hand, looks worried.

"Cathy?" he asks again. "Surely not the same Cathy who was friends with Jackson's sister?"

I throw him a puzzled look. Has he met Cathy before?

"Yes," Cathy answers, her own eyebrows creased. "How...?"

"Oh, Trisha used to talk about you a lot," Simon says.

Cathy's eyes grow wide. "You knew Trisha?"

"Yeah. Not much, though. I just met her a few times when she came to visit her big brother."

He pats my shoulder.

Right. I introduced Trisha to him when she came to visit me on campus. I didn't know they talked that much, though. Then again, I remember Trisha sneaking into my dorm once. I opened the door to my room and there she was, sitting on my bed and chatting with Simon. She could have talked about Cathy then, and I know for a fact that once she started talking about Cathy, she couldn't stop.

"So it is you, then?" Simon asks Cathy as he rubs his cleft chin.

Cathy spreads her arms. "In the flesh."

Simon nods. "Fascinating."

I notice him staring at Cathy again. This time, I clear my throat. Once is okay. Twice? Not so much.

"Cathy, why don't you have a table prepared for our friend here?" I say.

She smiles. "Sure."

I watch her as she walks off. Simon's gaze seems to follow her as well.

"Something wrong?" I ask him.

"No," he answers, but not convincingly. "She's just... not what I expected, is all."

My gaze narrows. "What do you mean?"

He turns to me. "I mean I always thought you'd marry someone... well, not someone who works for you."

Oh. Is that what's bothering him?

"I thought you said I was a lucky man," I remind him.

"Yeah, well, she is pretty," Simon admits. "But man, you need more than a pretty face to make a marriage succeed. Take it from me."

"Don't worry. She's more than that."

He frowns. "So you're bent on marrying her?"

"Why not?"

"I told you marriage isn't a good idea."

"To the right person, it is. And trust me, she's the right person."

I watch Cathy as she gives instructions to one of the waiters, who nods and scampers off. Afterwards, a customer from the next table calls her attention. For a moment, I worry that we might be getting our first customer complaint, but then I see the expression on the customer's face and realize she's probably giving her good feedback about the restaurant. Cathy's face lights up with pride. So does mine.

She is the right person.

"I hope you're right," Simon says.

I suppress a frown.

That's what he says, but why do I get the feeling he's hoping for just the opposite?

~

"Maybe he's just jealous," Cathy tells me later when we're back at the house.

She lies on her bed and lets out a yawn.

"He doesn't sound like he's happy."

"Nope," I agree as I type on my laptop.

And that reason did cross my mind. Still...

"Are you sure the two of you haven't met before?" I ask.

"Sure." Cathy gives another yawn.

Is she? But what if she did and she just doesn't remember?

I shake my head. As far as I know, Cathy clearly remembers nearly everything from her past, except for what happened the day or the night Trisha died and a few days after.

She couldn't have met Simon then.

"What? Don't you believe me?" Cathy asks.

"It's not that. It's just..." I place my hands on my lap and sigh. "I didn't like the way he was looking at you."

Cathy snorts. "Now you're sounding jealous."

She's right. I am. Worse, I think I am jealous, even though I can't put a finger on exactly why.

I frown. I've never felt like this before, and I don't like it. I don't like it at all.

I sit back and sigh.

"Well, maybe if you told me I'm the only man you adore, I wouldn't feel jealous," I say.

No answer.

"No? Then what about if you just tell me how you feel about me? How you really feel."

Still no answer.

I get out of the chair. "Cathy, I..."

I stop as I see her with her eyes closed. Her chest rises and falls with every breath she takes.

I scratch the back of my head. So she's fallen asleep, huh? And here I thought she was thinking that she doesn't love me, that we shouldn't be together after all.

I stand over the bed and pull the covers up to her shoulders. Cathy groans as she turns her head to one side but doesn't wake. A wisp of hair falls over her cheek.

I stare at her face as I gently brush it aside.

I'm sure she doesn't think that way. She might not have said so, but she must love me or she wouldn't still be here with me.

I let out a deep breath as I put my hands on my hips. Oh, what am I thinking? Where is all this insecurity coming from? It's not like me at all.

Besides, I shouldn't be feeling gloomy right now. The opening of the restaurant was a success. I should be feeling triumphant, on top of the world.

That thought makes me smile.

Right now, everything is still a circus, but once the chaos has died down, I'll be sure to celebrate with Cathy. We could even get away to relax, though maybe not too far away, just somewhere nearby with different scenery.

I touch my chin as I try to think of a place that meets that description.

A beach in Malibu, maybe?

CHAPTER 15

Cathy

I stand on the tips of my toes, which dig into the sand, and stretch my arms high above my head. As I do, I feel aches in my shoulders, in my lower back, and behind my thighs, just above my knees. I grimace.

The past week has been tougher than any I've ever known - day after day of going from the kitchen to the dining area, making sure everything is going as it should, of keeping customers happy even when they're waiting for hours with grumbling stomachs, of going over numbers and making reports. Some nights, I felt like I'd just been run over by a train, falling asleep seconds after my head hit the pillow.

Which is why I'm grateful for this break.

Just the sight of the beach - the sparkling blue of the ocean and the less dazzling, more tranquil blue of the sky behind wisps of cloud - is enough to invigorate my body and spirit. The soft sand soothes my aching, chaffed feet. The sound of the waves puts my heart at ease. The feel of the breeze against my cheeks sends my worries drifting away.

I close my eyes and breathe in the fresh, salty air. My lips curve into a smile.

This feels nice.

Suddenly, I hear a child's laughter. I open my eyes and turn my head to see Maisie in her red swimsuit, giggling as she chases after the receding waves and laughing even louder when they come rushing back to the shore.

A few feet away, Jackson stands watching, wearing just a white shirt and baggy shorts. I try not to stare at his chest outlined through the thin cotton. Ken stands beside him - she insisted on coming, and neither Jackson nor I had the heart to say no. They seem to be discussing something serious.

Something about work, maybe? But didn't they come here to escape work?

Oh well. I guess it just shows how passionate those two are about the restaurant, about what they do. I should try to be more like them.

But not today, I think as I gaze at the horizon. Today, I'm going to enjoy the beach. Just like Maisie.

I smile as I glance at her still playing with the waves. I walk towards her, thinking of joining her.

"Maisie!" I call her name.

She laughs. "Cathy, look! I'm a wave."

She turns around so that her back is facing the ocean and starts walking backwards. When the wave comes, she squeals as the water pools around her ankles. Then, as it recedes, she walks back some more.

"Okay, that's enough," I say after she takes a few steps.

She keeps going, though, and I suddenly realize she's being pulled by the wave, being swept to sea by the current.

I run towards her. "Maisie!"

Suddenly, a big wave comes in, washing over her.

"Maisie!"

I charge into the water but pause when it splashes above my knees, colder than I expected.

Cold. Dark.

Out of nowhere, a memory comes back - a memory of me swimming in a lake on a dark night. My head is above water but the rest of me shivers beneath it.

"Cathy!" Maisie shouts.

"Maisie!" I hear Jackson yell behind me.

I dismiss the flashback and swim towards Maisie. The water splashes on my face but I ignore it and reach for her hand. Once my fingers are wrapped around her wrist, I pull her against me and put my arm around her.

"It's alright, sweetie," I tell her.

I start to head back to shore where Jackson is waiting, but suddenly another memory hits me.

Trisha standing on the shore. She's talking to someone. I don't know who. I call her name but she doesn't hear me. My leg hurts and my body freezes. I can't move.

"Cathy!" Jackson pulls me out of the water.

He takes Maisie from my arms and hands her to Ken. Then he kneels beside me.

"Cathy, are you alright?"

I cough a few times from the water I've swallowed, then rest my head on the sand as I catch my breath. The big blue sky spreads out above me, but I'm thinking of a different sky - an ebony sky with a full moon hiding behind clouds and hardly any stars hanging over a lake...

"Cathy?" Jackson cups my face.

I look into his eyes. Trisha's eyes.

Trisha.

Did I just remember the last time I saw her alive? But why was she on the shore and not me?

My chest suddenly feels tight, and not because of the water. My heart feels heavy. A lump quivers in my throat.

Jackson strokes my cheek. "Cathy?"

The next thing I know, I'm sobbing.

~

"How do you feel?" Jackson asks me hours later as he enters my room with a sandwich, a bowl of sliced fruits and a bottle of whipped cream.

I glance at him from the bed and give him a slight smile.

"Better."

It's true. After unleashing all those tears which suddenly came at me from nowhere, my chest feels lighter. My head feels clearer, too, and while some sadness still lingers in my heart, I no longer feel burdened or overwhelmed by it. I'm calm now.

Jackson sets the tray of food down on the bedside table and sits on the edge of the bed. His eyes brim with concern as he places his hand over mine.

"I'm sorry," he says. "Thinking back now, I shouldn't have brought you here to the beach. Or anywhere with water. I should have known it would make you remember... what happened to... Trisha."

He means Trisha drowning. That's not what I remembered, though.

For a moment, I wonder if I should tell Jackson what I did remember, but I decide not to. They're just fragments of memories, after all, pieces of a puzzle that still don't make sense. If I tell him, I'll only make him worry.

I shake my head and touch his cheek. "It's not your fault. Besides, I'm okay now, so let's just forget about it. I'd feel worse if I knew I ruined our little vacation."

He smiles. "Okay."

"Where's Maisie?" I ask him curiously.

"With Ken," Jackson answers. "They're building sandcastles."

"So she's okay?"

He nods. "You know her. She bounces back fast."

I let out a sigh. "I wish I could bounce back that fast."

Jackson glances at the tray of food. Then his eyebrows furrow as he touches his chin. "Hmm."

I cross my arms over my chest. "What?"

His lips curve into a grin. "I might be able to help you with that."

My gaze narrows. I can tell he's thinking of something, probably something mischievous judging from that grin. But what?

"What are you thinking of?" I ask him directly.

Jackson grabs the bottle of whipped cream. "Say 'ah'."

I glance at the bottle and frown. What? Is he going to cheer me up by feeding me whipped cream? Is he trying to give me a sugar high? That's his idea?

"Come on," Jackson urges me. "Say 'ah'."

I give in and open my mouth. He sprays some whipped cream on my tongue. I close my eyes and swallow. The sweet, fluffy concoction goes down my throat.

"Now, wha - ?"

Jackson's mouth crashes down on mine as he cradles my face with both hands. When I part my lips, his tongue slips in. It caresses mine and an even sweeter sensation washes over me. A moan escapes my throat.

Jackson pulls his mouth away and licks his lips. "Yum."

I give him a puzzled look. "Yum?"

"Now, it's your turn."

He hands me the bottle of whipped cream and gets off the bed. He stands a few feet away and takes off his shirt. It falls on the carpet.

I swallow as I stare at the ridges of his bare chest. My gaze traces the dips and bulges of his abdominal muscles and follows that thin line of hair in between them over his navel and down to where it stops just above the waistband of his shorts. Then I bring my gaze back up to his face. The mischief in his eyes causes heat to flood my cheeks and my chest, extinguishing my breath. The hint of lust in them sends a shiver of excitement down my spine.

Now I understand what Jackson's talking about. I'm still not sure I want to do it, though. Or if I can.

"What? Not enough?" he asks.

Before I can answer, he hooks his thumbs into the waistband of his shorts.

My heart stops. Wait. He's not planning on un...

My thoughts evaporate as Jackson drops not just his shorts but also his briefs. They pool around his feet and he steps out of them.

Now he's completely naked.

And this time, my gaze lingers on his crotch. Even though he's not fully hard, I find myself fascinated by the rod of flesh hanging between his legs. It's a little darker than the rest of him, rosy, and the tip is especially pink. Whereas the rest of his body is ripped, that part of him is smooth, pretty almost.

Pretty? No, that's not the word. Magnificent. Enticing. Perfect.

My mouth waters.

Jackson places his hands on his hips. "Well?"

It amazes me how he doesn't seem the least bit embarrassed at showing me every inch of his skin. Then again, I suppose he has no reason to be, given how incredible his body now is.

If he's offering it to me, I guess I should accept.

I get off the bed. As I walk towards him, the corner of my mouth twitches up.

"Is that a smirk?" Jackson asks.

"No," I answer. "Just a grin."

"A wicked grin," he says.

I meet his gaze. "What? Are you the only one who can have one?"

"No. I'm just curious to know the reason for it."

I look at his chest. "I was just thinking how when I first saw you again, I wanted to see you in an apron. Just an apron."

"Aha!" Jackson cheers triumphantly. "So you already wanted me then, did you?"

I don't answer.

"So that's why you were staring," he adds.

"I wasn't..." I start to defend myself but stop. It doesn't matter anymore anyway.

I place a hand on his chest. "I never thought I'd get to see you naked, though."

"Should I put on an apron?" Jackson asks.

"No." I shake the bottle in my hand. "I think I have something better to dress you with."

I spray a dollop of whipped cream on each of his nipples. Then I put some more on his abdomen, one on each side and then in between. I circle his navel with the thick, white foam.

Afterwards, I step back to admire my work. Jackson, too, glances down.

"Not bad," he says. "Though I think you missed a spot."

His cock twitches.

I ignore him as I put the bottle down on the shelf. Then I stand in front of him.

"So now, I eat?" I ask.

Jackson grins. "Bon appetit."

I lick my lips. "Itadakimasu."

It's Japanese for "I gratefully receive" or "Thanks for the food", usually said before a meal.

Jackson chuckles. "Now, where did you learn that?"

I shrug. "I was doing some research on food customs around the world. I don't know a lot about wines, and I don't think I can do much about that, but I thought if I'm going to work at a restaurant, I might as well be more knowledgeable about food."

"Any chance you learned anything about how best to eat whipped cream?" Jackson asks.

"No," I answer. "But I have a feeling I'm going to find out."

I grip his hips.

"Now, stay still."

"Yes, ma'am."

I start with the whipped cream on his abdomen, dragging my tongue over hard muscle and making sure I get every drop. Jackson draws a deep breath, but otherwise I get no reaction. It's almost as if I'm licking a statue.

I feel a tinge of disappointment. I know I told him to stay still, but I was hoping he'd react just a little.

Guess I'll just have to make him.

I move up to his nipples, starting with the left one. They're not as prominent as mine, of course. Still, I decide to try what Jackson did last time with mine. I wrap my lips around the nub, sucking the cream into my mouth. Then I lick what's left, moving my tongue in a circular motion and then up and down, slowly and then faster.

I feel a tremor go through Jackson's body. A hiss escapes his lips.

Now things are getting interesting.

I do the same with his other nipple but don't get much of a reaction. I turn my attention to his navel, letting the tip of my tongue circle it as well before dipping in.

Jackson trembles. His hand grips my shoulder.

I look up. "You don't like it?"

"It tickles," he confesses.

That gives me an idea. I grip his hips as I continue teasing his bellybutton with my tongue even though there's no more whipped cream. Jackson grips me with both hands. His belly shakes. His laughter turns into snorts as he tries to suppress it. Still, some spill out.

"Cathy."

I know I should stop. I know I'm probably going to pay for this later. Still, I keep going.

This is too much fun to stop.

"Cathy." Jackson pushes me off when he's reached his limit.

I look up and see his face flushed. His shoulders rise and fall.

"Fine," I say.

I'm about to straighten up, but then I see his cock. It's harder now, pointing at me. Its wet tip is just inches away from my face and I can see the glistening liquid oozing out of the slit.

Again, my mouth waters. This time, though, I don't just swallow and look away. I go down on my knees and take a closer look. Unable to resist, I wrap my fingers around it and open my mouth to lick the tip.

Jackson lets out a louder hiss. He doesn't push me away, though, so I continue. I swipe my tongue against the tip of his cock, gathering the liquid there, which tastes slightly salty and bitter but not unpleasant.

Jackson's cock quivers in my hand. More of the clear liquid oozes out.

I leave it alone and lick the rest of him. I drag my tongue down his cock, then lick the thin skin between his balls. Jackson lets out a gasp. His fingers dig into my shoulders.

"Ticklish?" I ask him.

His eyes narrow. "Don't you dare."

This time, I take his advice. I drag my tongue back up and press the tip against the leaking slit. Jackson's hands shake.

I smile. I guess I've broken through his defenses now.

Who knew being on the giving end would be so exciting?

Indeed, my skin is buzzing, my heart racing. Jackson may not be doing anything to me, but his reactions are sending heat through my veins. I can feel myself getting wet as well.

I continue. I wrap my lips around his cock and take him inside my mouth. I feel the rod of flesh quiver on my tongue and I rub it.

Jackson lets out a curse. I'd like to see the look on his face but decide to focus on my task instead. I close my eyes and fit as much of him inside my mouth as I can. When the tip of his cock hits the back of my throat, I nearly gag. Jackson groans.

I pull away so I can recover. Then I try again.

"You don't have to do this, Cathy," Jackson tells me.

I ignore him. I tilt my head and his cock brushes against the roof of my mouth. Jackson lets out another curse and grips my shoulders harder.

"Fuck."

I hollow my cheeks and give a suck. He trembles in response. Then I move my head back and forth. I curl my lips to sheath my teeth and they rub against him. The friction fills my mouth with heat.

I move faster, so fast my lips feel like they're on fire. I can barely breathe, but I can hear that I'm not the only one having trouble with that.

Jackson's fingers grip my hair. He strokes it as his breaths turn to gasps, as I keep moving back and forth. Then suddenly, he pushes me away.

"Enough," he whispers as I look up.

The lust in his eyes sends a shiver of delight down my spine.

As his mouth claims mine, I can tell the game is over. He's all serious now. His tongue holds mine captive. His hands travel wildly over my body.

It feels like he might tear my clothes apart, so I take them off. I pull my shirt over my head. I push my leggings and my panties off. I reach behind me to unfasten my bra and let it slip off my arms.

Jackson pushes me down on the bed. His hand slips between my legs. One of his fingers slides inside me and I gasp. He pushes in another finger and moves both digits in and out. I start to tremble.

Jackson plants his mouth on my neck as he withdraws his fingers. His thumb starts to rub my sensitive nub and I begin to moan. My nails scrape across his back.

Then Jackson turns me around. I find myself on my hands and knees. He continues stroking me as he pushes two fingers inside me. I gasp, feeling them deeper inside me from this new angle.

He thrusts them a few times, then pulls them out and prods me with his cock instead. I grip the sheets and brace myself.

I hold my breath as Jackson enters me from behind, slowly but still faster than the last time. And this time, he doesn't pause. He keeps going until he fills me all the way, and when he does, my breath leaves me in a soft cry.

Is it just me, or has he grown bigger since the last time we had sex?

He grips my hips and starts to move. His cock rubs against spots inside of me that make my head spin. My vision starts to blur.

I close my eyes and throw my head back as I savor the sensation of Jackson's cock ramming into me. I don't know why, but there's something about this position that seems almost... primal. It feels as if Jackson is more in control and I have no choice but to surrender.

A few more thrusts and my arms grow weak. My face crashes on the bed. My hair sweeps over my cheeks. My moans spill out into the sheets.

Jackson moves even faster, rocking my body and the bed. His hands grip my swaying breasts and squeeze them. Then he reaches between my legs to tease my nub once more.

I clench fistfuls of the sheets and let out a cry as I come undone. My hips move on their own, pushing back against him. My toes curl.

Vaguely, I feel Jackson still moving behind me. As my hips grow still, he picks up his pace. He buries his fingers into my hips and gives a particularly deep thrust. His cock quivers inside me and explodes.

Afterwards, Jackson stays still for a while. So do I as I gasp for air. Even after he pulls out, I don't move. I know my ass is sticking out, but I'm too tired to care.

"If you're going to stay like that, I'm going to get hard again," Jackson threatens.

Only then do I lie on my back. I grab a pillow and hug it to my chest.

Jackson sits on the edge of the bed, his briefs and shorts already back on.

"Feel better?" he asks me.

"Tired," I complain as I close my eyes.

"Hungry?"

I open one eye and see the bowl of fruit in his hand. I'm about to say no, but then I realize I haven't eaten since breakfast. No, the whipped cream doesn't count.

"Maybe," I say. "But maybe I'll eat them without the whipped cream."

Jackson chuckles, "Sure?"

I sigh. "I don't think I'll ever be able to look at whipped cream the same way again."

He laughs, then turns serious as he touches his chin. "Maybe next time we should try chocolate syrup or honey."

I lift an eyebrow. "What?"

"Just kidding," he says.

He plants a kiss on my forehead. "Seriously, though, I'm glad you're feeling better. Maybe later we can take a stroll on the beach? Watch the sunset?"

I smile. "I'd like that."

This vacation may have started off on the wrong foot, but I suddenly have the feeling that everything will be okay now.

We'll watch the sunset. We'll have an amazing dinner. We'll take a moonlit stroll, maybe take a dip in the pool. And afterwards, who knows? Jackson and I might be able to find more creative ways to enjoy each other.

With him by my side, everything will be alright.

~

Something's not right.

My leg hurts. It feels like it's being twisted inside. It stops moving and I start sinking into the water.

No!

I fling my arms and thrash wildly, trying to keep myself afloat. I see Trisha on the shore and I try to call her name but my voice won't come out. My body feels heavier. My arms start to get tired.

I stop moving. The water swallows me whole. I fall on my back, sinking slowly. Above me, the light begins to fade. The bubbles coming out of my mouth grow smaller, fewer. My chest starts to hurt.

Am I... drowning?

Suddenly, though, a hand grips mine. I see the charm bracelet wrapped around it.

Trisha?

She pulls me out of the water and throws me on the shore. I'm safe.

"Thank you, Tri - "

I stop talking because Trisha isn't there behind me. She's nowhere in sight. When I look again, I see her hand sticking out of the middle of the lake. Then it sinks. The water turns into a whirlpool around her and sucks her in.

"Trisha!" I shout her name as I sit up on the bed.

Sweat dampens my back. My heart pounds so hard inside my chest it hurts.

"Cathy!"

Jackson rushes to my side and wraps his arms around me.

Still, I can't stop shaking. I know I was just dreaming, but that dream was too real. I know I'm safe, but fear still courses through my veins.

"Cathy, what's wrong?" Jackson asks me as he clutches my shoulders. "Tell me."

I grip my chest as I look at him. I swallow the lump in my throat.

"I think... I killed Trisha."

CHAPTER 16

Jackson

What did Cathy mean when she said she killed Trisha?

I ponder the thought as I flip a piece of leftover salmon on a pan.

A few days have passed, but it still bothers me. It still seems to bother her, after all. She hasn't been herself since that night. Yes, she wears a smile for Maisie. She acts strong in front of Ken. She goes about her duties and tends to the diners in the restaurant as if nothing has changed. Yet when she's all alone - or she thinks she is - she either seems on the verge of tears or has a far-off look in her eyes. What is she looking at? She's also been eating less. She's not in the mood for sex. She takes long showers with the door locked. One night, I woke up and she wasn't beside me. I found her wandering in the garden like a ghost.

What on earth is going through her head?

Surely Cathy can't believe she killed Trisha? I don't. I don't even know what that means.

It's not like Trisha was murdered. She drowned. Tragic, but plain and simple.

As far as I know, a man found Cathy on the shore of the lake and called an ambulance. My cousin was alerted. She and some of her friends headed into the lake to look for Trisha and they found her body. She was already dead. The coroner who came to the scene with the cops pronounced that she died from drowning almost instantaneously. He repeated the same to my mom and I when we went to the morgue to get her body.

Trisha drowned. So how can Cathy say she killed her? Does she mean she drowned Trisha?

Impossible. And absurd, so absurd I don't even want to think about it.

So why does Cathy think it? Why does it bother her so much?

"Um, chef," one of my cooks interrupts my thoughts.

I turn to him. "Yes?"

"That salmon is done, I think."

I look at the pan, and sure enough, the salmon has started to turn brown. I turn off the fire and try to take it out of the pan to save it, but it already seems stuck. As I move the spatula back and forth, it crumbles.

There goes lunch.

I let out a sigh as I step away from the stove. "Throw it in the bin."

"Yes, chef."

I walk out of the kitchen, scratching my head. I went there hoping to take my mind off things. Apparently, I can't. That burnt piece of beautiful salmon in the trash bin is proof of it.

There's only one thing to do - to get this thing off my mind once and for all. And there's only one way to do it.

Talk to Cathy.

And if she tries to turn me away again? Well, I just won't let her.

~

"I'm not going to stop asking until you tell me what's wrong with you, Cathy." I go after her as she walks down the garden path. "So you might as well tell me."

"Nothing," she says without stopping or glancing at me. "Nothing's wrong."

"We both know that's not true. Ever since you had that nightmare, you haven't been yourself. Something's weighing on your mind."

"I'm fine."

"No, you're not. If you were, you wouldn't be running away from me."

Cathy stops in her tracks. Her shoulders droop. Then she turns to face me but doesn't meet my gaze. Instead, she crosses her arms over her chest and looks to her side.

"I'm not running away from you."

"Yes, you are." I stop in front of her. "You still are."

I take her hand in one of mine and touch her cheek with the other. Finally, her hazel eyes look into mine.

"Tell me what's wrong, Cathy," I whisper as I stroke her cheek. "Please."

For a moment, she stands still and silent, her gaze locked with mine. I stand still as well, without saying another word, patiently waiting for her answer. Finally, she places her hand on top of mine and parts her lips, but just as I think she's about to say something, she clamps them shut again. She pushes my hand away and steps back. When our eyes meet again, hers brim with pain.

"Why can't you just leave me alone?" she hurls the question at me, her voice raised.

I stay calm. "Because I don't want you to go through this alone, whatever it is. I'm here for you, Cathy."

"Well, it's got nothing to do with you."

"Nothing?" I step forward and narrow my eyes at her. "Is that what I mean to you? Nothing?"

Cathy doesn't answer.

"Cathy, you're my fiancee," I point out.

"Your fake fiancee," she reminds me. "Have you forgotten?"

Is that how she still thinks of herself?

"Well, you're my girlfriend," I tell her.

After all, she's been living with me, sleeping in the same bed with me.

Cathy looks at me. "Am I?"

I frown. "Is that what this is about? Are you pushing me away because you don't want to be with me anymore? Because you don't feel the same way for me as I do for you?"

Again, she doesn't answer.

"Well, I don't care," I tell her. "Because you can't push me away. I'm not going anywhere."

I reach for her hand.

"I love you, Cathy."

She pulls her hand away. "Well, you shouldn't. I don't deserve your love."

My eyebrows furrow. "What? How can you say that?"

"You only fell in love with me because I was Trisha's best friend."

"That's not true."

"It is. If I wasn't, you'd never have met me. You know what? I wish you hadn't. I wish I wasn't Trisha's best friend. Then I wouldn't be feeling like this now, like I'm being torn apart over and over."

She clutches her shirt with trembling hands. The sight drives a thorn into my chest.

"Don't say that." I put my arms around her. "You being Trisha's best friend is the best thing that ever happened to her."

She shakes her head. "No, it isn't. If she hadn't met me, she'd still be alive."

I pull away. "What do you mean...?"

Cathy looks away. Why? Why does she seem so dejected? And why won't she tell me the reason?

"Cathy..."

She turns her back to me. "You should really just leave me alone."

I frown. That again.

"Listen, I don't know what you're going through right now, but it will pass. Everything will be alright."

"How would you know? You don't know how I feel."

"I would if you told me."

"You wouldn't understand."

"I could try."

Cathy doesn't answer.

I draw a deep breath. "Fine. If you won't tell me, I'll just guess."

Nothing.

"You feel like you're being dragged back into the past again, don't you?"

She still says nothing, but I get the feeling I'm right.

"That's fine. You were able to let go of it once already. You can do it again."

"I can't!" Her shoulders tremble as her hands clench into fists at her sides. "Can't you see? I've tried to get away but it's no use. Because the fear, the nightmares, they're all in here."

She points to her head as she turns to face me, then places her hand over her chest.

"And here. I can't get away from them."

"But you can," I tell her. "Let me help you."

"You can't!" Cathy shakes her head. A tear trickles down her cheek. "You shouldn't even try. If you do, your life will just be ruined. Yours and Maisie's. You'll just die because of me."

I grab her arm. "Cathy, what are you saying?"

"Leave me alone!" She wrenches her arm away and looks into my eyes. "There's nothing you can do for me, Jackson. You can't protect me. Your love can't save me. You should just give up on me."

I shake my head. "No. I - "

"For Maisie's sake," she cuts me off as she steps beside me. "I don't belong in her life. Or in yours."

She walks past me and goes back into the house, leaving me even more confused than before.

~

I'm still mulling over last night's conversation in frustration when the doorbell rings. I frown.

Who can that be? Betty? She always seems to pop up at the worst times.

I walk to the door.

Well, if it's her, I'll just tell her that I'm busy, which isn't a lie. I'm about to wake Maisie up to bring her to daycare since Cathy is long gone. I don't even know where she is.

I square my shoulders and open the door, ready to unload a piece of my mind on the person on the other side. To my surprise, though, it's not Betty standing there, nor anyone I've seen before.

Three men stand on the front steps, all of them dressed like cops. The sight of their black uniforms makes me tense instinctively.

The last time I talked to cops was right after Trisha's death. Something bad had happened then. I have a feeling something bad's about to happen now.

"Mr. Jackson Holloway?" One of the cops, the one with the mustache, steps forward.

"Yes," I answer.

He shows me his badge. "I'm Sergeant Danny Watts from Sausalito PD. These are Officers Roger McMillan and Henry Knox from the town of Staggart in Wisconsin."

Staggart? That's the name of the town where Trisha died. Why did police from there come all the way here?

"I believe there is a Cathy Jeffries living here," Sgt. Watts says.

Cathy?

"She's not here at the moment," I tell him. "May I ask why you're looking for her, though? Is this about Trisha Holloway's death?"

They don't answer.

I swallow the lump in my throat. "If this is about my sister, I deserve to know."

The two officers from Staggart look at each other, then nod.

"Yes," Officer McMillan says. "It's about your sister."

"And what do you want with Cathy?" I ask.

"We have papers from the prosecutor's office," he answers. "Ms. Jeffries is being summoned to court to answer to the charge filed against her."

"What charge?"

Officer McMillan draws a deep breath. "The slaying of Trisha Holloway."

CHAPTER 17

Cathy

I killed Trisha.

The thought goes through my head over and over as I gaze out the window of the hotel room.

I've had a feeling I did ever since I had that nightmare. Even so, I didn't want to believe it. That's why I felt so torn.

Now, though, I have no choice. Someone else thinks I killed Trisha. According to the papers from the prosecutor's office, a new witness has come forward saying that I did. And now, I have to prove my innocence.

The problem is, I don't know if I can.

I gaze down at my lap, cross my arms over my chest and clutch my shirt. What if I really killed Trisha?

"Cathy?" My mom sits up on the bed and rubs her eyes. "What are you doing out of bed? It's..."

She glances at the clock on the bedside table.

"...just past one in the morning."

I don't answer. I just pull my knees against my chest and wrap my arms around them.

I didn't want to bother my mom. The last thing I wanted was to cause her more trouble. I didn't have a choice, though. I knew I needed a lawyer to tell me what to do, and the only lawyer I knew was Mom's friend Gina. I had no choice but to call her and tell her what happened. Hours later, she appeared at my side.

Now, it's her and me again here in this hotel room in Milwaukee, two hours away from Staggart.

Just her and me against the world. Again.

"What's the matter?" She walks over to me after tying her robe around her waist and strokes my hair. "What are you thinking of, baby?"

I throw my gaze past the window once more. The leaves of the trees rustle in the breeze.

"Gina sent papers to the prosecutor's office, didn't she?"

"Yes."

"Saying I'm innocent?"

"Yes."

I hug my knees a little tighter and bury my chin between them. "But what if I'm not?"

My mom kneels in front of me and grabs my ankles. "Sweetheart, what are you saying?"

"I remembered something from that night," I tell her. "All this time, I've been wondering how I could have drowned when I always thought I was a good swimmer. Now, I understand."

"What did you remember?"

I pat my leg. "I had a cramp."

My mom rubs my leg. "Well, it happens to the best of swimmers. It's hardly your fault, is it? And it definitely doesn't mean you're responsible for Trisha's death."

I get out of the chair and start pacing the room. "But what if she tried to save me and that's why she drowned? I remember something else, too, you know. I remember seeing Trisha on the shore. What if I was the only one swimming and then I got a cramp so she had to come into the water and save me?"

"Fine. Let's say that's what happened. That still doesn't mean you're responsible for her death."

"But don't you see? It means that she drowned because of me."

My mom shakes her head. "No."

"It's possible, Mom."

"No."

"It could very well be what happened."

"Or not." She grabs my hand. "Maybe you had a cramp but it lasted only a minute and you were able to go back to shore."

"Then why did I almost drown?"

She shrugs. "Maybe Trisha chose to go swimming after you and she started drowning and you tried to save her but you couldn't?"

I fall silent. If that's the case and I couldn't save her, doesn't that still mean I'm responsible for her death?

"Or maybe you and Trisha were both in the water. She started drowning. You tried to help her but you got a cramp. You went under water but then your cramp went away and you were able to get to shore but she didn't. At least, that's what I've been thinking."

It is?

"But I remember seeing Trisha standing on the shore," I point out.

"Maybe you went into the water ahead of her," my mom says with a shrug. "But she followed you moments later."

"Because I asked her to."

"Or maybe you went into the water out of curiosity, you got out because you decided it wasn't a good idea to swim in a lake at night, but then Trisha dragged you back in. That sounds more like her. I mean, she was always the daring one, wasn't she? Wasn't she always the one dragging you along and you were the one pulling her back?"

I look at her. "Are you saying it's Trisha's fault that I almost drowned? That she drowned?"

She touches my cheek. "Sweetheart, it was no one's fault. It was an accident, okay? That's what this is, an accident. It's not a crime. The fact that someone's making a case out of it is absurd."

"But we don't know for sure that it's an accident, right?" I tell her. "At least, I don't."

I cross my arms over my chest and walk to the window.

"I still don't remember exactly what happened that night, after all. And maybe I never will."

I look up at the night sky. The nearly full moon gleams like a silver plate in the midst of a dark tapestry.

If only the moon could talk, maybe it could tell me what happened that night.

"Maybe you can," my mother says softly.

"Can what?"

"Remember."

I turn around. "What do you mean?"

She sits on the edge of the bed. "Years ago, after you had... problems with your memory, I started doing a bit of research. I found out that memories are actually never lost. Some people just have a hard time retrieving them. And some of them manage to succeed through hypnosis."

My eyebrows furrow. "Hypnosis?"

"I was able to get in touch with a hypnotherapist. He was confident he could help you recover your repressed memories.

I was about to invite him over, but that day, for the first time, I saw you smile while you were out in the garden, and then I thought it was better if you didn't remember."

I narrow my eyes at her. "Are you saying you could have helped me remember what happened but you didn't?"

So all this time that I've been agonizing over questions regarding the past, I could have had answers?

"You weren't ready to remember, Cathy," my mom tells me. "And then you started moving forward and I thought it was unnecessary, that maybe it was a blessing in disguise that you didn't remember."

"A blessing in disguise? Mom, you have no idea how many times I felt so broken just because I couldn't remember how Trisha died, or how many times I thought I was a failure because I couldn't remember my best friend's final words."

"Would that really have helped you?" She stands up. "Cathy, you were already living in the past, in the dark. You were already suffering so much."

"Because I couldn't remember!"

"So you're saying if you remembered, you wouldn't have suffered more?"

I don't answer. I can't give her the answer she wants. I can't say that knowing how Trisha died wouldn't have made it hurt more, or that remembering the last time I saw her, the last things she said to me, wouldn't have made me even more reluctant to let go of her. But years have passed. I'm stronger now.

"Even if you did remember, it wasn't going to bring Trisha back. Whether or not you remembered, you'd still have been lost and broken because you lost your best friend."

"I know that," I tell her. "I know that getting my memories back isn't going to bring her back. I know that this hole in my heart is not because of what I can't remember. Still, I want to remember. I want to know how I lost my best friend."

Maybe I didn't want to in the beginning, but I do now. I want to remember everything.

My mother sighs. "Fine. It seems the only way for you to believe that you're not responsible for Trisha's death is for you to remember what happened."

My eyes grow wide. So she'll help me remember?

She grabs my hand.

"Come back to bed. Tomorrow, I'll call that hypnotherapist."

~

"Now, close your eyes, Cathy," the hypnotherapist tells me in a clear but gentle voice.

I obey.

"Take a deep breath and relax. Picture your heart slowing down. Picture your muscles becoming loose and limp. Let yourself drift away. Imagine your mind as a vessel, a glass becoming empty of every thought. Now, bring yourself back to the lake. Tell me, what does it look like?"

"Black," I answer. "It's dark. I can barely see it."

"What do you see?"

"The moon. It's a full moon, but it's hiding behind some clouds."

"Do you see Trisha?"

"Yes."

"Where is she?"

"Beside me. She's wearing a turtleneck and a tank top. Black. The turtleneck is white and the tank top is black. Her hair is loose. Her hand is tucked into the pocket of her jeans. She's wearing her charm bracelet."

"What is she doing?" the voice asks.

"She's standing. She's smiling. Wait, she's talking to someone."

"A boy? A girl?"

"A boy. A boy in an orange sweater. Orange like marmalade. He's smiling at her. He's touching his chin."

"Do you talk to this boy?"

"No. I go into the water. It's cold, but I keep going."

"Where is the water up to now?"

"My knees. My waist. I bend my knees and the water goes up to my shoulders. It's cold."

I wrap my arms around myself as I shiver.

"I launch myself into the water and start swimming. My arms hit the water. My legs move behind me. There's no current. It's like I'm in a pool. I keep swimming. But then pain shoots up my leg."

I wince from the pain.

"I get a cramp. I can't swim anymore. I look at the shore and Trisha's there. I try to get her attention but she's not looking at me. She's drinking from a bottle. I splash around. My body's getting heavier and heavier. I start sinking. I go under water. I can't breathe. It hurts. It hurts all over. And I'm so scared. I don't want to die. Someone save me. Someone..."

"That's enough," I hear my mother's voice, clear as a bell, ringing through the air as I feel her arms wrap around me.

I open my eyes and find myself back in the hotel room. I'm not in the water anymore. My body still feels heavy, though. My chest still hurts.

"Shh." My mother rubs my back. "It's okay now. You're safe now, sweetheart. Mommy's here. Everything's okay now."

I say nothing as tears trickle down my cheeks. I don't believe her, though. How can everything be okay now that I know that I nearly drowned? I nearly drowned but I didn't die. I didn't die and Trisha did, even though I was in the water and she was on the shore, which means that Trisha saved me. She died saving me.

Just as I thought, she died because of me.

I grip my mother's shirt as I start to sob. How can I still say I'm innocent?

CHAPTER 18

Jackson

"You don't think Cathy is a murderer, do you?" Ken asks me without looking up from her tablet as she examines the contents of the pantry.

I pause to glance at her with slightly arched eyebrows. I'm surprised she knows about Cathy's case. I didn't tell her about it. Then again, Ken has a lot of connections.

I think of correcting her - Cathy is being charged with manslaughter, not murder; there's a difference - but I say nothing as I transfer the bottles of olives from the box on the floor to the shelf. I know what Ken means.

Could Cathy have taken someone else's life?

I've been wondering about the same thing for the past few days, ever since those cops showed up at the house. The papers from the prosecutor's office say the caretaker of one of the cabins near the lake where Trisha drowned, a man named Gary Pitts, came forward and said he saw what happened that night - that Cathy deliberately held Trisha's head below water while they were in the lake. It came as a shock to me, of course. I still find it hard to believe or even imagine. Even so, I can't help but wonder if it might be true, especially since Cathy told me herself that she thinks she killed Trisha.

What did she mean? Could she really have drowned Trisha?

I wish I knew. I wish I could talk to Cathy one more time and understand what's going on with her. But I can't. She's gone now, off to Staggart to deal with the charges made against her.

She didn't even say goodbye. Besides, I'm not supposed to talk to her, not now that I've received my own papers from the court asking me to share my testimony regarding what happened to my sister.

I let out a sigh. The distance between us just seems to be getting wider and wider.

"Hey." Ken puts her tablet down. "Don't tell me you're not going to help her."

"I don't think there's anything I can do," I answer as I grab another bottle of olives. "Besides, Cathy doesn't want my help."

Ken snorts. "Did she really say that, or are you just saying that because the two of you broke up?"

I glance at her curiously. Broke up? Who said anything about that?

"What?" Ken shrugs. "Everyone here knows the temperature between the two of you has gone cold."

I place the bottle on the shelf. "We didn't break up. Why would we when we're not together? She's not my fiancee for real, remember?"

"You mean you didn't propose to her for real?" Ken asks. "Or at least, ask her to be your girlfriend?"

Come to think of it, maybe I should have. Well, even if I had, she'd still have left.

"It doesn't matter," I tell Ken. "She doesn't love me."

She never said she did.

"Really?"

"And yes, she said she doesn't want my help."

"So what? You're just going to give up on her?"

I don't answer.

Ken snorts. "I guess you're not as much of a man as I thought you were."

I frown. "What do you want me to do, huh? Tell the judge that Cathy had nothing to do with my sister's death even though I wasn't there when it happened and she doesn't remember it?"

Ken looks at me with wide eyes. "Are you seriously thinking Cathy is capable of murder?"

"It's manslaughter, not murder," I correct her this time. "Which means it was accidental."

Ken puts a hand on her hip. "So you think Cathy accidentally killed your sister?"

"I'm just saying I don't know what really happened."

"You know Cathy," Ken points out. "You know her better than I do. You knew her even before all this shit happened and you got to know her even more these past few weeks. That's why you fell in love with her."

I say nothing.

Ken shakes her head. "If after all that, you think she could kill someone, then maybe you shouldn't be with her."

I sigh. "Well, she doesn't want to be with me anyway."

To my surprise, Ken grips the front of my shirt. "Stop it, Jackson. Stop wallowing in self-pity and act like a man. So what if your relationship with Cathy doesn't have a label? That doesn't mean you don't have one. So what if she hurt your feelings? This isn't about you. Right now, Cathy needs you. The woman you love needs you, and if you don't make an effort to be there for her, if you let her feel alone at a time like this, you're going to regret it. You can feel sorry for yourself all you want then. The question is: Do you really want to?"

I don't answer.

Ken lets out a deep breath as she lets go of my shirt. "Sorry about that, boss. I guess I just got... carried away."

"It's okay." I smooth the front of my shirt. "I understand what you're talking about, but should I really do anything for Cathy if she asked me to leave her alone? Isn't that just me meddling, making things harder for her?"

"If you love her, yes," Ken answers. "And no, it's not meddling. Meddling is when you try to interfere with the affairs of strangers. When it comes to the things that concern the people you care about, then it's just... caring. How is that going to make things harder?"

I don't know. I don't even know why I'm thinking of it. Maybe I'm not thinking clearly. Maybe it's my wounded pride talking. But Ken's right. This isn't about me.

"Hey." Ken places a hand on my arm. "I know with Evelyn, you didn't do anything, not just because she asked you not to but because you couldn't do anything. But this time, with Cathy, you can. You can do something for her. You can help her."

I look at Ken. Again, I realize she's right. There was nothing I could do to keep myself from losing Evelyn. I was helpless. But that's not the case with Cathy. It's not too late. Or so I hope.

"What should I do?" I ask her.

"You should figure that out, silly." Ken pats my arm. "Don't worry. I'm sure you will."

~

I'm still trying to think of what I can and should do as I watch Maisie sleep on her bed.

Thank goodness she's sleeping peacefully.

Two nights ago, she woke up with a nightmare, screaming for Cathy. And when there was no Cathy to comfort her, she became even more upset, crying for nearly half an hour before she was able to go back to sleep. Even during the day, I can tell she misses Cathy. She keeps asking about her. She keeps asking where Cathy is and when she'll come back, and whenever I tell her I don't know, the corners of her little mouth droop.

How can Cathy say she doesn't belong in Maisie's life when Maisie loves her so much?

"Don't worry, sweetheart," I whisper as I stroke Maisie's hair softly. "I promise I'll bring Cathy back."

She told me to give up on her for Maisie's sake, but it's precisely for that reason that I'm not going to.

"I'll find a way to bring her back."

Just then, Maisie stirs. She stretches one arm and tries to kick off her blanket. For a moment, I fear she might open her eyes, but she doesn't. She just turns on her side and throws her leg over a pillow, then tucks her hand beneath her cheek.

I smile. What is it about kids that they can't keep their blankets on or stay still while they sleep?

There's something endearing about it, though, and I can't help but plant a kiss on the top of Maisie's head after putting the blanket back on her. As I do, I catch a glimpse of something shiny peeking from beneath her pillow.

I pull it out and hear a clink as the charms of the bracelet jingle.

Cathy's bracelet. The one Trisha gave her.

I place it on my palm. As I run my fingers over the charms one by one, I remember the times I watched Cathy and Trisha together and another smile forms on my lips. They really were best friends. You could tell from just one look. They were different, sure, but they got along perfectly. Why, they only fought once as far as I can remember. They brought out the best in each other. They cared so much for each other. Why, they'd even risk their lives for each other.

My eyes grow wide. That's it. That's what I'll tell the judge. I'll tell the judge about what great friends Cathy and Trisha were and convince her that Cathy would never have hurt my sister. Who knows? Maybe I'll be able to convince Cathy, too.

I slip the bracelet back under Maisie's pillow and quietly leave her room.

It's time for me to get Cathy back.

~

When I get to the courtroom, Cathy is already there, dressed in a grey blazer over a black and white dress. The moment I see her honey hair, a smile coats my lips. It turns upside down, though, when I see the circles under her eyes and realize that she's already lost weight in the span of just several days. This whole ordeal must be harder on her than I thought.

When our eyes meet, hers grow wide. My heart leaps from my chest, seemingly pulling me towards her so I can feel her next to me and wrap my arms around her. When she turns away, though, my heart sinks all the way to my feet, keeping them in place. The frustration of not being able to hold her in my arms drops from my shoulders to my hands, which curl into fists.

I pull my gaze away from her and it falls on the judge's podium at the front of the room instead. The sight sobers me.

Right. I can't really go to Cathy right now, and she can't really talk to me even if she wants to. We're in a courtroom, involved in a case which has to be dealt with before either of us can move forward.

From the corner of my eye, I see Cathy's mother. She waves and gives me a smile. I can tell she wants me to sit with her in the row behind Cathy but I simply nod and take a seat on the opposite side, two rows back. I can chat with her later, but for now, I have to fulfill my role as a witness for the prosecution.

I unbutton my suit jacket before I sit. As I slip my hands into the pockets, I gaze at the empty table ahead. Moments later, two men occupy it, one who looks like he's halfway through his sixties and another in his early forties. The younger man wears a suit, the older a khaki jacket over a red and white plaid shirt. A woman in a black dress and coat takes her place beside Cathy. I'm guessing she's Cathy's lawyer. Then the court officials enter the room.

"Evidentiary hearing for the manslaughter charge against Cathy Jeffries now in session," one of them announces. "The honorable Judge Diana Vaughn presiding. All rise."

I stand up with the rest of the people in the room, then sit down after the judge, a woman with short salt and pepper hair and gold eyeglasses, takes her seat. She calls the lawyers to her podium for a word. Then the old man is called to the stand.

He limps his way there and states his name - Gary Pitts. His hand trembles slightly as he raises it to swear that he'll tell the truth. His features look pained.

Why? Doesn't he want to be here? Then again, I suppose no one does.

The prosecutor, who looks more relaxed - I guess he does want to be here - stands in front of Mr. Pitts.

"I'll go straight to the point here. Mr. Pitts, can you tell the court why we're here - what you saw at around 10:30 on the night of July 16, 2008?"

Mr. Pitts glances at Cathy, then turns to the prosecutor.

"I saw two teenage girls swimming in the lake," he says. "I remember thinking it was foolish of them, but then most teens are."

"Mr. Pitts, kindly stick to the facts and keep your opinions to yourself unless asked for," the judge says.

He nods. "One of the girls had dark brown hair, the other lighter brown. They weren't just swimming. They were playing, splashing around. Then they stopped. I think they started drowning."

"You didn't try to help them?" the prosecutor asks.

I was wondering the same thing.

"I wanted to, but my leg was bad even then. If I had tried to help them, I would have drowned."

"What happened next?"

"The girls tried to swim to the shore. One of them, the one with light brown hair, was panicking more than the other. She pushed the other girl's head under the water."

CHAPTER 19

Cathy

I clutch my skirt as my heart stops. Behind me, I hear my mother gasp.

No. It can't be.

"She kept pushing the other girl's head down as they swam to shore," Mr. Pitts goes on.

Each of his words feels like a dagger being plunged into my heart.

"When she got to shore, the other girl was no longer moving."

I clasp both hands over my mouth to hold back a sob. My stomach churns. I feel the weight of a hand on my shoulder and another on my back, but otherwise I feel numb.

"So there were two girls in the lake," the prosecutor says. "One came back to shore and the other didn't?"

"That's right."

"And this girl who came back to shore, the one you saw pushing the other girl's head down and seemingly using her body like some kind of lifesaver..."

Gina stands. "Objection, Your Honor."

"Sustained," the judge replies before casting a warning glance in the prosecutor's direction. "No need for dramatics here, Mr. Addison."

The prosecutor clears his throat. "The girl you saw survive that night, is she here?"

"I think so."

Mr. Pitts glances at me. I look away.

"I can't say for sure that I know what she looks like now, but I read about those girls later and I remember the one who died was T...Trisha Holloway and the one who survived was Cathy Jeffries."

I shake my head in disbelief. I know I'm the one who survived and Trisha didn't. I know that until this moment, I thought I was responsible for Trisha's death. Now that I've heard it from someone else's mouth, though, I can't bring myself to believe it. My mind and heart rage against the thought of it.

I didn't kill her. I didn't.

Gina squeezes my hand.

"It will be alright, Cathy," she whispers.

Will it?

"That will be all," I hear the prosecutor say.

Gina leaves the table.

"Mr. Pitts, you're a caretaker for one of the cabins around Lake Staggart. Am I right?" she asks as she approaches the old man who just said I killed Trisha.

"Yes."

"For how long?"

"I started in 1998 and I stopped around 2011."

"And during this time, you lived at the cabin?"

"I had my own place next to the shed," Mr. Pitt says.

"Which you shared with your family?"

"No. I'm divorced."

"So you stayed there alone. No one can say whether or not you were inside your room on the night of July 16, 2008?"

I lift my chin as I feel the first glimmer of hope. That's right. Mr. Pitts could be lying.

Mr. Pitts pauses. "No, but - "

"Your Honor, I have here the testimony of a guest saying he saw Mr. Pitts leave his residence before 10 PM on July 16, 2008," the prosecutor says.

He lifts the paper in his hand.

Gina frowns. "You couldn't have submitted that beforehand?"

"I submit it as evidence now, Your Honor," the prosecutor addresses the judge. "In support of Mr. Pitts' testimony."

"Very well," the judge says.

My shoulders sink further. I guess Mr. Pitts is telling the truth after all.

The prosecutor hands the judge and Gina copies of the document.

Gina looks at it. "Anything else you'd like to submit?"

The prosecutor shakes his head.

Gina brings the document to the table. I try to sneak a glance but she slips it under her laptop and goes back in front.

"Was it your habit to take a walk outdoors late at night when you were staying at the cabin, Mr. Pitts?" she asks.

"No," he answers. "It wasn't a habit. But when I can't sleep and the moon is out, I do sometimes take a walk."

"Even though you have a bad leg?"

"Yes. My doctor says exercise is good for me, that my leg would get worse if I sat still."

"So you took a walk on the night of July 16, 2008?"

"Yes."

"And you happened to pass by the lake?"

"Yes."

"And you saw two teenage girls swimming?"

"Yes."

I gaze down at my lap and fuss with my skirt.

"You're sure you saw them?" Gina asks. "Even though there are no lights around the lake and the nearest cabin was on the other side of the shore, about a mile away?"

"The moon was full," Mr. Pitts says. "It was out."

My hands grow still. Not really. It was coated with clouds.

"And the girls had a lantern perched on a tree branch," Mr. Pitts goes on. "One of those battery-powered ones. Red."

"Just like the one found at the scene," the prosecutor adds.

I frown.

"So you're sure you saw them?" Gina asks.

"Yes." His answer makes my chest ache.

"Has your vision always been good?"

"Objection, Your Honor." The prosecutor is on his feet again. "I've already submitted a report from an ophthalmologist saying Mr. Pitts' vision is excellent and has always been so."

"Sustained," the judge answers. "Next question, counsel."

"You weren't drunk that night?" Gina asks.

"No. I don't drink when there are guests," he answers.

Which means his vision was really good and his memory better than mine.

"And did you see anyone else?" Gina asks next.

"No. Not then."

My eyebrows go up. There was no one? Not even that boy I remember seeing with Trisha? Where did he go?

"And you're positive you saw Cathy pushing Trisha's head below water?"

"Yes."

I swallow.

"I understand why you didn't help them, but you didn't even shout at them? You didn't tell Cathy to stop what she was doing?"

"Objection, Your Honor," the prosecutor protests once more. "Mr. Pitts is not the one on trial here."

"But his testimony is the basis for the charges against my client," Gina answers.

The judge nods. "I'll allow it. Answer the question, Mr. Pitts."

"I was... in shock," he says.

"And even after those two girls reached the shore, you didn't try to help them or even check on them?"

The prosecutor stands up. "Objection, Your Honor."

"Sustained," the judge says. She turns to Gina. "Do remember what you're trying to prove here, counsel."

Gina nods. "I only have one last question. Why, Mr. Pitts, didn't you come forward before? Why only now, eleven years later?"

I lift my head to look at the witness. I've been wondering the same thing.

Mr. Pitts bows his head. "I... kept quiet because, well, because what happened was tragic and I was thinking that even if I spoke up, it wouldn't change anything. It wouldn't bring that girl back to life. I know the other girl didn't mean it and she was so young. I didn't want her to have a hard life."

"But you changed your mind?" Gina asks him.

"I'm not saying it never bothered me. It did, but I just... held back. But I'm getting old. And I have grandchildren. And I was thinking I'd want to know if someone tried to hurt them. I thought the girl's family would want to know."

He glances at Jackson. I do the same but look away as soon as our gazes meet. I knew he was asked to be here but I was surprised to see him just the same.

"So you just wanted to come clean?" Gina asks Mr. Pitts. "Unburden your conscience?"

"Yes."

Gina nods and turns to the judge. "That will be all, Your Honor."

Judge Vaughn looks at Mr. Pitts. "Thank you, Mr. Pitts. You may leave the stand now."

A police officer helps him down.

"Next witness?" the judge asks the prosecutor.

He glances behind him. "I'd like to call Jackson Holloway, the victim's brother, to the stand."

I draw a breath.

Jackson walks up to the podium in his crisp suit. I try not to stare at him as he states his name and swears to tell the truth.

How am I supposed to face him now?

The prosecutor stands in front of the podium. "For the record, I'd like to say that Mr. Holloway is also Ms. Cathy Jeffries' fiance, but - "

"Not anymore," Jackson interrupts.

My breath catches. I hear my mother gasp behind me as I try to regain my composure.

Right. I broke up with Jackson. Our engagement is over. Then again, we were never really engaged. I'm not even sure what we were.

So why does my chest hurt?

"Okay." The prosecutor seems baffled. "Let that be on the record, then."

He clears his throat. "Mr. Holloway, Trisha was your younger sister. Am I right?"

"Yes."

"Was she a good swimmer?"

"Yes," Jackson answers. "But not as good as - "

"She and your... former fiancee were friends, right?" the prosecutor cuts him off.

Jackson nods. "The best."

"They never fought?"

"Objection, Your Honor." Gina stands up. "I don't see how this is relevant. The charge is manslaughter, which means there is no need to establish motive."

"I'm simply trying to establish that the accused can be violent," the prosecutor argues.

Me, violent?

"Very well," the judge answers. "I'll allow it."

Gina sits down with a sigh but gives me a smile. "It will be okay."

"Answer the question, Mr. Holloway," the prosecutor says.

"Not as far as I know, no. I mean, they'd have arguments, but - "

"So you're saying Ms. Jeffries never hit your sister with a tin can because she got frustrated over the ending of a book she read?"

My eyes grow wide. How on earth did the prosecutor know that?

Jackson looks surprised as well. He falls silent.

The prosecutor moves closer to him. "Mr. Holloway?"

"If you didn't know it happened, you can say so," the judge says.

I tug Gina's sleeve. "I..."

"I know it happened," Jackson starts to speak. "I was there."

He was?

"Cathy had just finished reading her book. Trisha was waiting for her to finish it. They started talking about the book. Cathy was upset because of who the main character ended up with. Trisha didn't think it was so bad. They started talking about guys, teasing each other. Then Trisha grabbed a cookie from the can and threw it at Cathy. She threw it back. They just started throwing cookies at each other..."

I grin at the memory.

"Then when the cookies ran out, Cathy reached for the can. She threw it at Trisha but Trisha dodged and the can landed on the shelf. The problem was later on when they were laughing about what happened. Trisha hit the shelf and the can fell on her head."

I clasp a hand over my mouth as I snicker. I can't help it. That was just so funny.

The prosecutor doesn't seem to think so, though. His expression looks even more serious than before. Again, he clears his throat.

"Mr. Holloway, maybe make your answers shorter next time?" he suggests.

"Sorry," Jackson quickly apologizes.

"Well then. Did - ?"

"But I just wanted to show everyone here that Cathy never tried to hurt my sister," Jackson says. "She would never have done such a thing."

Gina grins. The prosecutor frowns.

"Mr. Holloway..."

Jackson turns to the judge. "Your Honor, may I speak? I swore to tell the truth and nothing but the truth, and I'd like to do that now."

The judge glances at her watch and nods. "Very well. You may address the court."

Jackson draws a deep breath. "Cathy and my sister, Trisha, were best friends. It's true they didn't always agree, but they were always there for each other. Trisha, adventurous as she was and reckless sometimes, would get into trouble and Cathy would pull her out of it. Or Cathy would feel reluctant to do something and Trisha would push her into it. When my parents got divorced, Cathy was there for Trisha. When Cathy had an appendectomy, Trisha wouldn't leave her side. Would you believe my sister offered to donate her own appendix because she thought Cathy needed it?"

Gina chuckles. My jaw drops. Trisha never told me that.

"One summer, a rattlesnake wandered into our yard," Jackson goes on.

Oh, this I know.

"Trisha was terrified, but Cathy rushed between the snake and her. She was ready to give up her life for her best friend."

I purse my lips. I still don't know how I did that. I guess I just didn't want to lose Trisha no matter what.

Jackson turns to the judge once more. "What I'm saying, Your Honor, is that Cathy Jeffries would never have tried to push Trisha's head under water. And I'm not saying this because she was my fiancee but because I saw how much she loved my sister."

I smile as his words fill my chest with a reassuring warmth.

"Your Honor," the prosecutor protests. "This is all Mr. Holloway's opinion. He doesn't know what happened. Gary Pitts does."

Jackson opens his mouth. "But - "

"Mr. Holloway, I thank you for your story," the judge says. "But no one's alleging that Cathy tried to kill your sister or that she meant it. The charge is manslaughter, which means there was no malice, just that someone died as a result of what someone else did or didn't do."

I frown as my hopes crumble.

Jackson stands up. "But - "

"But Mr. Pitts doesn't really know what happened," Gina interrupts as she, too, gets out of her seat.

The prosecutor turns to her. "Are you calling my witness a liar?"

Gina ignores him and turns to the judge. "Your Honor, I have just received information that I would like to submit into evidence. Early this year, Mr. Pitts' granddaughter was diagnosed with leukemia. His family was struggling to find funds for her treatment, but a few weeks ago, two days before the prosecution filed the charge against my client, his granddaughter was admitted to a modern and very expensive treatment program. I find that suspicious."

My eyebrows arch. Gina is saying that Mr. Pitts was paid off?

The prosecutor gapes. "Your Honor, this information is irrelevant and the defense's insinuations are absurd."

"Ms. Levinson, where did you get this information?" the judge asks Gina.

"I have medical documents, Your Honor," Gina answers.

I throw a puzzled look at her back. She does?

The judge turns to Mr. Pitts. "Mr. Pitts, is this information true?"

He stands up and scratches his head. "I..."

"I would like to call Mr. Pitts back to the stand," Gina says. "That way, he can tell us all the truth under oath. And nothing but the truth this time."

"No need." Mr. Pitts shakes his head. "I'll tell the truth. It's true. My granddaughter, Meg, is sick, and now she's being treated. Someone was kind enough to help."

"In exchange for what?" Gina asks.

"Objection, Your Honor," the prosecutor protests.

"I..." Mr. Pitts fidgets with the hem of his shirt.

"I know you're worried about your granddaughter, Mr. Pitts," Gina tells him. "I know you'd do anything to save her. But what good would that be if you made another person, an innocent person like my client, suffer?"

The prosecutor shakes his head. "Your Honor, what is this?"

The judge gives Gina a warning glance. "Counsel..."

"I... take back what I said," Mr. Pitts says suddenly. "I'm not sure I saw..."

For a moment, his gaze meets mine.

"I'm not sure I saw anything. It was dark and I might have made a mistake. I..."

The prosecutor turns to face him. "Mr. Pitts!"

"Order!" Judge Vaughn smacks her gavel.

The room falls silent and those standing take their seats.

"I don't know what's going on here, but clearly, this is a waste of time," the judge says. "I'm not going to waste another second. The charges against the accused are dismissed. This case is closed. Good day."

She smacks her gavel one more time and leaves the room. The prosecutor bolts, too, seething in frustration and sneering at Mr. Pitts over his shoulder. The old man limps towards the exit with his head hanging low.

I almost feel sorry for him.

As for how I feel about myself, I don't know. I'm still trying to figure out what just happened.

One moment someone was saying I killed Trisha and the next he was saying it was all a lie. So I'm not responsible for Trisha's death?

"Hey." Gina pats my shoulder. "Keep that head up. Everything's alright now."

I give her a smile. "Thank you."

I have a feeling that if not for her, someone would be dragging me to jail right now.

"Thank you, Gina," my mother echoes. "I owe you."

"No." She shakes her head. "I owed you. And now, that debt is paid."

My mother gives her a hug.

"Congratulations."

I turn my head and see Jackson standing in front of me. Is it okay for me to face him now?

I tuck a strand of hair behind my ear and look away. "What for? I didn't win anything."

"But now the charge against you has been dismissed," he says. "Not that I ever thought it wouldn't be."

The corners of my lips turn up into a soft smile. "Thank you for all those things you said. For trying to convince everyone that I would never do a thing to hurt Trisha."

"They weren't the only ones I was trying to convince."

I lift my head and meet his gaze. The warmth in his eyes takes my breath away.

"I don't understand." I shake my head. "I thought we broke up. I pushed you away. I - "

"Do you really think you can get rid of me so easily?" Jackson asks me as he places a hand on my cheek. "I've wanted you for so long."

I blush.

"Besides, you might have broken up with me, but my feelings for you haven't changed."

My eyes grow wide as the warmth on my face spreads to my chest. My heart does somersaults. Jackson... still loves me?

I place my hand over his and press his palm against my cheek as I put all the warmth in me into a smile.

He takes my hand. "Shall we get out of here and grab something to eat? You look like you could use some food, and I happen to know this great restaurant in Milwaukee."

CHAPTER 20

Jackson

"This is good."

I watch Cathy as she gobbles up her second serving of risotto with wild mushrooms, tomatoes and bits of venison braised in red wine.

She looks like she hasn't eaten in a month. Well, I suppose it has been about a month since she had that nightmare and started getting restless and acting distant. Thankfully, that seems over now. Or so I hope.

"You should serve something like this at the restaurant," Cathy recommends.

"You mean steal my friend's recipe? No, thank you." I take a sip of wine.

She eats a few more spoonfuls, then sets down her spoon. "How is the restaurant? Are there still a lot of customers?"

"Of course," I answer. "The lines are still long during lunch and dinner."

Cathy's face turns serious. "I'm sorry I left so suddenly."

"It's fine. You couldn't help it. You had a case you had to deal with."

Her eyebrows crease. "But I left even before..."

"It's fine," I assure her. "Everything at the restaurant is going as well as can be, though of course not as well as when you're around."

She snorts as she picks up her spoon. "I'm sure everything's perfect. What could possibly go wrong with Ken there?"

I shrug. "I burned a piece of salmon. And a piece of steak."

Cathy's eyes grow wide. "You did not."

"I did." I take another sip of the wine before setting it down. "Well, not for the customers, just for me, but yeah. That wouldn't have happened if you were around."

I meant it as a compliment, but Cathy's frown lets me know she takes it differently.

"I'm sorry."

I shake my head. "My point is that I need you there. The restaurant needs you, and I think even Ken needs you there."

"She must be mad at me for disappearing like that."

"No." I recall the last conversation I had with her. "She's worried about you. She wants you back as soon as possible."

Cathy wipes the corner of her mouth with the table napkin. "Then I'll be sure to make things up to her when I get back."

"You do that."

I should thank her, too. If not for Ken's advice, I wouldn't be here now.

Cathy takes a sip of water. "How's Maisie?"

"Ken brings her to and from daycare and the Hendersons watch her at night," I answer. "She misses you terribly, though. She keeps that bracelet you gave her above her pillow."

"Trisha's bracelet," Cathy mumbles.

"And she's been asking about you all the time. See, you've already made a home in her heart. In both our hearts."

Cathy says nothing, though I think she's also recalling that argument we had before she left. I hope she doesn't think the same way now.

I reach for her hand. "Cathy..."

Suddenly, she pulls her hand away and clasps it over her mouth. Pain and worry flicker in her eyes.

"Cathy?"

"Sorry," she mumbles before taking off in the direction of the bathroom, running so fast that she hits the back of one of the chairs and makes a few heads turn in confusion.

Some of them turn back towards me with questioning glances.

I ignore them and pick up my glass of wine. As I bring it to my lips, my gaze falls on Cathy's bowl, which only has a little bit of risotto left in it.

Did she get food poisoning? Nonsense. Fred makes sure every dish that goes out of his kitchen is perfect. Maybe Cathy just ate too much too fast.

I let out a sigh and take a sip. Whatever the reason, I hope she's okay.

~

"Cathy, are you okay?" I ask outside the bathroom door of the hotel room.

She looked fine when she came back to the table after spending nearly fifteen minutes in the bathroom at the restaurant, so long that I nearly went after her. She didn't want to eat more risotto, but she still had dessert - strawberry and lemon panna cotta. She seemed to enjoy it, too.

I thought she was fine, but as soon as we entered the hotel room, she rushed to the bathroom again. She's been in there ever since, probably for nearly twenty minutes now.

I knock on the door. "Cathy?"

When she still doesn't answer, I open the door. To my relief, I find her in the shower. A cloud of steam fills the stall.

It's no wonder she couldn't hear me.

I step inside and move closer so my voice can reach her. "Are you alright?"

She looks surprised to see me but nods. "I feel better now. Sorry about that. My stomach just started revolting against me."

"Well, you did eat a bit too much," I tell her.

"I guess." Cathy shrugs. "Were you waiting for me to come out? I'm sorry. I just thought I'd take a shower to freshen up and smell better."

"It's fine."

I fall silent as my eyes follow the drops of water raining down on Cathy's hair and trickling down her naked body. Even through the steam and the glass, I can see some parts of her clearly - her firm breasts, perfectly round with her nipples sticking out just slightly, the soft curve of her belly, a plump cheek of her ass, a supple thigh.

The sight of her creates a lump in my throat and sends heat stirring in my crotch, making me realize I've been without her for too long. I swallow.

"I should go," I tell her.

As much as I'd love to stay, it may be too soon for me to be intimate with Cathy again. I don't want to scare her.

I'm about to walk away when I hear the door to the shower slide open. A moment later, I feel a wet hand around my wrist. I meet Cathy's gaze and see the invitation in her eyes.

Still, I hesitate.

"If you're just doing this because you feel like you owe me something for defending you or you're trying to thank me for taking care of you, it's okay. You don't have to - "

"I'm not," Cathy cuts me off. "I've missed you."

I look into her hazel eyes once more. This time, I see not just a request in them but also a gleam of desire. My cock throbs.

Oh, to hell with it.

I step into the shower with her without undressing. The warm water seeps through my shirt and trickles over my woolen pants.

Cathy tilts her chin up. Her breasts press against my chest as she wraps her arms around my neck. I place my hands on her arms and kiss her lips. She parts them and my tongue brushes against hers.

I feel Cathy shiver. Her nipples turn into stiff pebbles, poking my skin through drenched cotton. My cock thickens in response.

She messes my hair as her tongue plays with mine. I rub her shoulders, her arms, her sides. My palms graze the sides of her breasts and she moans into my mouth.

I cup those mounds of flesh I've had my eyes on since I entered the bathroom and press the pads of my thumbs against the stiff peaks. Cathy pulls her mouth away from mine and gasps against my neck.

She rests her head against one of my shoulders as she clings to both of them. I kiss her ear as my fingers twist her nipples and tug them gently. I move my mouth to her neck as I wrap an arm around her and slip my hand between her legs.

My fingers brush against dripping curls and soft folds of skin. I find the opening between them and slide a finger in.

Cathy's fingers dig into my shoulders. She lets out a soft cry.

I nibble on her neck as I move my finger in and out of her. The heat and tightness of her makes blood rush to my head, and to my balls.

God, I've missed her.

Suddenly, Cathy grabs my wrist and pushes my hand away. She begins to undo the buttons of my shirt but stops at the third. Her lips curve into a grin.

"What?" I ask her.

"Just as I thought, you look best in a suit," Cathy tells me.

I lift an eyebrow. "In a drenched suit?"

"That, too."

She presses her mouth against mine again as she continues with the rest of the buttons. I decide to help her.

After the buttons are all undone, Cathy peels the wet layer of cotton off my skin. I unbutton and unzip my pants. I let them fall around my knees then pull them off. I throw them out of the shower and hear them fall wetly on the rug. I'm about to take off my underwear as well, but Cathy beats me to it. She kneels on the mat and pulls my boxers down. My erection springs free.

The sight of it seems to make her forget her task. I remove my boxers as she wraps her fingers around my cock. She brushes her lips across the length, then opens her mouth and starts to lick the tip.

The sight of Cathy relishing my cock like a tasty treat sends adrenaline pumping through my veins. The exquisite expression on her face with her eyes closed steals my breath.

The sensation of her warm, wet tongue swiping against my sensitive skin over and over makes my hands tremble. I grip her shoulders and let out shallow breaths as I, too, savor the experience. Within seconds, I feel myself become fully hard.

Cathy wraps her lips around the tip of my cock, takes me inside her sinful cavern of a mouth and sucks. I throw my head back. Her mouth can't accommodate the entire rod of flesh, but the friction from her lips and tongue as she moves her head back and forth is enough. Each time the leaking tip of my cock collides with the roof of her mouth, I shiver and hiss.

Fuck. Now, this is sublime service worthy of a Michelin star.

Cathy moves her head faster. One of her hands cradles my heavy balls. The other grips my ass.

I place my hands on the top of her head and let my fingers become entangled with her damp hair. I stroke it to prevent myself from holding her head in place, which a part of me has the urge to do.

Hold her head in place and pound into her sweet mouth.

She fondles my balls gently and moans around my cock. I feel it quiver against her tongue. The excitement buzzing through my veins intensifies. My balls grow even heavier and my cock feels on fire.

"Cathy." I pull her hair and try to push her off me as I feel the pleasure about to reach its peak. "Let go. I'm com - "

She doesn't let go, though, and it's too late. The pleasure hits. My cock explodes inside her mouth. My hips jerk as they take a life of their own. My fingers dig into Cathy's scalp as grunts, gasps and curses leave my lips.

"Fuck!"

When it's over, I take a moment to catch my breath. Then I take my hands off Cathy's head and step away. A trail of white liquid oozes out of the corner of her mouth and trickles down her chin. Her cheeks look like they're full of it.

"You don't have to swa - "

Cathy looks me in the eye and does precisely that - swallows. She wipes her mouth with the back of her hand, then licks her lips.

I place my hand on my neck and sigh. "What am I going to do with you?"

"What?" She gets off her knees and gives me a puzzled look. "Is it wrong for me to swallow?"

"Not wrong, but I didn't want you to."

"Why not?"

"It's..."

Well, Evelyn didn't like it. Then again, Cathy isn't Evelyn.

"What if your stomach gets upset again?" I ask her.

"No, it won't," she assures me.

She wraps her arms around me and kisses me on the lips. I taste myself on her mouth.

I turn her around. "Now, it's your turn."

I throw her hair over one of her shoulders and plant my lips on her nape as I pull her against me. I squeeze her breasts and rub her nipples. Cathy gasps.

I keep playing with one as I reach between her legs. A thrill goes through me as she parts them.

Again, I slip a finger inside her. She's wetter now. I put in another and push them both upward. Cathy lets out another gasp. Her hands grip my arms as she trembles.

I lick her ear as I move my fingers in and out. Then I pull them out entirely and search for her sensitive nub. I know I've found it when Cathy throws her head against my shoulder. I tease it and she starts letting out soft cries that bounce off the tiles. Her hands grip my hips.

I alternate between sucking on her neck and licking her ear as I strum her. The music she makes goes straight to my cock and makes it swell again, poking her lower back. Then I fix my lips on Cathy's neck as I move my fingers faster. Her knees shake. Her cries grow louder.

Cathy gives a particularly loud one as she comes undone. She thrashes against me, her head nearly colliding with mine. Her nails dig into my skin.

After she grows still, I wrap my arms around her to keep her from falling. I rest my cheek against hers as I wait for her to catch her breath.

"You're hard again," Cathy finally speaks.

"Think we can go one more time?" I ask her. "I can stop if you want me to, though."

At least, I can wait until she finishes her shower. Then I'll come back in here and jerk myself off.

She turns her head to meet my gaze. "I think I can take it."

I give her a mischievous grin. "Oh. We've become naughty now, have we?"

"It's all your fault."

"Very well. I'll take all the blame. Anything to please you."

I capture Cathy's mouth as I slip my hand between her legs once more. I push two fingers inside her and they slide right in.

She's ready.

And so am I.

I break the kiss, put my hand on her back and push her down gently.

"Spread your legs and place your hands on the mat," I tell her.

She obeys. "Like this?"

I nod and grip her hips. "Ready?"

"Ready."

I lower my hips and push my cock inside her slowly. I resist the urge to fill her with one thrust and do it inch by inch instead. I let out a hiss as I feel her silky sheath wrap around me.

Cathy lets out gasps. Other than that, nothing. She doesn't move, either.

Good. It's my turn to move.

Finally, I'm completely inside her. I pause to catch my breath.

"Are you okay?" I ask.

"I don't know," she answers. "This isn't very comfortable."

It's not the answer I was hoping to hear.

"Why don't we try this? I'll lift your hips and you wrap your legs around my thighs."

"What?"

"Ready? One, two, three."

I bend my knees and lift Cathy's hips. She takes her feet off the floor and wraps her legs around my thighs. Then I start with my thrusts. Cathy moans.

"Comfortable?" I ask without stopping.

"Not really," Cathy answers. "I feel like a vacu - ah!"

She lets out a cry as I thrust deep inside her.

"I think the word you're looking for is 'wheelbarrow'," I say between shallow breaths.

"Well... I... don't... want to... be one."

So she says, but then she gives out another cry.

I go for a few more thrusts before I lower her legs gently. I pull out of her, grab her arm, and jerk her to her feet.

"Let's do this instead."

I turn Cathy around to face me. I kiss her mouth as I grip her hip. My other hand reaches for her thigh.

"Grip my shoulder and lift your leg," I tell her. "Put your foot on the ledge."

Cathy obeys. As soon as her leg is up, I place my hand under her thigh and push my cock back inside her.

Cathy lets out a soft moan.

"Better?" I ask her.

She looks into my eyes and nods. "Yes."

I seal her lips as I jerk my hips anew. She moans into my mouth.

My hand moves from her hip to her ass. This angle isn't as deep as the one earlier, but I have more control of my movements, and I take full advantage of that as I pour power into my thrusts. My breath starts to come in gasps. The kiss gets sloppy.

Cathy pulls her mouth away and moans against my shoulder. Her silky sheath grips my cock wonderfully. Her body trembles.

I keep thrusting into her. I'm close. Judging from the way Cathy is trembling and the sounds she's making, she is, too.

I move even faster and Cathy lets out a cry. Her nails dig into my shoulders. A moment later, she tightens around me and I groan as I manage a final thrust. I spill myself inside her as my fingers clutch soft skin.

She puts her leg down on the floor and rests her body against me as she catches her breath. I wrap an arm around her and stay still as I catch mine. I hear Cathy's heart beating against me, its rhythm in sync with my own.

When it's slowed down, I grip Cathy's hips, pull out of her, and wrap my arms around her again.

"Are you okay?"

"Yes," she answers. "I'm just starting to feel a little cold."

Me, too.

"Well, then..."

I go under the showerhead and pull her to my side. The warm water feels good on my skin.

"Shall we continue our shower?"

~

"That's probably the longest shower I ever took," Cathy says as she dries her hair with a towel.

"But admit it," I tell her as I pull on a shirt. "It was one of the best."

She grins. "Fine."

I walk over to her and plant another kiss on her lips. Afterwards, I stroke her cheek as I gaze into her eyes.

"What?" Cathy asks me.

"You're beautiful," I tell her. "You always were."

She snorts. "By the way, how did you know about that incident with the cookies and the tin can? I didn't see you there."

I chuckle as I sit beside her. "I was watching from the stairs."

She frowns. "You should have joined us."

"Nah." I wave a hand. "The two of you were having enough fun. Besides, there were only enough cookies for two."

Cathy laughs, then suddenly turns serious. "How did the prosecutor know about that? Mr. Pitts couldn't possibly have known that."

I shrug. That thought has been bothering me as well. The only ones who knew about that incident were me, Cathy and Trisha. How come the prosecutor knew about it? Who told him?

"He didn't seem to know what really happened, though," Cathy remarks. "When you gave the details of the story, he looked rattled. It wasn't what he expected."

"Well, he did want you to turn out to be the villain," I say.

Cathy lets out a deep sigh. "I still think I am, you know. I still think I'm responsible for Trisha's death."

I frown. Aren't we done with this?

"Before the hearing, I met a hypnotherapist and I remembered some more things. I remembered that I was drowning and that I was trying to call out to Trisha, who was standing on the shore, talking to some guy."

My eyebrows furrow. "Guy?"

"I'm not saying I killed her. I don't think I pushed her head under water or used her as a lifesaver or anything like that."

"Of course not."

"But I think she went into the water because of me. She tried to save me and she did, but somehow she died in the process." Cathy looks into my eyes. "If that's what really happened, then I'm still guilty of manslaughter, don't you think?"

I reach for Cathy's hand. "No. I don't think that's manslaughter."

She doesn't look convinced.

"And if that's what really happened, then I don't think it's too bad. It only means that Trisha was your best friend until the very end. I'm sure she didn't mean to die. I'm sure she didn't want to leave you alone, but I think she died happy knowing that she saved you."

Cathy's eyebrows crease. "You think so?"

"I know so." I squeeze her hand. "She wouldn't want you to blame yourself. That would discredit her final heroic act. It would make her feel like she didn't save you. But she did save you, Cathy. She got you to shore. The best way you can repay her is by getting back on your feet and moving on."

Cathy says nothing.

I touch her cheek and look into her eyes. "Trisha was a best friend to you. Now be the best person you can be for her."

For a moment, Cathy's expression doesn't change. Then she smiles.

"Thank you, Jackson."

I answer by touching my forehead to hers and giving her a tender kiss. She kisses me back and turns her hand over in mine. Our palms touch and our fingers entwine.

After the kiss, I look at her hand. "You didn't throw the ring away, did you?"

"No," Cathy answers. "I left it in the drawer of the bedside table in my room. That's where I put it at night. I didn't put it back on in the morning."

I nod.

"Do you want it back?" she asks me.

"No," I tell her. "I want you to hold on to it."

"But..."

I hold a finger to her lips. "Cathy, I love you, so I'm going to do this properly. I want you to be my girlfriend. I want to marry you someday."

Cathy's eyes grow wide. "You're proposing?"

"I'm telling you how I feel and what I want. I'd like you to do the same."

Cathy draws a deep breath. "I..."

I put my finger back on her lips. "You don't have to answer right away. I'll wait. Just think about it, okay?"

She nods. "Okay."

I lift her hand to my lips. Then I put it back on her lap and stand up. I go to the closet and grab a pair of pants.

"Where are you going?" Cathy asks me.

"I just need to buy some stuff for the restaurant," I answer. "You stay here and rest."

"Okay."

~

It takes me only half an hour to get all the cheese I want, and I'm on my way back to the hotel when I see Simon sitting in a cafe. He's busy typing something on his laptop, so he doesn't notice me.

"Simon," I call out to him.

He jumps. As soon as he sees me, he closes his laptop and throws me a smile.

"Hey. What are you doing here in Milwaukee?"

"Business," I give him the simple answer.

I don't want to have to explain about Cathy's hearing. Besides, Simon may be a business partner and an old friend, but I still don't consider him close enough to give him all the details of my personal life.

He glances at the shopping bags I'm carrying. "Cheese. I guess that's a chef's business in Wisconsin."

"Yep," I agree. "What about you? What are you doing here?"

Simon shrugs. "Business."

"I see."

He taps his fingers on the lid of his laptop. "How's Cathy?"

I grow still. I know he's just making small talk and it's an innocent question, but I can't forget how interested he seemed in her that last time. Is he still interested in her?

"She's fine," I say.

"So she's handling the break-up well?"

My shoulders tense. How did he know I broke up with Cathy?

"We didn't really break up," I tell him.

"Really? I thought the engagement was called off."

I narrow my eyes at him. "Who told you that?"

I notice him pause to think for a moment. "From the website, the one with your groupies."

I frown. How would they know, though?

"Anyway, it's good that you're still engaged," Simon says.

"Is it?" I ask him suspiciously. "I thought you didn't want us to get married."

"I'm against marriage, not against you finding happiness," he says defensively. "Both of you deserve it after what happened to Trisha."

Again, my gaze narrows. I don't know why, but I find it annoying to listen to Simon talk about her.

"I know you met her, but you didn't really know her, so I'd appreciate it if you didn't mention her anymore. To me or to anyone else."

Simon nods. "Okay."

"Thanks. I have to go."

I start walking off, then stop.

"Oh, and one more thing."

"What's that?"

I glance over my shoulder. "Stay away from my fiancee."

With my warning delivered, I take my leave. After a few steps, I let out a breath of relief. I've been wanting to tell him that since the last time I spoke to him. I'm glad I was finally able to.

Cathy may not have agreed to be my girlfriend or my fiancee yet, but I love her. I'm not going to let anyone take her away from me.

Because I'm still hoping she'll say yes.

CHAPTER 21

Cathy

Jackson really loves me, huh?

I hold the diamond ring between my thumb and my forefinger and examine it against the sunlight drifting in through the window. It glistens.

It really is a beautiful ring, and I have to say I've grown used to wearing it. I can't keep wearing it, though, not until I've told Jackson how I feel about him.

How do I feel about him?

I press the ring against my chest as I think of the answer.

I like him. That's for sure. I like his smile. I like his laugh. I like how thoughtful and caring he is. I like his body.

I shake my head. No, that's not right. I don't just like his body. I - what's the word? - am in awe of his body and all the things it does to mine. Just the thought of Jackson naked makes me blush. The memory of his kisses sends a thrill down my spine.

So I like him. I enjoy his company, in bed and out. I admire him for being a great chef. I'm proud of everything he's accomplished. I look up to him. I admire him for being such a great father to Maisie. I feel like I've known him forever and I want to stay by his side.

Does that mean I love him? Or does that mean we're just best friends who have amazing sex together?

What is it exactly that makes a couple a couple?

I put the ring back in the drawer and let out a sigh.

I wish Trisha were still around. Maybe she could answer my questions and tell me what to do.

Then again, I know that if Trisha were still around, she'd leave the decision to me. She'd approve of me being with Jackson, I think, but she'd tell me to follow my heart.

In the end, it's still up to me.

My thoughts are interrupted by the sound of footsteps racing down the hall. A moment later, the door opens.

"Cathy!" Maisie shouts.

She flings herself into my arms.

"Maisie, darling." I squeeze her tight. "How have you been?"

She pulls away to give me a wide smile. "I'm glad you're back. I've been waiting for you."

"Have you?"

"Are you bringing me to daycare today?" she asks.

"No," I answer.

Maisie frowns.

I touch the tip of her nose. "I'm bringing you to the park. Your daddy insisted that I take one more day to rest."

Maisie's face lights up like a Christmas tree. "Yay!"

She throws her arms up in the air and wraps them around me.

"I love you, Cathy."

My eyebrows arch. How can a child say that with such certainty when I can't? Is it because she doesn't know what it means?

I place my hands on her shoulders. "Maisie, what do you mean?"

"I love you," she repeats. "It means I'm going to make you my mom."

Her words fill my chest with warmth and my mind with clarity.

She's right. That's what love is - a choice. It's not what you feel. It's what you choose to do.

And I think I know what my choice is.

I brush the wisp of hair from Maisie's cheek and smile. "I love you, too, sweetheart."

She gives an even wider smile.

I pat her head and get on my feet. "Let me just change, okay? I just - "

I stop as a wave of nausea washes over me. I grip the edge of the bed as my legs wobble.

"Cathy?"

I sit on the edge of the bed and touch my forehead. "Sorry, sweetheart. I just need a minute."

Worry gleams in her eyes. "But what's wrong?"

"I don't know. I just... Lately, there have been times when I don't feel so well."

"So why don't you go to a doctor?"

I look into Maisie's eyes. Why not indeed? It's the only way for me to find out if there's something wrong, and if there isn't, then at least I can finally get some peace of mind instead of worrying and making other people worry.

I touch her cheek. "Why not?"

~

"I have the results of your tests here, Ms. Jeffries." Dr. Ivers glances at the papers on his desk. "Are you ready to hear them?"

I cross my fingers before nodding.

Please don't let it be cancer.

"I'm ready, Doctor."

He draws a deep breath. I hold mine.

"Ms. Jeffries, you're pregnant."

My jaw drops. No shit.

That didn't cross my mind at all. Now that he's said it, though, everything makes sense. The nausea. The headaches. The appetite. And the fact that my period hasn't arrived yet.

Then of course, there's the fact that I've been having so much sex.

I touch my forehead. Why didn't I think I was pregnant?

"Ms. Jeffries?"

"I'm fine," I tell the doctor.

I actually am relieved. And happy. I can't explain it, but right now, I feel like I'm about to burst with joy.

I'm pregnant.

"Thank you, Doctor." I stand up and shake his hand.

"Congratulations, Ms. Jeffries." He hands me some papers. "Here are your test results, a prescription for your prenatal vitamins, and a schedule for your prenatal check-ups."

"Thank you."

I walk out of his clinic with a spring in my step.

I'm pregnant. With Jackson's child. I can't wait to tell him. Now, I have two pieces of good news to tell him.

I pause. Wait. I can't just tell him this plainly. This is special, so I have to plan a special way to tell him. Thankfully, I already have an idea, and I know just the person who can help me with it.

I take out my phone and dial Ken's number. She answers after the third ring.

"Cathy?"

"Ken, I need a favor. But first, I have a secret to tell you."

~

It's a hard secret to keep, I realize as I color pictures with Maisie in the living room.

I haven't told her about it. I just said the doctor said I was okay. But I already feel restless. What about when Jackson comes home? Will I be able to keep my mouth shut then?

The sound of the doorbell makes me jump. I force myself to take a deep breath before walking to the door.

Who can that be? Jackson? Did he forget his keys? Or maybe it's Ken.

It's neither, though. Rather, it's a woman in her forties in a grey dress.

"Is Mr. Jackson Holloway in?" she asks.

"Not yet, no," I answer. "How can I help you?"

"Kindly see to it that he gets these papers." She hands me an envelope. "It's important."

"Of course."

She leaves. I go back inside the house and close the door. On my way back to the living room, I can't stop staring at the envelope.

Papers? What papers?

The envelope isn't sealed, and unable to restrain my curiosity, I take a peek. As I realize what the documents are, I nearly fall to the floor.

No!

CHAPTER 22

Jackson

"What is the meaning of this?" I throw the papers on the coffee table in Betty's hotel suite.

She flips a page of the magazine on her lap. "Those papers are exactly what they say they are. Andy and I are petitioning the court for full custody of Maisie."

"Why?" I ask through gritted teeth.

Ever since I read the notice of custody hearing, I've been simmering like a pan of poached fish.

Betty, on the other hand, seems the epitome of serenity. There's not a wrinkle on her face.

"Why don't you take a seat, Jackson?" she asks me without meeting my gaze. "Would you like some water? Coffee? Whiskey?"

I place my hands on my hips. "I want to know why you're trying to take Maisie from me. I thought you were going to leave us alone."

Betty sighs. "I thought so, too. After I spoke to Cathy, I thought it would be fine to leave Maisie in your care and hers."

My eyebrows arch. She spoke to Cathy?

"But then I found out that Cathy was charged with manslaughter and all the trust I was putting in her vanished. You can choose to live with such a woman if you wish, but I will not let my granddaughter live with her."

So it's about that, is it? I draw a deep breath.

"Yes, Cathy was charged with manslaughter, but there was no basis for it, which is why the judge dismissed the case."

"But can you honestly say she didn't kill your sister? She can't remember what happened, right? That's a clue right there. She can't remember because she doesn't want to remember, and she doesn't want to remember because - "

"She can remember," I cut Betty off. "She can remember more now, and she remembers that she nearly drowned and my sister saved her. End of story."

"So it's because of her that your sister died?" Betty asks.

I shake my head in dismay. "It's not because of her. It was my sister's choice to save her best friend."

"But the fact remains that if not for her recklessness, your sister would still be alive." She flips another page of her magazine. "I will not let such a person be responsible for my granddaughter."

"It was an accident," I point out.

"And exactly why do accidents happen, hmm? Because someone was reckless. Are you going to wait for something to happen to Maisie before you realize how dangerous this woman is? Well, I won't."

She's about to turn another page, but I grab the magazine from her lap. I toss it on the coffee table on top of the court documents. I've had enough of her toying with me.

"Cathy is not a dangerous woman," I tell Betty.

"Really? If you think she's such a good woman, then why did you break up with her?"

I frown. She knows that, too? Wait. She wasn't the one who told Simon, was she?

"I didn't break up with her," I say in a calmer voice. "I just thought we shouldn't rush to get married."

"Because you have doubts about her?"

"No. I love her."

"But does she love you?"

I don't answer.

Betty snorts. "See. She doesn't love you. She told me the same thing when I spoke to her."

She did? No. I don't believe it.

"What I'm trying to say is that Cathy isn't just an innocent woman," I tell Betty. "She's a good woman. Just like Evelyn."

"I don't care. I'm Maisie's grandmother and I want what's best for her. Cathy just isn't good enough."

"And I'm her father," I point out. "I'll decide what's best for her."

"No." Betty stands up and shakes her head. "The court will the next time we meet."

She starts to walk out of the room. My shoulders sink in defeat.

"Don't do this, Betty," I ask her. "Don't put Maisie through this."

Betty turns her head. "You're the one who's putting her through this. I'm just trying to save her."

God, she's stubborn.

"Betty..."

She disappears into another room, closing the door behind her. I think of banging down that door. Instead, I grab the papers and the magazine on the coffee table and hurl them at the wall in frustration.

"Fuck!"

~

"She wouldn't listen to you?" Cathy asks me when I get back home.

"No." I pace her bedroom. "She's pushing through with the case. She says the next time we meet will be in court."

"Did she say why?"

I don't answer. I stop in front of the window and touch my neck.

"Jackson?"

"She said she doesn't want Maisie to live with you," I reluctantly tell her.

Cathy falls silent as she sits on the edge of the bed. Her chin drops.

"What did you tell Betty last time?" I ask her. "I didn't know the two of you spoke."

She shakes her head. "Nothing. I... I don't remember anymore."

I have a feeling she just doesn't want to tell me, but I don't insist on hearing it.

"It's fine," I say. "It doesn't matter anyway. Betty has already made up her mind. I'll have to fight her to keep Maisie."

Cathy stands up. "But surely the court will let you keep your own daughter."

I shake my head. "I don't know. I'm not exactly a perfect father, Cathy. I'm not even sure I'm a good one."

"Nonetheless, you are her father," Cathy tells me. "And you try your best."

"But don't you see?" I drop my hands to my sides. "Effort counts for nothing. It's the results that the court will look at. The judge will see that when Maisie was ten months old, she was rushed to the hospital because of an allergic reaction to the caviar I fed her. That when she was one and a half, she fell down the stairs. That when she was three, she nearly cut off her finger with one of my knives. The judge will know that I've been renting houses and moving from place to place, that I'm busy with work and that Maisie has had so many nannies I've lost count. The judge will learn that I lost Maisie in a playground just recently. All of those things show that I'm not fit to be a father."

Cathy says nothing. She looks at the floor, deep in thought. I bet even she is shocked by all the mistakes I've made trying to take care of Maisie.

I draw a deep breath and head to the door. "I'm going to the garden for some air. Don't follow me. I need to be alone."

I need to think of a way to keep my daughter. The possibility of losing her is driving me crazy. If I do lose her, I don't know what will become of me.

~

As I head back to Cathy's room after an hour, I feel a little calmer. I still don't know what I'm going to do, though. maybe I'll sleep on it. Who knows? Maybe in the morning, a solution will come to me.

I open the door. To my surprise, Cathy is still awake. She's not even in her pajamas. She's sitting on the edge of the bed. A suitcase sits at her feet.

A suitcase?

"What's going on?" I ask Cathy.

She stands up. "I'm leaving."

"What?" I let out a sigh as I scratch my head. "Cathy, please. It's been a long day. Whatever this is, we'll talk in the morning."

"No." She shakes her head. "In the morning, I'll be gone."

I narrow my eyes at her as I realize she's serious. "Why are you doing this?"

Cathy draws a deep breath. "You told me to give you an answer, to carefully think about what I want. This is my answer. This is what I want - to leave. I don't want to stay here with you, Jackson. I'm not ready for a serious, long-term relationship, and I'm not ready to... be a mother. And managing your restaurant is just too stressful for me."

My eyes grow wide because I can't believe my ears. Is this what Cathy really wants? Have I been burdening her all this time?

"I'm sorry, Jackson, but I'm leaving," she tells me. "And you can't stop me."

My heart sinks. My face falls.

"So it's true. You don't love me, after all."

"No."

That single word feels like a cleaver cleanly chopping my heart in two.

So, all this time, Cathy's just been - what? Tolerating me because I'm Trisha's brother?

Then again, that's like her. She's always been too kind. Right now, though, that kindness feels like the cruelest thing in the world.

"I was going to wait a bit," Cathy adds. "But it seems like things are going to be a mess around here, so I'll just go. The sooner I leave, the better."

I nod. There's no point in her staying now.

She hands me a piece of paper. "I wrote Maisie a letter to say sorry for leaving. It's up to you whether you give it to her or not."

I take it reluctantly. I know it will break Maisie's heart. Still, I think it's only fair that I give it to her.

"And here's your ring." Cathy drops the diamond ring on top of the note on my palm. "Thank you for letting me wear it."

I say nothing. Letting her wear it? I was the one who asked her to wear it. No. I made her wear it. All this time, I've been selfishly imposing my feelings and desires on her. I guess it's for the best, then, that I set her free.

Cathy grabs the handle of her suitcase. "Goodbye, Jackson."

"Goodbye."

She walks past me and heads out of the room. The soft click of the door closing behind her feels as loud as the sound of a boulder being dropped on top of me, leaving me in pieces, too shattered to move.

I've loved Cathy for years, and just like that, she's gone.

Gone.

CHAPTER 23

Cathy

The wheels of my suitcase don't make a sound on the carpet as I pull it behind me, just as my tears trickle silently down my cheeks, just as my heart doesn't make a sound while it continues to shatter inside my chest.

I place my hand over my chest and try to breathe.

I had no idea leaving Jackson and Maisie would hurt this much. But what choice do I have? If I don't leave, those two are going to be separated. I can't let that happen.

Love is a choice. You can choose to be with the people you love and make them happy, or you can choose to be away from them to make them happy.

If I have to leave Jackson and Maisie so they can be together, so be it. This is my fault anyway. It's because of all those mean things I said to Betty that she's trying to tear them apart. Jackson already lost his sister because of me. I'm not going to let him lose his daughter, too.

I wipe my tears and draw a deep breath.

I'm not going to let this family get torn apart because of me. First, I'm leaving this house. Then I'm talking to Betty.

~

I ring the bell at Suite 1209 and wait for someone to open the door. After a minute has passed, I ring the doorbell again. After the third ring, I hear footsteps approaching the door. A maid opens it.

"Yes?"

"I'd like to speak to Mrs. Ducant please," I say.

She scratches her head. "Mrs. Ducant is already asleep. You should - "

"I'm not leaving until I speak with her."

The maid's sleepy eyes grow wide.

"Please," I say more calmly. "I only need a few moments of her time and then I'll never bother her again."

"Do you promise?" I hear Betty's voice as she emerges from the shadows.

I let out a sigh of relief.

"Good evening, Betty. I'm sorry for coming to see you so late, but I'd like to talk."

She crosses her arms over her chest. "You're not going to ask me if you can sleep here, are you?"

"No," I assure her. "Can I come in for just a bit, though?"

For a moment, Betty stays still. The maid turns to her, waiting for her decision. Finally, she nods.

"Fine. Come in."

I step inside Betty's suite. She turns on a lamp and sits on the couch. I sit on a stool.

"You can leave," Betty tells the maid.

The maid nods and leaves us alone.

"Well?" Betty asks me. "What were you going to say?"

I place my hands on my lap and square my shoulders. "First, I'm sorry for everything I said to you last time."

Betty glances sideways. "What's said is said."

"And second, I want to tell you I'm leaving Jackson and Maisie."

Her eyebrows crease. "For good?"

I swallow the lump in my throat. "Yes. So please don't tear them apart. We both know a child deserves to be with her parents. Maisie may no longer have a mother, but she still has a father who loves her very much. Surely, you can see that, too."

Betty says nothing.

"I won't bother them or you again, so please promise me you'll let Jackson and Maisie stay together."

Betty narrows her eyes at me. "Why should I promise you anything?"

"I'm not asking you to do it for me," I answer. "I'm asking you to do it for them, for the family your daughter left behind."

"Don't you dare talk about my daughter."

Still, I go on. "I know what I said last time, but I also know that you loved your daughter. All mothers do, in their own way. Jackson told me that you didn't know about her illness until it was too late. That must have hurt. Not so much that your daughter kept something important from you or that she chose to sacrifice her own life without consulting you. But because you weren't able to be there for her during her final months. She was suffering, dying, and you weren't there."

"Quiet," Betty reprimands me.

"I understand how you feel. Evelyn probably didn't want you to suffer, which is why she didn't tell you. She didn't want to cause you trouble, but since you're a mother, you feel it's your right to suffer for your child. You're her mother, so you don't mind being troubled. You feel that by denying you that suffering, she denied you motherhood itself."

Betty says nothing. She looks away.

"But now you have another chance to be a mother, a chance to be a grandmother. Don't waste it by making Jackson and Maisie suffer. Please. I'm sure that's not what Evelyn would want, either."

Betty glares at me. "How would you know what my daughter would want? You don't know her."

"But somehow, I feel I do," I say. "Maybe because I love the same people she loved. I don't want them to suffer. I'd rather be the one to suffer then see them get hurt."

Again, Betty falls silent.

I stand up. "Please don't let our sacrifices be in vain."

Betty doesn't look at me. She points to the door.

"Leave. Now."

I remain standing.

She turns to cast her cold gaze on me. "Leave!"

I walk towards the door. Outside, I pause.

I've done what I came here to do. I've said what I came to say. It's up to Betty now, whether she will listen or not, though I definitely hope she will.

I look up at the ceiling.

Please help your mother make the right decision, Evelyn. Don't let her tear your husband and daughter apart.

I close my eyes.

I'll leave all of them to you.

Because now, there's nothing more I can do for them. I've done all I could.

I open my eyes and place a hand over my tummy.

And now, I have to do what I can for me and my child.

"We can do this," I whisper.

I'll go back home so Mom and Hal can help me. I don't want to trouble them, but hey, that's what families do. I'll find a job. I'll raise my child as best as I can.

I yawn. But first, I need to find a place to crash.

~

I wake up in the morning feeling refreshed. The motel room is small, especially compared to that hotel suite Betty is staying in. And it's not luxurious at all. But at least the room is clean and the bed was soft so I was able to sleep well. Then again, maybe I was just tired.

I decide to take a shower before leaving. As for breakfast, I'll grab it before I start driving home.

I open my suitcase so I can find something to change into only to frown when I realize my clothes are a mess. Of course they are. I just threw my stuff into the bag, after all, once I'd made up my mind to leave. I wanted to be done packing before Jackson returned to the room.

I fold the clothes now and arrange them into piles. I stop, though, when I see an orange sweater I've never seen before.

I hold it up.

This one's too big to be mine, which means it's Jackson's. Maybe he brought it to my room once and it got mixed up with my clothes.

I sniff it. Yup, definitely smells like him.

Oh well. I guess I'll keep it as a souvenir.

I start to fold it but stop again as my head throbs.

An orange sweater.

Suddenly, my memories of the night Trisha died start tumbling back. The red lantern perched on a branch. Trisha in her turtleneck and tank top. Trisha standing on the shore talking to a boy in an orange sweater with a C on it, exactly like this one. A boy with eyeglasses and a cleft chin.

Eyeglasses. Cleft chin.

Now where have I seen someone like that before?

My eyes grow wide as I remember.

Simon. Jackson's friend Simon. No wonder he knew Trisha. No wonder he looked like he'd seen me before.

But if Simon was there, what happened to him? How come he never told Jackson that he was there the night Trisha died? How come he didn't try to save me or Trisha?

I have a bad feeling about him. I also feel like I should tell someone. Who? My mom? Jackson?

I decide to call Jackson first since he's the one who knows Simon. I know he probably doesn't want to hear from me again, but I still have to tell him. I'm about to press the button to make the call when I hear a knock on the door.

Thinking that it's the manager bringing me the receipt he wasn't able to issue last night because of a problem with the printer, I open the door. It's not the manager standing outside, though, or anyone I know.

It's two men in their late twenties to mid-thirties, both wearing caps and sunglasses. One of them has a fancy looking watch, the kind that isn't just a watch.

For some reason, that sends an alarm off inside my head. I'm about to close the door again but one of the men steps in and pulls out a gun. He presses the barrel against my side and I gasp.

"Cathy Jeffries, you're coming with us."

CHAPTER 24

Jackson

"Are you coming with me to the farm or not?" Ken asks.

"No," I answer without glancing away from the view of the garden outside my bedroom window.

Since yesterday, I haven't had the energy or motivation to do anything else, so I've been staying at home, in my bedroom mostly, because it reminds me of Cathy the least. I thought I'd be okay with her leaving since she didn't love me. I thought I'd be setting both of us free. Instead, I feel even more of a prisoner, tied to the past, caged within myself.

Strange. I don't remember feeling this way after Evelyn died.

I'm about to bring my mug of coffee to my lips when Ken grabs it from my hands. To my surprise, she takes a sip.

"Coffee," she says. "I'm surprised there's no whiskey in here. A bit might do you some good."

I say nothing. I have thought of drinking, but I don't want to risk having anyone come over to find me drunk. That's the last thing I need with Maisie's custody hearing under way.

If there's anything I should do, it's spending time with her instead of sending her to daycare. Our days together may very well be numbered, so I should make the most of them. Yet I can barely stand to look at her gloomy face. It's the face she's worn ever since she read Cathy's letter.

Ken sets the mug down. "How long are you going to stay here sulking, hmm?"

I shrug.

She sighs. "You know, I was hoping I wouldn't have to kick your ass this time. I was going to wait for you to come to your senses. But forget it. Every minute you sit here feeling sorry for yourself is another minute Cathy is slipping away from you, and I can't stand it."

I give her a puzzled look. "What do you mean slipping away? She's gone, remember? She left me."

"Which is why you have to go after her."

I snort. "Why should I? She wanted to go."

Ken slaps her forehead. "Are we going to have the same conversation about Cathy leaving and you giving up on her again?"

"But this isn't like before," I tell her. "Last time, Cathy left because she was dragged into court. This time, Cathy left of her own free will. She wanted to leave."

"Let me guess. She told you that."

"Yes."

"And you believed her?"

"Of course," I answer. "Why wouldn't I?"

Ken draws a deep breath. "Seriously, you can be so stupid sometimes."

My eyebrows crease. "What?"

What exactly did I do wrong?

"The day Cathy left is the day that Betty told you she was going to sue for custody of Maisie, right?" Ken asks me.

"Yes."

"Cathy left shortly after you talked to Betty?"

"Yes."

"And let me guess. Betty told you she was going to get Maisie because she didn't want Maisie to live with Cathy because Cathy isn't good enough for her. And then you told Cathy that, right?"

"Right."

"And then she left?"

"Yes."

Ken raises her hands. "You still don't see the connection?"

What connection?

She sighs. "You told Cathy that Betty was going to get Maisie because Betty didn't think she was good enough to be Maisie's mother. Cathy left shortly afterward, telling Maisie to take care of you."

I narrow my eyes at her. "You read Cathy's letter to Maisie?"

"No. Maisie told me about it yesterday," Ken answers. "Can't you see? Cathy left because she didn't want to be the reason you and Maisie have to live away from each other. She gave way."

I shake my head. "I already told her before that I was going to keep them both no matter what."

"But that was before Betty filed a case," Ken says. "Can you honestly say that you can still keep Cathy if you would lose your daughter because of her?"

So Cathy sacrificed herself for me and Maisie? No. I don't believe that. Cathy knows I don't like sacrifice, not after what happened to Evelyn. She knows how helpless I felt. Why would she want me to feel that way again?

"Cathy left me because she doesn't love me," I tell Ken.

She lets out another long sigh. "There you go again, making lies out of self-pity."

"It's not - "

"Cathy loves you. That's why she left."

"That doesn't make sense. If you love someone, why would you leave them?"

"You would if you felt like that was the only way for them to be happy," Ken answers. "Maybe that's how she felt."

I shake my head. "I still don't believe you."

"Fine." Ken puts her hands on her hips. "I wasn't going to tell you about this, because Cathy swore me to secrecy, but since circumstances have changed and you're acting like an idiot, I think I have to break my vow."

I look at her curiously. "What secret?"

"Cathy was going to arrange a romantic dinner for you at the restaurant," Ken tells me. "She was going to cook herself."

My eyebrows go up. "She was?"

"Convinced now?"

I don't answer. I want to believe Ken. I want nothing more than to believe Cathy loves me. But I'm still afraid it might not be true.

"Fine. I'll tell you the rest," Ken says.

"The rest?"

"The dinner was just the means. She was planning it because she wanted to tell you something. Something important."

I frown. "You're keeping me in suspense here. I thought you didn't want to waste time."

"She was going to tell you she loves you and that she accepts your proposal!" Ken blurts out.

My eyes grow wide. No way.

"And she was also going to tell you that she was pregnant."

"Pregnant?"

Ken nods. "Mm-hm."

Cathy's pregnant? The thought makes my heart skip. So that's why she's been feeling sick lately.

"Now tell me she doesn't love you and doesn't want to be with you."

I look at Ken but say nothing. I can't say that now, not now that I know what Cathy was planning.

"Are you sure she's pregnant?" I ask Ken.

"What? You think she'd lie about that? You think I'd lie about it?"

No. They wouldn't, which means that Ken is right. Cathy only left because she felt she had to, which is likely because of the custody case.

Well, right now, I don't care about that. Yes, I'm still worried about losing Maisie, but I'll find a way to keep her. I'll find a way to keep her, Cathy and our baby. I'll find a way to keep them all. I'm not losing anyone anymore.

I get out of my chair.

"Finally, you're getting off your ass," Ken says. "Where to?"

I grab my phone from the bedside table. "I'm going to go after Cathy, of course."

~

First, though, I have to find Cathy, and right now, I can't. Her phone is dead. She isn't at her mother's house - I can tell Nina isn't lying about that - and she isn't at her old apartment. I've called all the hotels for miles around and they don't have her listed.

I slam my fist into the living room wall. Where can Cathy be?

Suddenly, I get an idea. Maybe I can ask my fans, my groupies to help me?

I grab my laptop and log in to their website. I'm about to click the button to post a new topic when I read the one on the top of the page.

Chef Jackson's Engagement.

My eyebrows crease. Didn't Simon say that he saw on the website that I broke off my engagement? But it doesn't say that here. Could they have posted it and removed it?

I look at the list of removed topics but find nothing about me and Cathy breaking up.

I frown. I guess Simon did get that information from Betty. Or did he?

Suddenly, my phone rings. I grab it, thinking that it might be Cathy calling, but it's an unknown number I see on the screen. I answer the call hoping it could still be her.

"Hello."

"Mr. Holloway," a man speaks to me from the other end. "This is Lyndon Barnes, the private investigator you hired."

Now that he's introduced himself, I do recognize his voice.

"What is it?" I ask. "Is it important? Because I'm a little busy right now."

"I just wanted to tell you that I found out who's paying for the treatment of Alexandra Pitts."

Right. I did ask him to do that because I was curious as to who would want Cathy to go to jail.

"And?"

"It's an IT company owned by a Mr. Simon Hessler."

Simon? My eyes grow wide. Why would Simon want to send Cathy to jail? Wait. Is that why I saw him in Milwaukee? Was he in contact with Mr. Pitts or the prosecutor? Is that how he knew my engagement to Cathy was called off?

I frown. I'm getting a bad feeling about this.

"Mr. Holloway?" Lyndon asks.

I hold the phone firmly against my ear. "Mr. Barnes, I want you to give me every piece of information you have on Simon Hessler."

CHAPTER 25

Cathy

"I knew it was you." I glare at Simon as he enters the room where I'm being held captive.

He grins. "Then I'm glad I didn't disappoint."

He pulls the chair from the corner and sits on it.

"I'm sorry I couldn't come sooner. I would have, but I had stuff to do at work. I trust those men outside have followed my instructions and treated you nicely?"

I show him my bound wrists. After three days, the rope has started to chafe my skin.

"Is this your idea of treating someone nicely?"

He lifts the bottle of beer in his hand to his lips. "Well, at least only your hands were tied."

I frown. If only I could get a shard of that bottle, I'd be able to free myself.

"Why did you have me brought here?" I ask Simon.

I can try to escape later, but first I want to know what he wants from me - and more importantly, what his role was the night Trisha died.

"Well, for one, I thought you'd love the place. After all, there is a lake not far from here."

I did see it on my way here.

So I am right. He was there the night Trisha died.

The guy in the orange sweater.

"And the other reason?" I ask.

Simon takes another gulp of beer. "Well, that lake is where I'll dump your body."

His words send a chill down my spine, but I keep my shoulders square.

"You're going to kill me?"

"Yes," he answers plainly. "Soon."

A knot forms in my stomach, but I force myself to calm down.

Don't panic, Cathy. If you panic, you'll lose.

"But first, you and I are going to have a bit of fun," Simon says.

A wicked grin appears on his face. Fear grips my nape.

He sets his bottle down near the leg of his chair and stands up. I back up against the wall.

"Don't come any closer," I warn him even as I try to keep my voice from shaking.

"Now, now." He walks towards me with a lecherous look in his eyes. "Why don't you be a good girl and play along? Don't you want to enjoy this? This is going to be your last bit of fun, after all."

I quickly look around for a weapon but find none. Those thugs swept this place clean of anything that could be used for escape or self-defense.

There's only one thing to do - run.

I dash to another corner. "Stay away from me."

Simon frowns. "Run away from me again and I'll call the men outside to hold you down and spread your legs for me. I might let them have their share of fun, too."

My knees shake. The knot in my stomach grows tighter. Now what?

Think, Cathy. Think of something.

Simon comes closer. His grin grows wider.

"You were the guy in the orange sweater," I blurt out.

He stops. His eyes grow wide.

"You remember?"

I nod.

Simon strokes the cleft in his chin. "I guess I made the right decision, then. I was surprised when I heard you had amnesia. And disappointed. I thought the reason why you never told anyone about me was because you were scared. When I found out you could remember what happened one day..."

"You got scared," I finish the sentence for him.

He taps his fingers on the windowsill. "I knew I had to do something, so I did. I paid Mr. Pitts to go to the prosecutor with that story. Needless to say, that didn't work out. Well, I've dealt with him already."

My eyebrows arch. Does he mean he had the poor old man killed? The fear in my veins steels into anger.

"You're a despicable coward," I spit at him.

"It would have been better for you if that plan had worked," Simon tells me. "You'd be in jail, but at least you'd be alive. Now, I have only one way left to get rid of you."

I should be trembling at his renewed threat, but I'm not scared anymore.

"Why are you so desperate to get rid of me, hmm? Is it because you killed Trisha?"

Simon says nothing.

"Tell me," I urge him. "You're going to kill me anyway."

He pauses for a moment, then gives in. "Fine. I was partly responsible."

I give him a puzzled look. "Partly?"

"I wanted Trisha from the moment I saw her when she came to visit Jackson at campus," Simon says. "When I saw her in Staggart, I was overjoyed. I thought it was finally my chance to have her. But did she give me a chance? No. So I slipped a drug into a drink and I gave that to her."

I feel the blood drain from my face. Drug? He drugged Trisha?

"I was supposed to take her back to my room after she passed out, but then you started drowning and she had to go save you."

I tense.

"And then she realized she'd lost her bracelet, so she went back into the water. That's when the drug took effect and she drowned."

My hands clench into fists at my sides. So Trisha drowned because of the drug Simon gave her? She died because of it?

"So you see, it's partly my fault and partly yours. We're accomplices. But I'm afraid that also makes you a loose end."

"How dare you say this is my fault." I step forward. "You're the one who drugged her."

"Yes, and if you hadn't drowned, she would still be alive. I would have brought her to my room, had my fun with her, and then brought her back to you."

The thought of his filthy hands on her sends me seething with rage. "You son of a bitch."

"But I didn't get to have my fun with her, so I guess I'll just have it with you."

He walks towards me. I run to the chair without thinking and grab the bottle of beer from the floor. I break it on the back of the chair and threaten him with the biggest piece.

"I'll kill you for what you did to Trisha."

"No, you won't." Simon grins. "And now that you've run away from me again, I have to call the boys."

I grow still as he puts his fingers in his mouth to whistle. But no sound comes out. Instead, I hear a shout from outside.

"Police. Put down your weapons!"

Relief washes over me.

The police are here. I'm safe.

Or so I think until I see the panic on Simon's face. He runs towards me. I prepare to stab him with the glass shard in my hand.

Then all of a sudden, the door opens. Jackson crashes in. He tackles Simon and knocks him out with a single punch. Seconds later, cops follow.

I drop the shard in my hand and sink to the floor as my knees give way. My eyes close and I draw a deep breath.

It's over.

CHAPTER 26

Jackson

"Are you sure you're alright?" I ask Cathy once more as I drive her home. "Simon didn't hurt you?"

"No," Cathy answers.

Good. When I found out that Simon had a lakeside property, all the alarm bells in my head went off. I kept thinking he had drowned her, that she was gone, and the fear just kept gnawing at me, causing knots in my stomach and every muscle of my body. When I saw the thugs around Simon's cabin, I was actually relieved because it meant she was still alive.

Thank God she's alive.

I glance at her stomach. "Just to be safe, maybe we should have a doctor check on you and the baby."

Cathy looks at me with wide eyes. "Ken told you?"

I nod. "Only because I was being stubborn and refusing to go after you."

She directs her gaze straight ahead. "So you came after me because you found out I was pregnant?"

"That's not the only reason," I tell her. "I realized I should never have let you go in the first place."

Cathy shakes her head. "But I chose to go. And I can't go back. If I do, Betty will - "

"I will deal with Betty," I promise her. "And whatever happens, I'm not going to let you, Maisie or our baby go."

I place my hand over hers.

"Trust me."

Cathy falls silent. Then she nods as she places her hand over mine. "Okay."

I smile. "For now, let's just go back to Maisie."

~

When we get back home, though, Betty is waiting there. I frown. What? Did she find out I left Maisie alone again? Is she here to take her away already? Well, I won't let her.

I pat Cathy's shoulder. "You can go in ahead to Maisie."

Betty looks at her. "No, she can - "

"Go," I tell Cathy.

She looks at Betty as she walks past her but says nothing.

I stand in front of Betty. "What do you want? If you're still going to insist on the hearing because you think Cathy is responsible for Trisha's death, then let me tell you now that she isn't. My sister was drugged and the man responsible is now in jail, where he will rot for the rest of his life."

Betty nods. "That's good news. I didn't show up here to insist on the hearing, though."

She didn't?

"In fact, I came here to watch my granddaughter... and also to tell you that I'm not going to sue for custody anymore, not now or ever."

My eyebrows go up. Is Betty serious? It sounds too good to be true.

"So you're going to let Maisie stay with me?" I ask.

"You're her father, after all. Besides, she's going to have a mother now. And as much as I hate to admit it, I think she's going to have a good one."

Betty starts to leave. I remain rooted where I stand, still in shock.

"Betty." I turn around once I've recovered. "May I ask what made you change your mind?"

She glances over her shoulder. "What do you mean, change my mind? It's only natural for me to sacrifice my own happiness for that of my granddaughter. I am a mother, too, after all."

With that, she walks to her car. I watch her leave, shaking my head in disbelief. I don't know what happened. I'm glad, though. It feels that puzzle pieces are falling into place.

I run inside the house to tell Cathy the good news. I find her with Maisie in Maisie's bedroom, both of them with huge smiles.

"Betty said she'll leave us alone," I announce. "She'll let us be a family."

Cathy's eyes grow wide. "She did?"

I nod. "She even said you were going to make a good mother."

Cathy smiles.

My eyebrows crease. "Wait. Did you talk to her?"

"Is Cathy going to be my mommy now?" Maisie asks.

I lift a finger. "That reminds me."

I run to my bedroom to get the diamond ring. When I come back, I go down on one knee in front of Cathy.

"I know I didn't ask the first time, so I'll do that now," I tell her as I present her with the ring. "Cathy Jeffries, I've loved you for most of my life. I don't want to ever be without you. Will you marry me and be the best mother to my children?"

"Will you be my mother?" Maisie adds.

Cathy takes the ring from my palm and slips it on. Then she pulls me to my feet and looks into my eyes.

"Yes, Jackson Holloway. I will marry you and love you for the rest of my life."

My heart leaps. Beside me, Maisie cheers. I wrap my arms around Cathy and give her a quick kiss. Then I carry Maisie in my arms.

"And I will gladly be your mother." Cathy gives her a hug.

"Yay!" Maisie throws her hands up.

"Oh, and one more thing," Cathy says as she catches my gaze. "Your father and I have something to tell you."

EPILOGUE

Cathy

Three years later...

I linger in the doorway as I watch Maisie and Trish sleeping in their beds. Maisie snores softly as she hugs her pillow, her blanket off. Trish is still tucked in, sleeping soundly with a stuffed unicorn on either side of her. They may not look like it, but I know they're sisters. And that they'll always love each other. The thought brings me comfort and makes my chest swell with joy.

Jackson touches my arm. "What are you doing?"

"Shh."

I hold a finger to my lips and close the door gently before turning to face my husband.

"I was just watching them sleep. It gives me a sense of peace."

Peace. After all these years, I finally have it. Peace. And hope. And wonderful children. And an amazing husband.

He grins. "Well, now it's our turn to go to bed."

Jackson scoops me up in his arms and carries me to our room. There, he drops me on the bed and pins me down with a kiss. I wrap my arms around him and shiver with delight as I feel the heat from his tongue all the way to my toes.

He unties the sash of my robe and runs his hands over the lace chemise I'm wearing. His palms cradle my breasts. His thumbs press down on my nipples.

I pull his shirt off him and slip my hand beneath his boxers. My fingers brush against his hard cock and a thrill goes through me. It quivers against my palm in turn as Jackson gasps.

I take it out of its cotton prison and lick it until it's completely hard, savoring every inch of him and the unique taste of him. Then I wrap my lips around the tip and suck him into my mouth. I puff my cheeks and let him slide across my tongue as I move my head back and forth.

Jackson hisses. His fingers become entangled with my hair.

When my lips start to grow numb, I pull away. I take Jackson's boxers off and take off my own underwear, then I push him down on the bed and position myself above his wet cock.

Some nights, it's Jackson's turn to do whatever he wants. Some nights, like tonight, it's mine.

I flatten my palms against Jackson's chest and lower my hips. The tip of his cock enters me and I gasp.

Even after all this time, I still can't get used to this feeling, and that's fine, because each time Jackson enters me, I feel like it's the first time - or should I say the second time?

I let out shallow breaths as I take his cock inside me inch by inch. Jackson, on the other hand, seems to be holding his breath. Once he's completely sheathed inside me, I bend over for a passionate lip-lock. Then I straighten up and take off my chemise.

Jackson sits up. He takes one of my nipples between his lips and I gasp. He rubs the other with his fingers.

I savor the playful sensation for a moment before pushing Jackson back down. I hold his arms down and capture his gaze, then start moving my hips.

Back when my stomach had grown big, this was my favorite position. It still is, because this way, I can control my pace. I can get lost in my rhythm.

I lose myself to it now. My eyelids fall shut and my body moves on its own. Up and down. Up and down. My hips rock and my shoulders sway. My breasts bounce.

When I'm tired, I stop and Jackson grips my arms. He starts to move his own hips beneath me and a different pleasure takes over. I throw my head back as I ride it. With each dizzying gallop, I inch closer to the peak of pleasure.

Just as I'm nearly there, Jackson pushes me off and down on my back. He grips my thighs and enters me with one thrust. A cry escapes my throat.

As much as I like being in control, I also like it when Jackson takes control. Even more so when he loses control because of me.

That seems to be what's happening now. His eyes are half lidded, dilated pupils peeking beneath them. His thrusts become erratic.

After a few more, the pleasure washes over me. I feel like I'm drowning, but there's no fear, only exhilaration. I cling to his shoulders as I'm swept away. Moan after moan spills from my lips.

Jackson follows moments after. He grunts as his cock fills me with an explosion of warmth. I tighten around him and milk him of every drop.

Afterwards, we stay still, catching our breaths and waiting for the haze to fade, relishing having our bodies connected. Then Jackson pulls out. He wraps his arms around me and plants a kiss on my forehead, my favorite kiss of all. I snuggle against his chest and smile.

"Do you think our new restaurant in Melbourne will be successful?" Jackson asks as he breaks the silence first.

"I know it will," I answer. "After all, Ken is there to make sure everything goes well."

I still help with managing some of Jackson's restaurants, but my priority now is taking care of my children.

"You know, Maisie and Trish sometimes remind me of Trisha and me," I tell Jackson. "I hope they will be best friends forever."

"I think they will be."

He takes my hand in his. Our fingers entwine. Our platinum wedding bands collide.

I look into his eyes. "And you will be my best friend forever."

I know that I lost the one I used to have, but now I have a new one, someone who knows me inside out and loves every bit of me, someone who always makes me feel like the best is yet to come. Just like now.

I close my eyes as I feel his heart beat in my ear.

I can't wait for what's to come.

~The End~

If you LOVED Kitchen Boss, be sure to check out Protector!

PROTECTOR SNEAK PEEK

Ex-Firefighter. Current Boss. Future (Pretend) Husband.

"Save me."

I saw that plea in Robyn's tear-moistened chestnut eyes the moment she stepped off the back of my truck naked, shivering, bruised and scarred.

How could I refuse?

Her gaze calls out to the hero in me.

Her touches awaken the man.

Each brush of her body against mine starts a fire I can't put out.

F*ck yeah, I'll protect her.

I'll go through flames for this woman.

I'll even marry her and father her child.

And brand every inch of her skin as mine so her monster of an ex won't ever touch her again.

She belongs to me now.

And I will keep her from harm.

But can I still protect her when my darkest secret is her greatest fear?

https://www.ashleepriceromanceauthor.com/product/protector/

Prologue

Xander

"Silent night, holy night..."

"Dashing through the snow in a one-horse open sleigh..."

"Fa la la la la la la la la!"

The familiar lyrics of holiday tunes merge into a medley with no rhyme or rhythm above the roar of my motorcycle engine. The strings of colorful lights on the windows blur into a seamless spectrum.

I tighten my grip on the throttle, urging my vehicle to go even faster. The icy, sobering wind sweeps my hair back and numbs my hollowed cheeks.

Damn Tracy for hiding my helmet. As if it wasn't bad enough that she turned off my phone.

The rotten smell of burnt turkey drifting out of an apartment window puts a grimace on my face. Moments later, the aroma of cranberries and perfectly cooked turkey makes my mouth water.

If Tracy had only cooked good turkey like she promised she would, instead of making that excuse for a meatloaf, I would have drunk less. As it was, I had to open a second bottle of wine to cleanse my palate of the rubbery aftertaste.

It was probably part of her strategy to get her hands inside my pants faster. Not that I minded that, though now is neither the time nor the place for reminiscing about that particular episode.

The clamor of church bells, ominous to my ears instead of jubilant, reminds me of the gravity of my current situation. A family is going inside as I drive past the church, and I catch a glimpse of the nativity set on the altar through the open door. For the first time in a long time, I utter a prayer.

Please let me make it in time.

The city's fifty-foot Douglas fir looms over the horizon, then towers over me in all its dazzling glory as I drive around it.

It's an enchanting sight, a reminder of all the warmth and magic the holidays bring.

Unfortunately, tragedies don't take holidays. Even tonight, on Christmas Eve, hell is threatening to break loose.

I only hope that I can shut it down before innocent lives are lost.

Please, please…

The plea gets derailed from the tracks of my thoughts as I hear the wail of the sirens riding on the breeze. My eyes grow wide as I see a curl of smoke blotting out a portion of the night sky. The stench of smoke reaches my nostrils and my jaw clenches.

No.

As the burning building appears before my eyes, the fire worse than I expected, my heart begins to hammer. I crouch on my motorcycle, practically hugging the vehicle as I go even faster, as fast as it allows me to go. The engine roars in protest. The wind stings.

The tires screech against the pavement as I finally stop in between the crimson fire trucks. I let the bike fall as I get off and march to the nearest truck.

"Xander?"

Chester peers at me through narrowed eyes as he speaks between ragged breaths. His charred suit tells me he's just come out of hell. His slumped shoulders are the sign of defeat.

I frown.

"What are you doing here?" he asks.

"Captain said all units," I briefly explain as I grab a set of gear. "Are Martin and Jessie inside?"

"Yeah." Chester nods. "I was just there, too."

But as usual, you chickened out. Coward.

"Xander, you should know…"

"Bolt." Capt. Rick Morrison appears from behind the truck. "What are you doing?"

I zip my suit up. "Getting ready to go in, sir, like you asked."

"I asked you that more than an hour ago," he tells me with a disapproving frown and both hands on his hips. "I didn't hear from you. I assumed you were too busy making out under the mistletoe to help out."

I swallow the bitter lump in my throat. "I'm here now, sir."

"I've already told the team to get out. The building won't hold much longer."

I lift my head to give him a puzzled look. "But there are still dozens of people left in that building. We can't just abandon them."

He shakes his head. "It's too late to save them."

No.

I slip on my boots, grab my helmet and run towards the building.

"Bolt!" The captain calls after me. "Don't go in there! Do you hear me? That's an order."

Fuck it.

"Are you crazy?" Chester shouts behind me. "Don't try to be a hero, man."

No. He's got it wrong. I'm not trying to be a hero. I never have. The only one I'm trying to save is myself.

"Xan—"

The explosion in front of me drowns out Chester's voice and every other sound. The thunder buzzes in my ears. The force of it pushes me back and I end up on the pavement. My helmet flies from my hand.

For a moment, I can't move. When I finally try to get up, I notice the pain over my eye. I touch my forehead and feel something damp.

Blood.

A flaming felt Santa ornament a few inches away from me draws my attention. Around me, more burning debris rain down from above.

I grab it and put out the flames with my own hands before clutching it to my chest. As I turn my head towards the fresh pile of charred rubble, my heart stops.

My ears clear just in time for me to hear the echoes of my own scream.

Chapter One

Robyn

Faster!

The command from my brain sends my heart pounding like a war drum. Adrenaline pumps through my veins and my legs spur forward. Long blades of grass tickle my knees.

Faster!

Through a gap between the branches, I catch a glimpse of the sun barely staying afloat in a sea of clouds. None of the weak sunlight filters through the trees to splotch the ground beneath my feet, and no heat scorches my bare skin.

Good. With no sunbeams bouncing off my copper locks, it should be easier to blend in with the trees and the bushes.

A breeze sends the leaves shuddering and sweeps my hair across my face. The thin tendrils stick to my cheeks. Instead of brushing them off, I wear them like a gossamer veil as I continue running.

A stronger breeze blows against my back and an involuntary shiver crawls up my spine. I wrap my arms around my breasts in an effort to ward off the cold.

....

Get Protector here and find out what happens next.

https://www.ashleepriceromanceautho
r.com/product/protector/

GET MORE FROM ASHLEE PRICE

Amazon lists millions of titles, and I'm happy you discovered
this one.

But if you'd like to know when I release a new book, instead of
leaving it up to chance, sign up for my newsletter.

I'll send you an email when my latest release goes live.

https://www.ashleepriceromanceaut
hor.com/signup/

KITCHEN BOSS MERCH

Tote Bag

Throw Pillow

Samsung Galaxy Cases

iPhone Cases

https://www.ashleepriceromanceauthor.com/pro
duct-category/ashlee-merch/